NINE BAR BLUES:
Stories from an Ancient Future

Praise

"Sheree Renée Thomas gives us a whirlpool of poem and story, a 'wild and strangeful breed' of cosmology that maps each star from Machu Picchu to Congo Square, from Legba to Medusa."

—Tyehimba Jess, author of *Olio*, winner 2017 Pulitzer Prize

"Through the lyrical lens of Thomas, this extraordinary collection carries us into the ancient, past and future of cosmic beings and humans enhanced by power inherited or genetic engineering. Filled with mesmerizing stories of a mysterious hole swallowing a town, night's refusal to lift over a river city, mutating water, hunger for Freedom, downloaded souls, music, music, music and so much more. An amazing book worthy of re-reading."

—Linda D. Addison, author of *How to Recognize a Demon Has Become Your Friend*, recipient of the Horror Writers Association Lifetime Achievement Award

"*Nine Bar Blues* is a song of deep folklore and apocalyptic myth. Here in these pages are women seized with second sight. There is loss and longing, days without sun and nights without dream...the balm of music and unfathomable magic."

—Sandra Jackson-Opoku, author of *The River Where Blood is Born*, winner American Library Association's Best Fiction of the Year Award

"Sheree Renee Thomas continues to demonstrate why she is one of the preeminent voices, a true griot, of the Black Speculative Tradition. With her well-crafted stories, her latest offering, *Nine Bar Blues: Stories from an Ancient Future*, will join the great tradition and pantheon of writers such as Walter Mosley's *Futureland* and Jewelle Gomez's *The Gilda Stories*.

—Reynaldo Anderson, co-founder of the Black Speculative Arts Movement

"*Nine Bar Blues* is a wondrous, musical delight. There's a transporting magic in every story, no, every page of this book. Be prepared to be stunned and to feel joy in equal measure."

—Rion Amilcar Scott, author of *Insurrections*, winner 2017 PEN/Robert W. Bingham Prize

For more information:
Third Man Books, LLC, 623 7th Ave S, Nashville, Tennessee 37203
A CIP record is on file with the Library of Congress
FIRST USA EDITION
For more about the book: http://thirdmanbooks.com/ninebarblues
password: thomas

ISBN: 978-0-9974578-9-6

Design and layout by Caitlin Parker

NINE BAR BLUES

STORIES
FROM AN
ANCIENT FUTURE

SHEREE RENÉE THOMAS

THIRD MAN BOOKS

STORIES

Space music'd be really something ...
but they don't have no gravity up there.
You couldn't have no downbeat!
Miles Davis

The whole of life itself expresses the blues...
in words and song
inspiration, feeling, and understanding.
The blues can be about anything pertaining to the facts of life.
The blues call on God as much as a spiritual song do.
Willie Dixon

The funk is its own reward.
George Clinton

ANCESTRIES

In the beginning were the ancestors, gods of earth who breathed the air and walked in flesh. Their backs were straight and their temples tall. We carved the ancestors from the scented wood, before the fire and the poison water took them, too. We rubbed ebony-stained oil on their braided hair and placed them on the altars with the first harvest, the nuts and the fresh fruit. None would eat before the ancestors were fed, for it was through their blood and toil we emerged from the dark sea to be.

But that was then, and this is now, and we are another tale.

It begins as all stories must, with an ending. My story begins when my world ended, the day my sister shoved me into the ancestors' altar. That morning, one sun before Oma Day, my bare heels slipped in bright gold and orange paste. *Sorcadia* blossoms lay flattened, their juicy red centers already drying on the ground. The air in my lungs disappeared. Struggling to breathe, I pressed my palm over the spoiled flowers, as if I could hide the damage. Before Yera could cover her smile, the younger children came.

"Fele, Fele," they cried and backed away, "the ancient ones will claim you!" Their voices were filled with derision but their eyes held something else, something close to fear.

"Claim her?" Yera threw her head back, the fishtail braid snaking down the hollow of her back, a dark slick eel. "She is not worthy," she said to the children, and turned her eyes on them. They scattered like chickens. Shrill laughter made the *sorcadia* plants dance. A dark witness, the fat purple vines and shoots twisted and undulated above me. I bowed my head. Even the plants took part in my shame.

"And I don't need you, shadow," Yera said, turning to me, her face a brighter, crooked reflection of my own. "*You* are just a spare." A spare.

Only a few breaths older than me, Yera, my twin, has hated me since before birth.

Our oma says even in the womb, my sister fought me, that our mother's labors were so long because Yera held me fast, her tiny fingers clasped around my throat, as if to stop the breath I had yet to take. The origin of her disdain is a mystery, a blessing unrevealed. All I know is that when I was born, Yera gave me a kick before she was pushed out of our mother's womb, a kick so strong it left an impression, a mark, like a bright shining star in the middle of my chest.

This star, the symbol of my mother's love and my sister's hate, is another way my story ended.

I am told that I refused to follow, that I lay inside my mother, after her waters spilled, after my sister abandoned me, gasping like a small fish, gasping for breath. That in her delirium my mother sang to me, calling, begging me to make the journey on, that she made promises to the old gods, to the ancestors who once walked our land, to those of the deep, promises that a mother should never make.

"You were the *bebe* one, head so shiny, slick like a ripe green seed," our oma would say.

"Ripe," Yera echoed, her voice sweet for Oma, sweet as the *sorcadia* tree's fruit, but her mouth was crooked, slanting at me. Yera had as many faces as the ancestors that once walked our land, but none she hated more than mine.

While I slept, Yera took the spines our oma collected from the popper fish and sharpened them, pushed the spines deep into the star in my chest. I'd wake to scream, but the paralysis would take hold, and I would lie in my pallet, seeing, knowing, feeling but unable to fight or defend.

When we were *lardah,* and I had done something to displease her— rise awake, breathe, talk, stand—Yera would dig her nails into my right shoulder and hiss in my ear. "Shadow, spare. Thief of life. You are the reason we have no mother." It was my sister's favorite way to steal my joy.

And then, when she saw my face cloud, as the sky before rain, she would take me into her arms and stroke me. "There, my sister, my second, my own broken one," she would coo. "When I descend, you can have mother's comb, and put it in your own hair. Remember me," she would whisper in my ear, her breath soft and warm as any lover. "Remember me," and then she would stick her tongue inside my ear and pinch me until I screamed.

Our oma tried to protect me, but her loyalty was like the *suwa* wind, inconstant, mercurial. Oma only saw what she wanted. Older age and even older love made her forget the rest.

"Come!" I could hear the drumbeat echo of her clapping hands. "Yera, Fele," she sang, her tongue adding more syllables to

3

our names, Yera, Fele, the words for one and two. The high pitch meant it was time to braid Oma's hair. The multiversal loops meant she wanted the complex spiral pattern. Three hours of labor, if my hands did not cramp first, maybe less if Yera was feeling industrious.

With our oma calling us back home, I wiped my palms on the inside of my thighs, and ignored the stares. My sister did not reach back to help me. A crowd had gathered, pointing but silent. No words were needed here. The lines in their faces said it all. I trudged behind Yera's tall, straight back, my eyes focused on the fishtail's tip.

"They should have buried you with the afterbirth."

When we reached the courtyard, my basket empty, Yera's full as she intended, we found our oma resting in her battered rocker in the yard. She had untied the wrap from her head. Her edges spiked around her full moon forehead, black tendrils reaching for the sun. She smiled as Yera revealed the spices and herbs she collected. I pressed fresh moons into my palms and bit my lip. No words were needed here. As usual, our oma had eyes that did not see. She waved away my half empty basket, cast her eyes sadly away from the fresh bloody marks on my shoulder, and pointed to her scalp instead.

"Fele, I am feeling festive today, bold." She stared at a group of *baji* yellow-tailed birds pecking at the crushed roots and dried leaves scattered on the ground. They too would be burned and offered tomorrow night, at Yera's descension. And we would feast on the fruits of the land, as my sister descended into the sea.

"I need a style fitting for one who is an oma of a goddess. My beauty."

"A queen!" Yera cried, returning from our *bafa*. She flicked the fishtail and raised her palms to the sky. "An ancestress, joining the deep."

Yera had been joining the deep since we were small girls. She never let me forget it.

"Come, Fele," she said, "You take the left," as if I did not know. Yera held the carved wooden comb of our mother like a machete, her gaze as sharp and deadly. Her eyes dared me to argue. She knew that I would not.

Together we stood like sentinels, each flanking oma's side. The creamy gel from the fragrant *sorcadian* butter glistened on the backs of our hands. I placed a small bowl of the blue-shelled sea snails, an ointment said to grow hair thick and wild as the deepest weed of the sea. Yera gently parted our oma's scalp, careful not to dig the wooden teeth in. Before I learned to braid my own hair, Yera had tortured me as a child, digging the teeth into the tender flesh of my scalp. Now her fingers moved in a blur, making the part in one deft move. A dollop of gel dripped onto her wrists. She looked as if she wore blue-stained bracelets—or chains.

I gathered our oma's thick roots, streaked with white and the ashen gray she refused to dye, saying she had earned every strand of it.

"This is a special time, an auspicious occasion. It is not every year that Oma Day falls on the Night of Descension. The moon will fill the sky and light our world as bright as in the day of the gods."

I massaged scented oils into the fine roots of her scalp, brushed my fingertips along the nape of her neck. I loved to comb our oma's hair. The strands felt like silk from the spider tree, cotton from the prickly bushes. Oma said in the time before, our ancestors used to have enough fire to light the sky, that it burned all morning, evening, and the night, from a power they once called electricity. I love how that name feels inside my head—*e-lec-tri-city*. It sounds like one of our oma's healing spells, the prayers she sends up with incense and flame.

Once when Yera and I were very small, we ran too far inside the ancestors' old walled temples. Before we were forbidden, we used to scavenge there. We climbed atop the dusty, rusted carcasses of metal beasts. We ducked under rebar, concrete giants jutting from the earth, skipped over faded signage. We scuttled through the scraps of the metal yard at the edge of green, where the land took back what the old gods had claimed. I claimed something, too, my reflection in the temple called Family Dollar, a toy that looked like me. Her hair was braided in my same simple box pattern, the eyes were black and glossy. She wore a faded skirt, the pattern long gone. When I flipped her over, to my surprise, I discovered another body where the hips and legs should be. The skirt concealed one body when the other was upright. Two bodies, two heads, but only one could be played with at a time. I tried to hide my find from Yera, but she could see contentment on my face. So I ran. I ran to the broken, tumble down buildings with blown-out windows that looked like great gaping mouths. I ran into the mouth of darkness, clutching my doll but when I closed my eyes, searching for the light, Yera was waiting on the other side.

That is when I knew I could never escape her. My sister is always with me.

Before the Descension, our people once lived in a land of great sweeping black and green fields, land filled with thick-limbed, tall trees and flowing rivers of cool waters, some sweet and clear, others dark as the rich, black soil. Our oma says when our ancestors could no longer live on the land, when the poisons had reached the bottom of every man, woman, and child's cup, they journeyed on foot and walked back into the sea, back to the place of the old gods, the deep ones.

But before they left, they lifted their hands and made a promise. That if the land could someday heal from its long scars, the wounds that people inflicted, that they would return again. In the meanwhile, one among us, one strong and true, must willingly descend into the depths to join the ancestors. This one, our people's first true harvest, will know from the signs and symbols, the transformations that only come from the blessing of the ancestors, when the stars in the sky above align themselves just so. Yera is that first harvest. She has wanted this honor her whole life. And from her birth, the signs were clear. Her lungs have grown strong, her limbs straight and tall, she does not bend and curve like the rest of us. My sister has the old gods' favor and when Oma Day ends and the Descension is complete, she will join the waters, and rule them as she once ruled the waters of our mother's womb, she will enter them and be reborn as an ancestress.

The ceremony has not yet begun and I am already tired. I am tired, because I spend much of my time and energy devoted to breathing. For me, to live each day is a conscious act, an exercise of will, mind over my broken body's matter. I must imagine a future with every breath, consciously exhaling, expelling the poison because my brain thinks I need more air, and signals my body to produce light, even though my lungs are weak and filled with the ash of the old gods. Unable to filter the poison quickly, my body panics and it thinks I am dying. My knees lock, and I pull them up to my chest and hold myself, gasping for breath like our oma said I did, waiting in my mother's womb.

Oma gives me herbs. She grinds them up, mortar and pestle in her conch shell, and mixes them in my food. When I was smaller, she made me recite the ingredients daily, a song she hummed to lull me asleep. But as I grew, the herbs worked less and less, and my sister did things to them, things that made me finally give them up. I have given so much to her these years.

And I have created many different ways to breathe.

I breathe through my tongue, letting the pink buds taste the songs in the air. I breathe through the fine hairs on the ridge of my curved back and my arms, the misshapen ones she calls claws. I breathe through the dark pores of my skin. And when I am alone, and out of my oma's earshot, out of my wretched sister's reach, I breathe through my mouth, unfiltered and free. My fingers searching the most hidden, soft parts of myself and I am *light air star shine, light air star shine, light—*

In the suns before Oma Day, I spent a lot of time sleeping. My breathing tends to be easier if I sleep well, and so I slept. My lungs are filled with poison which means there's no space for the light, the good clean air. I have many different ways to expel the poison, and meanwhile my body goes into panic because my mind thinks I'm dying, so between controlling the exhalation, telling my mind that I am not dying, inhaling our oma's herbs through her conch shell, I am exhausted since I do this many times a day. And then there is Yera. Always my sister, Yera. I must watch for her. I know my sister's movements more than I know myself.

This night, on the eve of Oma Day, which is to say, the eve of my sister's descension, I can feel Yera smile, even in the dark. It is that way with sisters. As a child I did not fear the night. How could I? My sister's voice filled it. Outside, the *baji* birds gathered in the high tops of our oma's trees. Their wings sounded like the great wind whistling through what was left of the ancestors' stone wall towers. They chattered and squawked in waves as hypnotic as the ocean itself, their excitement mirroring our own. And I too was excited, my mind filled with questions and a few hopes I dared not even share with myself. Would I still exist without my sister? Can there be one without two?

As more stars add their light to the darkness, I turn in my bed, over and over again like the gold beetles burrowing in our oma's soil. I turned, my mind restless while Yera slept the sleep of the ages. For me, sleep never comes. So I sit in the dark, braiding and unbraiding my hair and wait for the day to come, when my world would end again or perhaps when it might begin.

The past few days I've been aware that braiding makes me short of breath, and I realized that I am very, very tired. Last night I was going through my patterns, braiding and unbraiding them in my head, overhand and underhand, when I remembered what the elder had once said to our oma. That she had done a lot in her life, that she, already an honored mother, had raised *felanga* on her own, and it was all right if she rested now. And I thought that maybe that was true for me, the resting part, which is perhaps why today I feel changed.

"Hurry, child. Hunger is on me."

Our oma calls but even she is too nervous to eat. Her hair is a wonder, a sculpture that rises from her head like two great entwined serpents holding our world together. My scalp is sore. My hands still ache in the center of my palms and I am concentrating harder now to breathe. I rub the palm flesh of my left hand, massaging the pain in a slow ring of circles.

Yera has not joined us yet. She refused my offer to help braid her hair. "You think I want your broken hand in my head? You know your hands don't work," she said. I remember only once receiving praise from her for my handiwork. I had struggled long, my fingers cramped, my temple pulsing. I braided her hair into a series of intricate loops, twisting off her shining scalp like lush *sorcadia* blooms. Yera did not speak her praise. Vocal with anger, she was silent with approval. Impressed, Yera tapped her upper teeth with her thumb. Oma, big-spirited as she was big-legged, ran to me. She lifted my aching hands high into the air as if the old gods could see them. Now dressed in nothing more than a wrap, Yera's full breasts exposed, nipples like dark moons, her mouth is all teeth and venom. "You have always been jealous of me."

"Jealous?" I say and turn the word over in my mouth. It is sour and I don't like its taste. I spit it out like a rotten *sorcadian* seed.

She turns, her thick brows high on her smooth, shining forehead. "Oh, so you speak now. Your tongue has found its roots on the day of my descension?"

Inside, my spirit folds on itself. It turns over and over again and gasps for air, but outside, I hold firm. "Why should I feel jealous? You are my sister and I am yours. Your glory is my glory."

I wait. Her eyes study me coolly, narrow into bright slits. The scabs on my shoulder feel tight and itchy. After a moment, she turns again, her hands a fine blur atop her head. She signals assent with a flick of her wrist. Braiding and braiding, overhand, underhand, the pattern is intricate.

I have never seen Yera so shiny.

I take a strip of brightly stained cloth and hand it to her. She weaves it expertly into the starfish pattern. Concentric circles dot the crown of her head. Each branch of her dark, thick hair is adorned with a *sorcadian* blossom. We have not even reached the water and she already looks like an ancestor.

"Supreme," I whisper. But no words are needed here. I pick up the bowl of sea snail ointment and dip my fingertips into the glistening blue gel. My stained fingers trail the air lightly.

"Mother's comb," Yera says and bows her head. "You may have mother's comb. I won't be needing it anymore."

I smile, something close to pleasure, something close to pain. My fingertips feel soft and warm on her neck. They tingle and then they go numb.

Yera's mouth gapes open and closed, like a *bebe,* a flat shiny fish. Her pink tongue blossoms, juicy as a *sorcadian* center. Red lines spiral out from her pupils, crimson starfish.

"Sister, spare me," I say. "Love is not a word that fits in your mouth."

The *sorcadia* tree is said to save souls. Its branches helped provide shelter and firewood. Its fruit, healing sustenance. Its juicy blossoms with their juicy centers help feed and please the old gods. To have a belly full and an eye full of sweet color is not the worst life. As I leave our Oma's house, the wind rustles and the *sorcadia* in Oma's yard groans as if it is a witness. I gaze at the *sorcadia* whose branches reach for me as if to pull me back into the house. Even the trees know my crimes.

Silver stretches over the surface of the sand. Water mingles with moonlight, and from a distance it looks like an incomplete rainbow. Our oma says this is a special moon, the color of blood, a sign from the ancestors. The moon is the ultimate symbol of transformation. She pulls on the waters and she pulls on wombs. When we look at it we are seeing all of the sunrises and sunsets across our world, every beginning and every ending all at once. This idea comforts me as I spot our oma in the distance. I follow the silver light, my feet sinking in the sand as I join the solemn crowd waiting at the beach.

There are no words here, only sound. The rhythmic exhalations, inhalations of our people's singing fills the air, their overtones a great buzzing hum deep enough to rend the sky. Before I can stop myself, I am humming with them. The sound rises from a pit in my belly and vibrates from the back of my throat. It tumbles out of my dry mouth to join the others around me. Beneath my soles the earth rumbles. That night my people sang as if the whole earth would open up beneath us. We sang as if the future rested in our throats. The songs pull me out of myself. I am inside and out all at once. As my sister walks to stand at the edge of the waters, I feel as if I might fly away, as if every breath I had ever taken is lifting me up now.

A strong descension assures that straight-backed, strong limbed children will be born from our mothers' wombs, that green, grasping roots will rise from the dead husks of trees to seed a future. The others dance around this vision. When one descends, all are born. When one returns, all return. Each bloodline lives and with it, their memory, and we are received by our kin.

Music rises from the waves, echoes out across the sand, a keening. The elders raise their voices, the sound of their prayers join. I walk past them, my hair a tight interlocked monument to skill, to pain. The same children who laughed in my face and taunted me are silent now. Only the wind, the elders' voices, and the sound of the waters rise up ahead to greet me. The entire village watches.

Oma waits with her back to me, in the carved wooden chair they have carried out to face the waters. When I stand beside her, her fingertips brush the marks on my shoulder. Her touch stings. The wounds have not all scabbed over yet. She turns and clasps my hands, her eyes searching for answers hidden in my face.

"Fele, why, why do you do such things?"

Our oma's unseeing eyes search but I can find no answer that would please her.

"Yera," I begin but her *tsk*, the sharp air sucking between her teeth, cuts me off.

"No," she says, shaking her head, "not Yera. You, Fele, it is you."

They think I don't hear them, here under the water, that I don't know what they are doing, from here in the sea. But I do.

I wanted Yera to fight back, to curse me, to make me forget even the sound of my own name. I am unaccustomed to this Yera. This silent, still one.

"Fele!" they call. "She has always been touched." "I told her oma, but she refused to listen." "One head here with the living, the other with the dead." "Should have never named her. To tell a child she killed her sister, her mother. What a terrible curse."

They whisper harsh words sharp enough to cut through bone. But no words are needed here. I have withstood assault all these years, since before birth. This last attack is borne away by the ocean's tears. They say my Yera does not exist. That she died when our mother bore us, that I should have died, too. But that was then and this is now and we are another tale.

It does not matter if she is on land or that I am in the sea. We are sisters. We share the same sky.

Though some spells, when the moon is high and the tide is low, and my body flinches, panics because it thinks it is dying, I journey inland, to where the ancestors once walked in flesh, the ones we carved into wood. I journey inward and I can smell the scent of *sorcadians* in bloom, the pungent scent of overripe fruit, and feel my sister's fingers pressed around my throat, daring me to breathe.

Tiny *bebe* dart and nibble around my brow. They swim around the circles in my hair and sing me songs of new suns here in the blueblack waters. Now I am the straight and the curved, our past and our future. Here in the water, I dwell with the ancient ones, in the space where all our lives begin, and my story ends as all stories must, a new beginning.

THIRTEEN YEAR LONG SONG

"If I could have another life, I'd take it," he said, sitting upright in the straight back chair. "This one ain't worth ten cents to me. I'd like to do things for myself again. Would give everything I've got for that."

He was sitting on his porch, staring at a field so green, it almost hurt his eyes. Rachel, Doc's middle daughter, had cut the grass for him again, and this time, she hadn't bagged it yet. The grass lay in soft piles and clumps all along the neatly-trimmed rows. Suddenly, he wanted to jump again, to leap and roll in the mounds of grass like he did when he was little. If he could, he would scoot the red, peeling chair back against the leaning house's wall. If he could, he would leap clean over the front steps, scattering the piles like great clouds of green dust.

He sat there and remembered when his back was both iron and water, when his legs pumped like two pistons, and his feet flowed like the river beyond his acres; when his whole body carried him whenever and wherever he wanted to go. If he could, he would leap across the fence, which separated his land from the company's, and give those Viscerol folks a rough piece of his mind. Back in the day, he'd done more for less. But the world he lived in now didn't look like anything Doc recognized. Seemed like people had given up, even the earth itself. He gazed at his little patch of land and remembered how lush it had all been. Pollen got in his eyes, and the orbs, one brown and one blue, soon covered in mist.

Outside, the wind picked up a loose clump of grass, along with his wishes, and spun the green stalks into the air. A lazy *S*, the bottoms of the stalks waved like flags in the sky above him. He sat there in the chair, one hand balled into a tight fist, the other's nails dug into the rotten wood. Memory poured down on him like hard rain. Behind a curtain of pines and cypresses, a pair of eyes watched, and something listened.

A few days later, Doc rose, feeling more tired than he ever did. More tired than all those years ago when the nurses had stuck him so full of needles that he thought he'd turned into a pin cushion. "Y'all done drew so much blood, now you gon' have to give some back," he'd said, but the men had only smiled. Whatever they knew then, they didn't speak, and what they told him later he wished it was a lie.

Now Doc's whole body felt like he fell down the stairs and hit every step on the way down. He kept waking in the middle of the night with soil all over the thin white sheets and clumps of dirt all up in his hair. Doc didn't know what he had done or where he had gone. He took the dirty sheets and held them like dark secrets, balled them up like fists, and hid them under his bed. He tried to bathe, but he couldn't get himself in the lukewarm water before Rachel arrived. He could hear her fussing at the front door. His whole body flushed with embarrassment.

"Doc? Oh, Doc!" she cried and tossed the keys into the amber dish on the old phone stand. "Where are you?"

On Rachel's best day, her whisper was more of a shout.

Doc fumbled with his pants so long, he tired himself out, had to sit on the toilet seat just to catch his breath. He grabbed a yellow Bourbon & Bacon T-shirt and pulled it over his head. His beard got caught in the neck. Doc untangled it with his fingers, then stroked the white strands straight and smooth until the ends curled into cottony wisps.

"There's something in the blood," he muttered. Doc had known for over a dozen years that something more than memory coursed through his veins. His body was full of poison. They all were. Those with good sense had already gone and got out.

"Doc, you hear me?"

He took a deep breath before Rachel could come around the corner, bustling with those big hands that didn't know nothing about being ginger. He heard her hand jangling the knob at the door.

"Girl, why you always tryna bust in on me?" he asked. "You know this doxin got me moving slow."

"Dioxin, Doc," Rachel said and laughed. "And ain't nobody trying to see nothing you got!" She put her bike helmet away and fluffed her flattened hair.

He opened the door and waved away her helping hand. "I got more than plenty."

"Come on out of here, Daddy," she said, and chuckled, opening the window. "It's stuffy in here and too hot today to be fussing. I done cooked this food and I need you to eat it," she said, side-eying his linen-less bed, "so I can get on back to work."

"Y'all still protesting?"

Rachel sighed, forehead nothing but a crease. "Some of them still out there. Not as many as before."

"Ain't gon' do no good," Doc said. "You can't shame the shameless."

"Well, I don't know one way or the other," she said and bit off a hangnail. "It is good to know somebody still trying ..."

"Even if these muthafuckas ain't listening?"

"Daddy!" Rachel said. "Don't start up again. Last time you made a ruckus, your pressure went up."

"My pressure didn't go up, my patience just low!"

"Exactly! And either way, we got to get these coins, so ..."

Doc stiffened, lowered his voice. "I ain't mad at you, baby girl. You do what you can. And I appreciate it. I'm just saying ..."

"I know, Daddy. I know."

Doc stared out the window, frowning at the silhouette that overshadowed his land. He raised a clenched fist up and covered the water tower with his knuckles.

"Did you crank the truck?"

"Not yet," she said, and watched him lower his bony arm to tie his robe around his waist.

"When you gon' do it?" he asked. "When I finally get ready to go, I want to be able to get on down. Big Daddy can't crank hisself."

"Soon, Doc, you act like I'm getting my nails done here.

Let me clean up this kitchen *after* you eat, and then I'll start up Big Daddy. You and I both know that ole truck is just fine. Big Daddy gon' outlast both of us. Besides, you been up and about, I see. But you looking frail. Don't you want something to eat? Don't look like you ate all day."

Doc scratched his beard, avoided her eyes. "Not hungry."

"Doc, you got to eat. Can't be sitting up in here, nibbling on leaves, and that jug of water still half full." She clapped her hands, brass bracelets singing like wind chimes. "I'm going to fix you something extra, for later tonight. Put some meat on them bones," she said, and headed for the kitchen.

"Ain't nothing wrong with my bones," Doc whispered, muttering under his breath. "Ground is wrong." He mourned his garden and his empty fields, soured burial ground of what used to be. His last crops had come out so scraggly, he finally gave it up. Yield so bad, neither a weevil nor a worm would want it.

Anyone that knew him knew his family's roots had run deep in that land. Now he and Rachel and that rust heap he called a truck was all that was left. Outside, the wind whispered and sounded like somebody was calling his name. He wrapped the robe tighter around his waist and peered through the window. Nothing but shadows and wind. And that poison plant's tower.

He glanced over his shoulder and remembered the muddied linen he had hidden. No need to worry Rachel. Besides, he had no idea where he had been.

When Rachel came in with that smile of hers, the smile that never quite covered the worry in her eyes, he decided he would go ahead and eat whatever she had taken the time to make. No sense adding his worries to hers. The girl had enough.

"This is good," Doc said, licking his fingertip. "I don't think I could eat a mite more."

Rachel took the tray of pancakes from him and frowned. "You ain't ate nothing but syrup!"

Doc shrugged and drew the sheet around his shoulders. He couldn't seem to get warm. "I'm sorry, Slick Bean. Ain't had much appetite. Them hotcakes are good, but whatever I eat these days feels funny in my throat."

Rachel grunted. "Funny, huh?" She shook her head and eyed the empty Aunt Jemima bottle, as if she might answer back. "You ain't getting a fever, are you?"

Doc waved Rachel away. "Go on, girl. Don't want you to be late." He lay his head on the flattened pillow and closed his eyes, whispered all night in his sleep.

The radio coughed and sputtered. "... administration dismisses EPA scientists ... Toxic Substances Control Act of 1976 gutted ..." Doc reached up and turned the channel. "There's an old flame, burning in your eyes ... that tears can't drown, and makeup can't disguise ..." Alabama and a chorus of cicadas filled the front yard with song. Doc turned, confused. He climbed out of his bed, big toe searching for his house shoes.

He stood up. The wave of sound droned around him, the rhythm filling his head and clouding his eyes. The food Rachel had prepared him was resting on a plate on his nightstand. The window he swore he had closed was wide open, gaping like a dark mouth.

The hair on his arms rippled, and he caught himself from crying out. He hadn't been afraid for so long, he had forgotten how fear might feel. Rachel kept one of those drugstore cell phones for him, but he rarely used it because there was no one left to call. He thought about picking it up and calling Rachel, but he wasn't so sure what he would say once she answered. *Hey, daughter, a haint chasing me all through my sleep. Hey, daughter, I got mud on my clothes and mud all cross the bottom of my feet.* Rachel wouldn't understand none of that. And she had already started to watching him out of the corner of her eyes, when she thought he didn't notice. He knew what his most loyal child had been searching for, and he was determined to hold back the fatigue that kept calling him to linger longer in his sleep. Whatever was chasing him would have to come harder than that.

When Doc put on his knock-around boots and stepped out into the yard to greet the day, he liked to fell down when he saw the ruckus in his yard. A big-ass crack, zigzagging long like Moses in the mountain high, had separated what was left of his family's property. "Sweet geegee, great day in the morning," he said, and stumbled down the porch steps so fast, he nearly flipped over.

He had never, in all the long minutes and hours of his days, seen a sight like this.

The yard was all torn apart, as if a great hand from above had reached down and unzipped the dark earth. He walked over to the crack nearest him and eased over, his knee and his whole leg tense. Doc craned his head to see how far the hole went, and realized there was no bottom to see, just darkness leading down and thick, twisted roots and stones and things he wasn't sure he actually did see.

What he did recognize was the same source of all his and the town's troubles, that red-stained poison that the Viscerol plant had cursed them with. At one point, everyone and their mama had worked at Viscerol, and the money was good, too. But one by one, family by family, a sickness had come down on each of them, until finally, the only healthy families left had packed up their things and got on down the road. Only a few stubborn, hard scrabblers stayed on, Rachel included. That bloody water ran through each dark vein across the town, until only a few families remained. Rachel was all of Doc's own, the others, he knew, long gone, perhaps to sweeter grounds. Silver citadels of columns and pipes, smokestacks and tanks rose along the town's skyline like rusted spikes. "Relocate Fair Property Buy-Out" signs dotted abandoned lawns, jagged yellow teeth. Houses, once full of light and life, sat on their haunches, full of furniture, roofs lolling like broken baby dolls, doors flung open, bloated, wooden tongues.

Scavengers came to take what the families had not deemed worthy to carry on. Whole families had disappeared, it seemed, overnight, leaving all that they once owned behind to decay in the town's deadly dust. And now Doc stood, staring down into what he thought had to be the dark face of God's judgment. The Good Lord took man and put him in the garden to work and keep it, but from what Doc could tell, man had done a piss poor job.

And what had that hard, scrabble-back preacher said, before

he, too, showed his backside to Viscerol and the town, with its labyrinth prison-like plant that spewed poisons, and the giant water tower emblazoned with its red V? They had transgressed the laws, violated the statutes. They had broken the everlasting covenants, turned an ancient blessing into a new curse. Old Rev. Bowen had preached a word that day, as he took the church Bible and its baptismal altar with him. That they never should have let Viscerol build on their fertile land. That they should have turned those jobs down, and the money, too. Now newborns of townsfolk, who had been there for generations, were being born so sick, they had to carry the future away from there.

Doc didn't know what that was, rumbling deep inside the open door of earth, but he knew he didn't want to be standing around when whatever it was came busting through. He bolted up the steps as fast as his legs would carry him and knew exactly what he must do. He planned to be long gone, before the skies rolled up like a scroll and the heavens vanished like smoke.

"Doc! Oh, Doc! What is all this you got piled up in the truck?" Rachel stomped up the steps, the screen door banging shut behind her. Her bike lay on the ground, the rusted kickstand jutted out like a swollen tongue. The house was dark and the whole sky, too, but she could still see that Doc had emptied half the house and had it sitting up in the back of Big Daddy.

A groan met her before she walked in his room.

"What did you say, Doc?"

She put her helmet down and found him lying on his side in his bed, staring out the window. Rachel missed the times when he was a handful, when she used to get off work and find him, stumbling, mumbling in the dark, cranky as ever. Then he would cuss like a thief with an empty wallet, tell her story after story about some slight from the past, a friend who stole away from the broken, poisoned town without even saying goodbye, the neighbor who still had his good clippers and never bothered to acknowledge the debt. The other one, whose grass he cut as if it was his own, when the poison had made the man's skin peel off under the tainted bloodstained tap water. Thirteen years, he and his friends had suffered, undergoing varying stages of collapse and decay, until only Doc remained, steadfast and stubborn on his family's land. But it wasn't the land that worried her. It was his mind. Now it didn't even look like he was going to be able to hold on to that.

"Where have all the fireflies gone?"

Doc pointed a finger at the darkness outside. "There used to be clouds of them, all up through here. When y'all was little, you used to run out and try to catch them ..."

"In jelly jars, yes," she said, "I remember, Daddy. Why are you worried about fireflies? We ain't seen them in years, now. And why have you tired yourself out, packing up this old house by yourself? I told you, when you were ready to move, I'd be ready to move with you."

"'Cuz they gone like everything else."

"I ain't gone. I'm still here."

He turned to look at her. "Yes, you are. You and that old maple in the yard, the only things softening the heat. What you gon' do when my eyes close?"

"Oh, Daddy," Rachel said and brushed some lint out of her eye. "Why you always got to say that?"

Doc didn't answer for a while. He raised up on his elbow and craned his head, as if listening to a sound far off in the darkness. The wind whistled and the little strip of curtain fluttered like a moth's wing. Finally, he turned to her, his beard jutted out like a question mark. "Because I don't want you to be the last one left here."

Rachel rubbed her palms together, the sound like sandpaper. "What I tell you? When you leave, I leave." The moon rose from behind a cloud, the light spilling over the windowsill into the room of darkness, a sign and a symbol. "We got to leave soon. The ground ain't good."

Doc lay his head down and drifted off to sleep.

The next night, Rachel could hear the sound before she pulled up. When she dropped her bike and first walked up the gravel driveway, little husks crunching under her feet, she thought the sound was coming from the tree. She stumbled on an upturned root that hadn't been there before.

"Where did you come from?" she asked, and unsnapped the chin strap of her helmet, but the tree was silent. As she walked, the driveway sounded extra gravelly, almost crunchy. She thought she was moving carefully, but she tripped again. Not a root this time, but something hard, shell-like. Rachel turned on the flashlight on her phone and peered at the biggest husk she'd ever seen, liked to jumped right out of her skin.

"Lawd," she cried before she could catch herself, started laughing at her own fool self. Then she looked around and saw that the yard and the porch steps, all the way up to the front door, were filled with empty shells.

The warm spring night chilled her, the fine hairs on her arm prickled in alarm. She was fine until the air filled with a high-pitched, shrill-sounding song. The sound was deafening. Suddenly, everything about Doc's yard seemed strange and frightening. The driveway littered with hills of hollow husks, and the maple tree's branches that hung low in the darkness, as if weighed down by a burden only the wind could see. Hundreds of them, perhaps thousands, resting and waiting in the limbs, singing that song that made all of her flesh ripple and itch. A deep, pulsing sound like a great alarm, ringing through the dark scroll of sky.

And then she saw it. A wave of movement rushing up from what looked like the biggest hole she had ever seen. A mini-Grand Canyon ripped right open in her daddy's front yard. A few more steps to the right, and she would have been good and gone.

Rachel hunched her back, held her helmet like a weapon, and when a low humming buzzed her left ear, she flew up the front steps, practically barreling through the door.

"Doc!"

Inside the house, they covered the floor like a glittering, blue-green blanket. Rachel shuffled through them, trying not to cry out as they crunched beneath her feet. She found Doc lying there, wrapped up in his bedsheets, mud all over the bed, mud all over the floor. She called to him above the din, but he only turned his eyes away and would not answer. The more he refused to speak, lips sewed up, the more she found herself ripping at invisible seams. In her time, the town had seen its share of plagues, but this was a new marvel. And Doc didn't want to speak. He didn't even seem to want to be anymore. He seemed to be waiting, wrapped in his muddy cocoon, surrounded by the insects that cuddled him as if he was their own true kin. He held the sheets so fast that she'd grown weary and stopped wrestling with him. She patted his shoulder and left him to the mud, and the wind, and the rising moon.

Desperate for answers, she found herself breaking and entering. Shamed, Rachel asked for forgiveness as she crossed herself and climbed and picked her way through overturned piles of books, laid out like waterlogged corpses, all that remained of the town's old library.

After some time, Rachel discovered a thin volume, *Cicadas: The Puzzle and the Problem.* She forced herself to slow her breathing, to focus her eyes on the handwritten text. An entomologist's entry read, *Magicicada tredicula,* but by the time Rachel got to Doc's house, all she could remember was "magic Dracula," and something about thirteen-year-long broods and spirits. From the book's maps, no broods of cicadas had ever been documented anywhere near that part of the state, but given the damage already done, no telling what else the plants had unleashed on the town and its few remaining citizens.

"They can't sting or bite," she'd read at the library, her wheels now crunching as she pulled up to Doc's house. "They sing," the book said. "Their song can be a hymn-like trance, a lullaby that lulls weaker spirits to waste away, while others rejuvenate, are resurrected."

"They don't bite, huh, but they sho'll can swarm and scare the mess out of you," she'd thought. One of the books mentioned something about a divine test, a path to transformation. Rachel didn't have time for none of that. "Hush, loud bugs," she said as she slammed on her brakes. "Ain't no way in hell I'm finna let some devil dust bugs suck up my daddy's soul!"

Rachel was kicking the piles of shells out of her way, determined to get Doc, when the ground shifted and rumbled beneath her. "What did I say that for!" she muttered as she held onto the porch rail.

Low clouds of cicadas swept from the holes in the grass, hovered in the sky, headed for the maple tree. Rachel ran into the house and locked the door behind her but remembered the open window in Doc's room.

"Daddy!" she cried, racing to his bedroom. "I need you to get up." She reached for him but discovered that he was covered in a sticky film. If he wasn't her own father, scared as she was, she would have left him right there.

Rachel wiped her palms on her jacket and reached for Doc again. She unpeeled the cottony layers and tossed the dirty sheet onto the floor.

"I need you to help me, Daddy," she said. She spoke to him quiet, calm, like he did when she was a small child and had fallen and didn't want to get up. He had always been there for her; that's why she vowed she would always be there for him.

"We don't have to live in this place, no more. We can leave, Daddy. You can leave. We can go right now. Come with me."

She peeled the spider web-like substance from across his eyes. She was relieved to see recognition there.

"All right, Slick Bean," he said, as if waking from a dream, and reached for her outstretched hand. He held it, letting the warmth spread through his palms, and then he forced himself to rise.

❧

They waded through the carpet of husks until they were standing outside.

"Daddy, did you see that hole in the ground? I swear, I ain't never seen nothing like this in my whole life. You think it's fracking that did all that? Brought all these damn bugs?"

"Not all. I did it," Doc said as he leaned on her, letting her guide him to the green truck door. He didn't wait for her puzzled reply. "You know how it is! Here, people don't always say what they mean or mean what they say. They just be talking, thinking aloud. But sometimes, out here, the land be listening." He turned to the wind, the piles of husks, the moon and the shadows. "Can't a person think aloud sometime? Wrassle with a thought until they come up with their own good answer?"

He stood and pointed at the dark tower, the V lit up like a bright red scar.

"What's a good answer for this? How can we fight it?" he

shouted into the black mouth of earth. "We opened our mouths and welcomed them here with open arms, helped them build the very thing that would kill us." He turned to Rachel. "Some things you build, not so easy to tear down again. Now, what's the answer for that?"

The wind carried his cry through the air, and the question rested in the darkness around them, in the limbs of the tree.

And something else waited under the roots of the trees and beneath their feet. The wind rippled through the leaves, shook the maple's branches in answer. Loaded with emerald and red-orange cicadas, the branches swayed as the insects split their skins and struggled out. As the ground shook, they emerged from the dark, wet earth, emerged after a lifetime of waiting alone. Night after night, they had awakened. Wave upon wave, they came.

"The ground gon' sour?" Rachel asked as she opened Big Daddy's passenger door.

"Not the ground. Us."

The humming rose, a hymn that seemed to sing the world anew. Up from the jagged edge of earth, a great figure climbed out, six gigantic, jointed legs lifting it up and out of the land Doc and his people had once proudly claimed as their own. Iridescent wings unfolded from its wide, curved back. They glistened and sparkled in the night, unearthing mountains of soil and roots and old things not witnessed since the angel poured its first bowl over the sun, and the moon had opened like a great eye in the sky. Free from its dark sleep, the giant unfurled its wings and thrummed a deep tympani-drum sound that the little ones echoed and joined in, their song a bellowing in the air.

Rachel and Doc covered their ears and watched in wonder, as it raised its great, jewel-encrusted head and turned to them. It seemed as if a million eyes watched them from all directions, all at once, then within minutes, the creature stomped across acres of what had once been the town's most fertile land. The ground shook beneath its many feet, and the others raised their drumsong as it headed toward the Viscerol plant.

Safe in Big Daddy, Rachel and Doc stared at each other, not speaking in the airless truck. They held each other for a long, long time, and for an even longer time, it seemed like neither one of them breathed. Then they jumped, a startled, delayed reaction after they heard the thunder, a rush of mighty wings as the last of the Viscerol plant and its signature water tower crashed to the ground. The earth rumbled one final time, and Rachel and Doc shook in the truck that rattled like a great tin can. The wind howled, a loud keening, and the old trees lay low, then all was still and quiet, and the only thing they could see was the white mouth of the moon.

Rachel rolled the window down, hands shaking, the old handle squeaking. She started to crank the truck up, but Doc reached for the keys.

"Come on out and let me drive, girl," he said.

Tired as she was, Rachel didn't even have the strength to argue. She just shook her head and looked at him. "Daddy, you ain't driven Big Daddy in years."

Doc wiped a layer of gossamer threads from around his jaw and his throat. His hands looked smooth, sturdy. His heart felt ripe and strong. "When I leave, you leave," he said. "Step on out, Slick

Bean, and let's get up out of here."

Rachel stared at him, her eyes wide with wonder. "Doc?"

He hummed a happy tune as they drove off, some of that old country music Rachel pretended she couldn't stand. Big Daddy groaned down the road, only empty shells and withering husks remained. But above them and around them, hidden in the dark earth and in the green branches of trees, something like hope remained, listening and waiting for a warm spring night, and a mischievous wind to return again.

AUNT DISSY'S POLICY DREAM BOOK

"**W**ant some candy?" Aunt Dissy asked when I was seven. Delighted, I thrust open my hand.

"Let me see it," she said. She grabbed my hand before I could hide it in my pocket, forced me to reveal the map that was the dark life lines of my palm. Aunt Dissy shook her head and laughed, her face like water, rippling between a smile and a frown. "See here? I told your mama when you were born."

The women in my family aged like trees. To Mama, Aunt Dissy was like a grandmama, more big mama than sister. Aunt Dissy was strong and clever, nimble-minded and sure. She pointed at a dark groove, a short river rolling across my palm. "Your love line all broken, your life line zagging, too," she said. She traced the pattern with the red tip of her nail. "It's all writ right here," she said, her face resigned. "Cassie, you ain't never going to be lucky in love, and you sho'll ain't going to be lucky in cards either. But don't worry." She leaned over, blowing peppermint and something stronger in my face. My bottom lip trembled, her bright jewelry banged against her chest.

"You got the best luck of all, child, the best."

Luck? I was only in the first grade, and hope rose above my fear. Maybe if I raised my hand in class I would always know the right answer, I thought. Maybe if I didn't know, I could be invisible. Aunt Dissy stared at me, her eyes wide, knowing, bottomless mirrors. I wished I were invisible right then.

She dug her nail into the fat meat of my palm. I tried to focus my eyes on her thick silver ring, not the pain.

"You got the Sight." Her tongue held onto the "t," the word itself an incantation.

My face crumpled, my palm raw, exposed. For a moment, Aunt Dissy's eyes softened. She passed me one of her hard candies then stroked my palm with her rough, bejeweled hand, tugged at a loose plait curled around my ear. "If you don't understand right now, rest assured, babygirl. One of these nights you will find out in your sleep."

The red twisted wrapper fell from my hand. I stood petrified under the hard gaze of several generations of Aunt Dissys, hanging on the wall. Behind her heavy choker, I could see where there had been a deep gash in her throat. The scarred skin was raised and thick like a rope. Maybe the Dissys looked so sour because they were all cursed with the same "best" luck.

"Go on, play now," she said and frowned, as if she'd heard my thoughts, but I was frozen, didn't close my eyes for more than a few minutes for three whole days. Instead, I stared at the dark portraits that hung in heavy frames along the walls of every room. Imagined the navel names of the stern-faced women. Before, when I asked Mama about their names, she answered with one sharp word. "Dissy," she said and shrugged. So I fought off sleep making up a

litany of names and stories about the Dissys' mysterious lives. And
when the strain of wakefulness became too much, Mama found me
passed out under the sink in the back bedroom, owl-eyed and babbling.

"What did you do to her?" she asked and carried me away.
Aunt Dissy bit down on hard candy and grinned, the sound like crushed
bones. I didn't find out until much later that Aunt Dissy poured whiskey
in my tea, an old Dissy trick to force me to fall asleep. "The Sight's
coming one way or the other, Faye." Mama unbuckled my overalls and
put me to bed. "Even a mother's love can't change a child's fate."

Mama didn't speak to Aunt Dissy for six whole weeks. Didn't
matter no way. Aunt Dissy had told me something else that scared
me that first night. Peppermint couldn't mask the whiskey on her
breath, nor those words she had whispered, as if they were a gift.
"And with the Sight, you're going to live longer than the richest
woman, deeper than the sweetest love." Coming from Aunt Dissy's
lips, that didn't sound so good.

All day long Mama had tried to protect me, but when my eyes
closed, I was on my own. And like all the others born before, not long
after Aunt Dissy read my palm, the Sight came to me, just as she said,
deep in my sleep.

That night I dreamed my room was alive. The walls, the doors,
the ceiling pulsed and heaved as if they were flesh and breath. The
room rattled like the tail of a snake. In the night, dark as the inside of
an eyelid, I willed myself awake, refused to sleep for fear I would dream
the dream again. But when I grew weary of fighting off sleep, I woke to a
room that was collapsing all around me. Chips of paint floated down like
peeling flakes of dry skin, decayed flesh. The walls hissed and screamed.
I scratched the paint chips off of me, but they kept falling, dark and

jeweled snowflakes.

My body felt dry and prickly as the brightly colored paint stuck to me, covering my skin. I screamed as the chips crept over my arms, my legs, my throat and face. Only my eyes remained. I could see the dream world caving in on me, but I could not escape. Something or someone was holding me, holding my breath. It forced my mouth open, forcing me to swallow. I tried to swing and fight but my arms felt heavy, weighed down by the rainbow tiles that covered my flesh. Neither asleep nor fully conscious, I fought between worlds. I couldn't stop seeing. A mosaic mummy, I scratched and clawed and screamed myself awake. The skin on my throat, my arms, even my belly were in tatters.

I cried for my mother but it was too late.

The night the Sight came to me, the night it ripped my flesh into cruel tattoos, Mama died. I never forgave the Sight for taking my mama away from me.

Aunt Dissy claimed it was a heart attack. "Yo' mama has always been weak." She covered the mirrors and dressed my wounds with raw honey, forced me to drink a bitter tea. As I swallowed the peppery spice, she refused to let me see her. She wrapped my tattered body in cloths and locked me in my room. But it didn't matter. I already knew the look of terror on Mama's face. As the Sight's fire crept over my body, burned through my shredded skin, I let the pain take over, allowing it to numb the pain of me being left behind.

I never got a chance to tell Mama what I saw in my dream. Every night I waited for her, whispered her name as I tried to fight sleep, but Mama never came. Only Aunt Dissy. And the others. When the oldest came to me, the very first Dissy, I recognized her as if she had always been there, hovering in my room. She floated in the air above me, the look in her eyes like two open wounds. Her body was covered in what I thought at first to be tattoos. But she was riven in cuts and runes. Even her blue-black face. The others gathered around her, rubbed ashes into the wounds. They covered her with a dark stained robe and gently braided her hair, dabbed petals from bright flowers on her unblinking eyes.

As they worked, I recognized them from the portraits that filled the walls in all the rooms of Mama's house. The woman with the regal black bun and the high, lacy white collar that covered her neck, the Dissy in the long skirts, with bright ribbons that hung down to her knees. The other dressed in sack cloth, her head covered in a handkerchief. Still another dressed in a cloche hat, sporting glossy marcel waves and a fur-trimmed coat, wrapped around her glorious figure. I saw another Dissy wearing what might have been a lab coat. She puzzled me. I couldn't tell if she was a scientist or held court in someone's kitchen. All of them Dissys, the infamous line of women in our family, women whose minds wandered in the realm of the spirits, returned with the answers in their dreams. And from what I could tell, their stern faces staring back at me from heavy frames along the mirrorless wall, none of them had been full of cheer. Ever.

So many Dissys. And still others came, from times I could not recognize. They showed me things I didn't understand, led me to places past fear. And if I refused to sleep, they would sing in the wind. They would whisper in the rain. They would linger in the shadows, the walls of my house shaking, humming, hissing until I slept, until I wove their signs into stories, some I whispered to Aunt Dissy, some I kept to myself. And when I refused them too long, the dark circles under my eyes like black half-moons, they would carve the dreams into my skin. Signs and symbols haunted me, a bloody warning in the light of day.

I wore long sleeves for years. The others teased me, said I was sanctified. I never kept up with fashion, for fear that one of the guidance counselors would think I was a cutter, for fear that CPS might take me away. I covered myself until women in ink were as common as night and day, and then I set the scars free.

For most, dreaming marks the end of labor, a time for rest, reflection. For me, it marks when my labors begin.

My dreams held the fates of people I had not met, their lives netted with my own. And no matter what I did years later to try to change my 'luck,' my fate, what Aunt Dissy said was turning out to be true. She'd lived longer than nature allows, while my own mama had died fairly young. Aunt Dissy had seen more dreams than any single mind should ever have. Her body held the story, just like mine. And at the rate I was going, it looked like I too would carry her burden, the weight of the scars, the weight of years.

Longer than the richest, deeper than the sweetest love, she'd said.

But what's the point in living long if you're broke and lonely and all the dreams you hold are for everyone but you?

"Hey Slim." I jerk my chin up in the obligatory greeting and watch Mrs. Medina's green beanpole of a grandson bebop his way down the street. He has gotten to the age where he thinks he's grown. He has three long hairs on his top lip he calls a mustache and some knobby strands on his chin he calls a beard. He believes he is a man now and can make a play for me or any woman he sees. If he sees even the hint of a curve, no matter how old that curve is, he's practicing on you. It's almost cute. He has grown tall and strong and brown over this Indian summer, but the baby, the boy straining underneath the skin of the man, is all up in his face. I hear Katherine's little knock-kneed girls giggle as he struts by. His long arm waves as he gives them his back. Still wearing pigtails and bright bobos, they are too young to be *kee-keeing* in the manboy's face, but it's summer, such as it is, the ice cream man hasn't crawled by yet, and young hearts are for flirting, for loving, if nothing else. Or so I am told.

I stand in the shade of the fire escape, breathe in the scent of spices and my struggle herbs as the manboy disappears around a corner, down the brownstoned street. Aunt Dissy had the gift of green. Me, a different story. My rosemary looks dry, the peppermint and basil wilted, and the yarrow won't bloom. With my back to the kitchen, I can feel the spirits pulling the huge sky over me. The air feels heavy, humid with the weight of rain. Sheltered from the wind, my skin feels like ripe fruit about to burst. I haven't slept for nearly two days. A dry spell. Haven't had dream the first. Aunt Dissy's book sits on the kitchen table, atop its golden stand, its pages closed, judging me.

A lone black sock from the rough and tumblers upstairs just barely misses my head. That couple is always fighting. Everyone on the block already knows how that dream ends. I watch the sock sail down to the dirty street below, like a fuzzy feather, a sign or a warning. It falls in slow motion, a sign surely, but I don't know what it means. It's too early in the day and I can't tell which. The inside of my head itches. My eyes probably look like teabags. I'm afraid to look. In my mind I am two thousand miles away. My Sight is shaded up from the hot sun. Like a rainbow-tailed serpent, it won't budge until it's cool.

I close my eyes. Right now I don't want to see anything, don't want to hear, don't even want to feel. But I know he is standing outside the door before the bell rings.

"Come, sit down," I tell him and wave at the piano stool set up before my table. He sits as if the weight of his burdens has just sat down on the stool with him. His face and his thin shoulders worn down with worry, the remnants of his dreams linger in the wrinkles of a loose shirt that is too big for him. The man looks not much older than me, but I'm a Dissy—got more years than the stories in my skin can tell. I don't offer him a drink or a cool glass of water, don't want him to get too comfortable here. The hard, backless stool is perfect, uncomfortable by design. When I had that old cushy armchair, fools asked me questions late into the night. The frightened and the lonely. The vengeful and the resigned. My head hurt, my eyes stung, and my mind was weary with their dreams. I couldn't get them out of that seat.

You don't get what you want because you want it. The waxy skin of my palm, the faded scars, remnants of a jagged river, was proof that not everything is meant for you. No, not love or riches, health or success. With Aunt Dissy's words in mind, I enjoyed the comforts of flesh, the mysteries of skin. Pleasure came easy because I never expected more. While others gnashed their teeth and wept at the comings and goings of lovers, my heart drifted above dry land, tumbled into dark caverns like water, slumbered in the shadows. Intimacy gave the vastness of my loneliness a sheltering look. His is the face of a man who might turn on you at any time. As if he was just born, already wary of the world.

"If I ask a question, will you tell a lie or answer me true?" he asks.

"Depends on the question."

He leans on my table—I hate when they do that—presses his palms into the indigo Adire cloth so hard, that I can see the dark lines on his knuckles, the veins running along the top of his hand to his wrist.

"Do you have the Sight or do you just need money?"

I stare into his black pool eyes, unblinking.

"'Cuz if it's the latter, I can pay you for your trouble and save us both the time."

He's got an accent I can't quite place. Something with a river in it, deep and Southern.

Can he see my discomfort or am I invisible? What is the right answer?

A lie or the truth?

He is not the first to sit in my chair, nor the first to ignore the signs, to will the impossible. Trying to change one's fate is a lifelong Sisyphean task, but to change another's is like trying to move a brick wall by hitting it with your fists. In the center of this knotted thought, your desire, is the belief that if you will it, change will be. Rest assured, the people who come to me have bloody fists. They sit in my chair, much like him, with disappointment or hope or both peering from the shadows beneath their eyes. And they expect me to move the wall for them, expect me to make a lie a truth.

I watch his hands, now cupped in his lap as if they hold a message. The remnants of his dream waft off him like invisible smoke, snaking through the air over to me. I don't want to be bothered but my utilities are due. Mama may have left me the house but she left plenty of bills, too. Utilities and property taxes so high, I had to break down and take on worrisome tenants. The sock puppets upstairs.

"Yes and yes," I say. He thrusts five folded bills in my open hand. I slip them in my trusted bank, adjust my bra strap, pat my breast.

Listen, telling lies is easier than reading, and reading is harder than telling the truth. It had been hard even with Aunt Dissy at my side. She greedily watched me as I slept, combed through every detail of my most mundane dream. It became even more challenging without her, because I never thought I would be. Of all the Dissys who came to me, it's odd that Aunt Dissy never did. I waited for her those first weeks, but all I received from her defiant portrait was silence. And yet when she lived, I studied the ways and means, the art and the craft of reading dreams. And make no mistake, it is an art, the delicate task of mixing the truth with half-truths, but she joined Mama and the line of Dissys before she could tell me all her secrets. Before she died I wondered if she ever would. Her death was a final sign of disapproval. The signs and symbols of the old policy dream book remained a mystery to me.

Truth be told, mistakes were made. After one mother came, her belly hanging low, her forehead riven with anxiety, that night I dreamed of a large sumptuous table. Luscious fruit, sweets, and bread were piled high around two bright brass candelabras with candles. I was so relieved to see the fresh fruit, the loaves of bread. I didn't notice that while one of the candles was bright, the other flickered in the dark, almost spent. I told the woman she had nothing to fear. Her son, would be healthy, safe. So when she gave birth to twins, one who wailed in her arms, the other who shed no tears but was still warm, I counted her loss as my own. I grieved, for all I could see and for all I did not.

It was with her, that first mournful young mother, that I learned the power of nuance, the strength in ambiguity. Neither was for charlatans to hide, but for professionals to appreciate. Every square-toed soothsayer and two-boots traveler knew the universal sign for the conception of a boy, but I'd failed to see that the pair of candles in my dream meant that she would give birth to twins. A novice, I could see all the signs but I misread the symbols. Instead I'd spoken to the mother as if her child's fate was assured. A jackleg error is what Aunt Dissy would have said, a rookie rushing toward the finale instead of redreaming and working the scene.

Long after that mother buried her child, I wondered if he might have lived or if I could have better prepared her for the loss. But even if I had known, and told her that her son would die, she would have hated me still. Never to return. Each day I woke with that mother's grief running down my face. But tears wouldn't help me. They never did. I had learned the hard way, the danger in misinterpreting a dream. It was almost as painful as refusing to see a dream at all, and I wanted nothing more than to be rid of Aunt Dissy's burden, my 'best luck.' I tried every drug and remedy I could find, lost myself in the forgetfulness of flesh, hoping something or someone would grant me the release of a dreamless sleep. But still they came, surrounded me. Dreaming awake, the Dissys watched from their gilded portraits, silent on the wall, the dream book waiting, as always, on its stand.

"A copious record of others' subconscious travels," one Dissy had written in her crowded, sloping pen of the late 19th century, but

I could find nothing in Aunt Dissy's book that would offer me relief. With its smell of damp roots and weeds, its Old Testament-like list of names all handwritten by Dissys, reaching back generations, its hand drawn apocryphal images and inked sacred numbers, the dream book offered the key to others' fates, but for me it offered no answers at all. For all of its passages, handwritten and collaged, Aunt Dissy's dream book remained an enigma full of hidden, unwritten codes I struggled to decipher, blank spaces I filled with fear.

And it was clear that no Dissys dreamed of their own deaths, for where one scrawling hand ended, sometimes mid-sentence, another began.

"What you see is not writ," he tells me, "not like in the Book of Life," he says. "You can be wrong, can't you? Sometimes it ain't all clear?"

I lie to him. After he tells me everything, about the unseen woman who haunts his dreams and makes him lose sight of his days, the faceless phantom, the haint that sabotages every attempt at love he makes. A lost love, perhaps, an old flame, an unforgettable ex? Most people who sat in that chair had more than a sore bottom. They came with stooped shoulders, bent from carrying the dead weight of the past. A relationship that would not be resurrected. Memories that should be put to rest and forgotten. But this was a different kind of hopeless, one unknown to me. I closed my eyes and rubbed my forehead, a finger at my temple, lying because despite the smoky tendrils of his dream, I couldn't see a single thing. The serpent slumbered, spent.

Sky released rain. The day was leaving without me but this man was still here. I could feel the spirits around me, hear them pounding the streets outside my window, but I couldn't get this man out of my chair. His sadness was a long, unbroken note slowly descending into madness. Anything else I could say would sound reedy, hollow to his ear. I could tell from his face. He was one of those hard-headed, fingers-in-your-split-side souls. I would have to show him. This is where the cards become more than props.

I pull out the pouch. Its worn purple velvet is smooth in my hand, the royal yellow stitching now only reads "CROW."

"You're going to read Tarot?" he asks, incredulous. He glares at the discarded crystals and the bowl of red brick dust, both silent failures atop the lacy table. I have already tried everything. He is not impressed. "Been there, done that," he says. His old genteel Bojangles act discarded, too. "Death card comes up every time, don't mean shit."

He's right. Skeletons and bones, black knights on white horses. Mine is a great dying baobab, the tree of life, cut down with a bone ax. A Dissy from the 1920s called the weapon the Bonecarver. She even sketched the ax, a drawing I used to make my tarot. I stroke the purple velvet pouch, unloosening the yellow cord even as he protests. Death, the thirteenth trump, a major arcana, represents significant change. Transformation, endings, and new beginnings. I shuffle and reshuffle the deck, stall for time, hoping for some kind of inner vision. Nothing comes through, not even a dirty sock tossed out a window.

He shakes his head. He doesn't want to hear any of this.

"You got to close one door to open another," I say, stalling.

"Whatever. Just tell me what you see."

I'm tired. I drop the cards. He is closed to me. Just like Aunt Dissy. Distrustful and secretive, she never let me see her dreams. "That's the problem. I can't," I say. I can't look him in the eye. "I, I have to sleep with you."

His brow shoots up, his sad mouth almost turned to a half smile. "You what?"

"No." The words aren't coming out right. I feel like I'm already sleepwalking in a dream. "I mean I am going to have to sleep, to see..." my voice trails off. No sane way to explain it.

He studies me coolly. "You're telling me you're trying to go to sleep in the middle of the job? Go ahead then. I'll be here when you wake." That's not what I expected. I study his face again. Now it's my turn to protest, but he stops me, bloody fists still hitting that wall. "I don't know if I can explain it, but Mrs. Bannister—"

"Cassie. Mrs. Bannister was my aunt."

"Cassie," he said it as if it pained him. "It's really important that I get some closure here. I can't—" He stares at the backs of his hands. "I can't keep living like this. I was engaged. We, we could have been happy but I—I need to know who this woman is, what she is. I don't care about being with her or not. I just want this not-knowing to be over. So I can make a decision."

Something in his words tug at me. He is ripping up the whole damn script. Most people sitting in that chair wanted that other relationship no matter what. They wanted assurance. A sign that what they hoped for would come true. But this man didn't even know who he was pining for. This one just wanted closure. He wanted sleep at night—but don't we all? Wanted to know and to walk away—

or so he claimed. I wasn't yet sure if he was the letting go kind or, like my upstairs tenants, the kind with the stranglehold.

He told me how he first encountered her, in some old childhood nightmare of a dream that clearly scarred him for life. Typical guilty conscious mess. But as he spoke, suddenly the silvery threads of his dreams circled around his throat, coiled in the air, weaving and unweaving themselves like silk webs, shrinking then growing longer as they covered me, a gossamer cape until my eyes closed. A sea of blue green sapphires opened up and I stepped inside to see.

In this dream the ground is chill, wet underfoot, the air laced with sweet perfumes. Honeysuckle and moon musk sting my eyes; sibilant leaves prick my scalp from up above. I walk to an aged willow tree, groaning its complaints to a brook. Aunt Dissy taught me the language of trees. Sometimes they offer you real clues. Most of the time they're just bitching. This one complains about a bruise, a burden too heavy, a man named Iudas. Old dirt he needs to get over. I tune out the trees and adjust until my eyes grow accustomed to the darkness. I know the woman is there but cannot see her face.

She is hiding from me. I am not in the mood. "Look, lady," I call out, trying to keep up with her. "I'm not trying to get in your business or nothing, it's just that..." *Wait. Is this woman running from me? Oh, hell no!* As she flees, she's stripping, dropping whole swaths of cloth, brightly colored, glittering in the night. By now she is probably buck naked and there is no way I am following her into those woods. She is going to have to Hansel-and-Gretel on her own.

Night is never quite as dark as you think. There is always some starshine, some moonbeam, firefly glow. But not here. Wherever the woman disappeared to is like a black hole floating in the middle of the night. The backs of my eyes are itching, my eyelids and elbows twitching like a needle scratching on a record. I waver in the narrow band of zodiacal light, the faint luminosity of the horizon, the memory of a day that will not come again, the promise of a new one that has yet to begin. Ravens circle my head—a really fucked up sign—I swing at them and moonwalk my way back out of his dream. Like the others, he knows what he wants but he has no idea what he needs. He is asking me to peer into the darkness, asking me to see past what was to what could be. I tell him there is no harder work than imagining a future.

"Hold the deck," I command, eyes still closed. Time for some theater. He hesitates. "Don't worry," I say, opening my eyes slowly. "They won't hurt you." *Bless his heart.* He thinks I'm talking about the cards. He grips them, his sad mouth now a defiant frown. I take the cards from him, still warm from his touch, and spread them out in a fan. "Choose three." He studies the backs of the cards, his eyes narrowing at the design, a raven caught in the thick limbs of the blossoming world tree.

As I watch him decide, I wonder if I could love someone with the same unforgiving force that pushed forests from the deep ground. People think because they forget their dreams, that they are gone. They are not. The body holds them, the way rich soil holds water. Dreams are hidden somewhere deep in the bones, and flesh, and skin. The residue of his recurring dream hovered around him like a sweet musk, like sweat. With its scent I could feel the Sight stir inside of me, uncoiling again from the back of my brain like a waking snake.

He watches my face, unaware that I am still dreaming even as he sneers at me. He tries to look indifferent, but his eyes are now as sad as his mouth.

I try to recall the woman's shimmering steps. In the dream her path is the same. Down a road she doesn't want to travel, with branches for legs and twigs for hands. Raven's feathers pour from her mouth. A filthy starless sky of rain and blackbirds pierce the clouds, dark ribbons of flight.

I shake my head, try to think of another dream, something of comfort, of resolution, to cut off the images that unfold before me, a troubling silent movie. One of the Dissys, from the seventies, swore by iron and copper. A disc of metal to block dreams. The trick never worked for me. Even as I finger the heavy key around my neck, I can feel my Sight uncoiling and writhing in the air around me. And then they come. The wet mud shining underfoot. Trees twisting in the wind, the twig limbs reaching to grab his hand.

"Are you going to choose the final card or should I?" His voice sounds far away.

His hand covers mine and the shock of his touch pulls me from the vision, his dream.

"I know you saw her," he says. "I can see it in your face."

There's no telling what I look like. I want to speak, want to tell him how she hurts and for how long, but the words get stuck in my throat and slide down to the bottom of my belly.

How to tell him that she is lost to him? That the love he seeks is already a dry husk, gone for many seasons.

He must have thought he was reaching back into the past, that she would be as he remembered her, whichever spring it was when their future was green. Who is she? I do not want to know. I just know she does not want him.

All night, while sleep carries others to dreamland, I work at remembering, rewinding to study others' dreams, to rework the scene. But some signs you do not want to see. I told him a lie because the truth was too expensive. His presence fills the space inside my mind as he sits, arms crossed, legs tucked under him. I breathe through the odor of his sweat and desperation, my back curled, his final card hidden, face down on the table.

When he finally left, I stood on the fire escape, listened to the waves of bachata and kompa music floating up at a sky littered with stars. Night-time. I could still hear the children laugh and leap, shrieking through the darkness below, their shouts mingling with the sharp-edged call of car horns and crows. The ever present crows.

They knew.

The truth I would not admit to myself.

I had told him a sweet lie, a story pieced together of all the women I had ever known. Enough of the truth to make his spirit woman real, enough of a lie to make him release the cards and turn away. A lie stitched together with the threads of past lives, crossed stars, ill-timed fates, the worst kind of luck. Now the crows have come to pick it all apart.

"I'm not going to do it!" I cry. I run out to the terrace, kicking over my poor, struggle herbs. "I don't believe in you." The black circle slows. The sound comes not from outside, but within my ear. I scream. Regret every foolish word I've uttered. How stupid could I be? The circle of sound reverses itself. The murder of crows dives from the sky, but instead of cutting through the night, they circle inside my head. I back away, knocking over my thyme, and climb back inside. Slam down the window so I cannot hear. They shriek and call, wings clawing at the air. A cloud of them circled overhead, counterclockwise, haranguing me. Their beaks are sharp as needles, sharp enough to pierce the skin.

Bleeding or not, that night I refused to sleep, let alone to dream.

I snatch the cards off the table, hands shaking, I drop one. The Hanged Man, reversed. I stare at the figure entwined in lush green vines, surrounded by blood red flowers and gourd-like fruit, then stuff all the cards into the velvet bag. I double tie it, almost wishing it was a hangman's knot. If only it was that easy. I take the crystals and the bowl of dust and dump them into the trash. A red cloud rises into the air. I am done. *D. O. N. E.* Done.

I dig in my bra and pull out a couple of the crumpled bills he'd given me and grab my keys. Though I had never been up there before except to get late rent, it was time to see the sock puppets.

I stomp up the rickety stairs so they could hear me coming. The music, propulsive beats that make the whole floor shake, turns down before I even make it to the door.

"What's good?" a sleepy-eyed man asks. He has grown his hair out since last month, and his hair is half-braided. His girl lounges on a couch, frowning in the background. Piles of folded up laundry cover the floor.

"I need to stay awake."

He shakes his head. "Naw, sis, you sure? Look like you need to be sleep."

I hold my money out to him. He won't take it. I dig in my bra and pull out some more. "I don't want to dream."

He turns back to his girl, as if asking permission. She grabs a dress out of the basket and lays it flat across the couch. After she smoothes it out with the palms of her hand, she shrugs. Her purple twists dangle over her shoulders.

"I got you," he says, and disappears into a back room.

At first there was nothing. I slept the sleep of the ages. So much nothing I could dive into it. Hours and hours of nothingness. I had been resting, better than I had in a good, long while but then, just before dawn, the dreams—if I did not speak them, they would bleed into my waking thoughts. If I did not speak them, they would tear the veil away from their world into my own, rip and tear at reality, starting with my skin. Soon, nothing gave way to the Sight, the Sight becoming all I could see. The crows came to screech a warning. I had to tell him something. Enough of the truth to keep both him and the spirits away, or I would never have another day or night's peace.

Real hoodoos, sho'nuffconjurewomen can't be bothered with black cat bones in pockets or meetings at crossroads. Meetings take place in the mind, in the space where your soul sleeps, where all the signs are newborn, hidden from view. The night after I spent his money, the night after the crows shrieked my name, I hear the house split and crack. I open my eyes and see a zig zag scar across the ceiling above my bed. I watch it grow deeper, longer until I fall asleep. The crack grows while I dream. Then I see him.

"What the hell are you doing here?" I ask.

"What are you doing here?"

We avoid each other's eyes and shift on our sides. He is lying next to me, clutching my pillow as if it's his own. He is dressed in a T-shirt and some tighty-whities. I had pegged him for a boxer man. I'm not looking all that great myself. I am dressed in a jersey tank top that is so tattered, I should have been using it as a dust rag. I clutch myself self-consciously. My best bra is wet, hanging on the shower curtain pole, dripping by the sink. Neither of us admits that we've been keeping our own separate vigils in our sleep. We are so close, almost touching. I assume that this dream is another way for the Dissys to mess with my head, to tease me about latent lust, so I snatch the pillow back from under him.

"Hold up, that's mine," he says when his head bangs against the headboard.

"You're in my dream. My rules."

He looks confused. "Last night, I saw this crack in my wall and I..."

"Put your finger in it and it brought you here. Great. Jacking up my sleep." I snatch the quilt I sleep under year round and cover my boobs like a death shroud. "Go on back where you come from."

"I don't understand..."

He repeats syllables that make no sense to me. All I hear are the sounds of paper peeling back, a window's snap before it cracks, the shift of plaster under layers and layers of paint, the break...

"I'm going back to sleep," he says. "I mean, I'm waking up."

"Boy bye," I say and turn over.

With that he disappears.

A few nights later we wake to the sound of Mama's house breaking. Before I open my eyes, I know it is him beside me. Of all the people I could dream of waking up to, it's his ass. Not Mama, so I can tell her I'm sorry for not saving her life, for not seeing her dream sooner, not Aunt Dissy or one of the other Dissys, so I can tell them to kiss my ass, not an ex-lover I didn't really want to kick out of the bed, but him. Now I have grown accustomed to his scent. Irish Springs and strong minty toothpaste. He is using mouthwash before he goes to bed. I think I smell the hint of cologne or some kind of dime store aftershave. I am almost flattered that he has started to clean up for me.

He doesn't say anything about my ruined skin. My scars were like tree rings, bloody palm prints, maps of all the horrid dreams I'd ever had. He doesn't stare at them but he doesn't look away either. My scars are my shield. They remind me, even with so much death around, that I still live.

His eyes wonder briefly over the gown I had put on. It is the closest thing to a nightgown I own, and calling it lingerie would be a stretch. I have braided my hair neatly and hid the black satin bonnet I usually sleep with.

We spend the night plastering the cracks, caulking breaks and holes. We think if we make the repairs in our dreams, we will wake to fewer holes in our waking life. I suspect that neither of us can afford to regularly repair our houses. It sounds like he is almost as broke as I am.

This time the breaking sound is louder. We hope the walls will hold themselves. I don't know about him, but I definitely cannot afford to move. We clutch our pillows and hold our breath as the sawdust and plaster float down from the ceiling like fairy dust. I'm so tired in this dream, I can barely keep my eyes awake. There is nothing sexy about any of this. My house is dying all around me. It seems like each crack I fill reveals another gaping wound. We are afraid of what the house will do in our sleep, so now we rest in shifts.

When I wake after he's softly snoring, the front wall has moved. The door to my bedroom is gone altogether. Three of the Dissy portraits lay on the floor, facedown, silent as corpses. I panic. I feel trapped. But then I feel cool air tickle my scalp. The ceiling opens up and all the stars look in. I am more surprised at the sight of them than any of the other changes to my room. Suddenly the stars I never see in this city of light and noise and loneliness fill the night sky.

I need a witness. I shake him but he won't wake up. I look for paper and a pen. This is not something I want to write in Aunt Dissy's dream book. This is something I want to keep for myself.

We leave each other notes now. Not love notes ...just ... notes.

"The west wall, near the kitchen is going next. I think I heard it rumbling near the bookcase."

"A new set of stairs may appear out of nowhere."

"You overslept! There were more cracks in the hall. I woke to two sets of double doors before I could use the damn bathroom!"

I spend my days at the hardware store. I lug heavy panels, hammers and nails, cans of paint, brushes, and glue. My upstairs tenants don't even bother asking anymore. They know I'm not repairing their shit. They owe me two month's rent and are counting on losing their deposit. And how can I explain? I don't have the heart or the energy to kick them out anyway. I wobble into the brownstone and trip up the stairs, crashing into the walls. Cornrows pokes his head out the door.

"You OK, sis?"

I wave. Now they look at me like *I'm* the fuck up.

I scrape the old paint and smooth out rough edges. I can't remember what my mother's house looked like before, before Aunt Dissy moved in and came to take care of me. The only thing that remains the same are the walls of Dissys. And even they are changing. Their backs are still turned to me, but now I see here and there, a hand on a hip, the jut of a jaw, a bell-shaped hat turned to cover a side-eye in profile. I don't need to see the pictures or their poked out lips to know how much they disapprove.

Our hallways are now labyrinths. I say "our" because he and I now share the same dreaming hell—or purgatory. I can't tell which. We lurch through the house, shoulders stooped, eyes squinted up and frowning.

After a month of midnight renovations, the full moon returns again. To my surprise, the ravens disappear and the sky is washed clean. I turn away from the mirror and return to my empty bed that is not really empty anymore. I push his pillow over to his side of the bed. By now I know he likes to sleep with his back to the window.

In my dream, I see him as he cannot see himself. The landscapes of his spirit, as level and gentle as an open hand, without one fist for boundary. His goals and joys, memories and defeats are mine now. They lay glittering in small pools of green and brown and gray as he sleeps, continents on a bright unfolding map reaching out, unbroken across the sea.

I see myself, too, reworking a scene that is my own. Not buck naked this time, but wearing the shimmering scraps of clothing like rainbow strips of skin. Instead of running, I'm dancing, and all the breadcrumbs lead back to me.

I think I will tell him someday. On one of these nights when the wind sounds like the rustle of a blackbird's wings, when the stars look sharp enough to slice the black sky into ribbons. I will tell him of Aunt Dissy's book, of all the Dissys who are pretending not to watch us now, and of the woman whose face still holds my unimagined dreams.

NIGHTFLIGHT

Three o'clock in the morning, Old Mama Yaya walks at this hour unobserved, past tumbled-down apartment buildings, empty lots, and shuttered storefronts dark and asleep. She limps slowly in the streetlight, but there is another light. She looks up to her left, grimacing as if the gang graffiti has suddenly come to life, her gaze arcing toward the candle burning in the second-floor window. "Close your eyes, child," she mutters. "At this hour, even haints sleep." Adjusting her cart, she continues down the sidewalk, rattling as she goes.

The child sits at her makeshift desk made of cinderblocks and her daddy's old albums. Led Zeppelin, Muddy Waters, and Parliament Funk stare back at her. The child likes the album art, although she does not understand it. What does it mean *to get funked up?* She wants the *P-Funk,* too. She loves Minnie Ripperton's Afro, so lush and wild as a black sun. These are her friends, the music and the beautiful math behind the music. She imagines it as a kind of sacred geometry, a language that speaks to her when words are too difficult to say. It gives her the same feeling as when her daddy lifted her up into the sky, lifting her by her elbows, as beautiful as seeing a moonrise over stunted willow trees. In her daddy's hands she feels neither too fat nor too black. Skyborn, she is no ordinary, plain girl. She is a magician.

After the sun stopped shining in Memphis, Nelse decided that she was better suited to theory than to operations. After all, theory was not a product and Nelse was a ponderer. Her grandmother, who raised her after her father got shot in a failed home invasion, had called her a natural-born Figurer. All math was *figurin'* to her grandmother, and all math came easily to Nelse. She was inexplicably moved by it, the possibilities shifting like a multicolor Moebius strip, like the rainbow ribbons in her hair when her daddy's arms lifted her as a child, skyrocketing her into that other space. There she could sit with the cinderblocks that now looked like two ancient columns, sit with the paper Big Mama collected from the office building's trashcans, *'cuz most people wasteful and the rest ain't got no good sense.*

Theory allowed her to work mostly alone, and alone was how Nelse preferred life. There was less margin for error. When Big Mama would come home from the third shift at the factory, she would cry out in her tin-can voice, *Girl, don't tell me you been sittin' up figurin' all night, wasting your eyesight.* She would gather Nelse up in her arms, stare deep into her eyes as if trying to guess her future, then she would scold her once more, saying, *If you don't sleep more, you'll stunt your growth and have only one titty.* Nelse would pat her flat chest and giggle at this, then finally drift off to sleep, the beautiful equations and figures filling her head.

Big Mama was always saying funny things, but the words that meant the most to Nelse were, *Get yo' lesson, child, if you don't get nothing else.* And get is what Nelse did. Lying on her bed, the sky outside her window as dark in the morning as it was in the night, she wiped away the final remains of the odd, recurring dream and wondered why the sky used to turn perfect red at the end of the day. She wondered why the soap bubbles in her childhood magic wand formed in nearly perfect spheres, and why the human voice filled with emotion could urge a dying plant to grow or impact the cellular life of water. She wondered why a spinning top didn't fall over but instead slowly gyrated, its speed inversely proportional to the initial turn, why outer space goes on forever. And when the city did not burn up when the sun went out, she wondered how life continued to go on the way sap rose in the remaining trees, rose against gravity, the way the people rose, hoping to see that shine again, glimmering along the muddy river, hoping against probability, against fate.

The sky now was as muddy as the river. The first day the city woke and the sun had not, people stood out on their porches, circled the pavement around their lawns, and stared, just stared at the sky, as if willing the sun back. The young folk danced down the streets with flashlights, flirting and laughing loudly as if the sun had gone out for their pleasure. The sick and shut-in sat hunched at windows, clutching curtains, shaking their heads at these end days. Then the cell phones rang out until every line was busy. The media was in an uproar and the newly minted mayor had to be rushed to the Med after having a minor stroke. The children, those in public school and in private, were unashamedly happy. They leapt in their yards, jumped like grasshoppers until frightened mothers and fathers shooed them back into the houses. When the airwaves cleared, the mayor, mildly recovered, finally made a speech. Memphians were to get duct tape and garbage bags and seal all their windows and doors. This could be the result of a terrorist act, directed at the good citizens of Memphis. Who would do this, why, and what for were the questions that needed figuring. No one had answers.

Not the Shelby County Center for Emergency Preparedness, nor the governor and the congressmen, even the President and the CDC could not explain why the sun had gone out only in Memphis. Some said it was because the city had given up its charter, others said it was a Chickasaw curse for building on the bluffs and bones of the city's first inhabitants. And then there was some who blame every crooked thing on Voodoo Village. Whole families went by car, truck, and foot across the arched bridge, zooming across I-40 like hell had opened up behind them. Barbecue pits, student loans, and 30-year mortgages, even some marriages and Elvis, great day in the morning, Graceland!, were left behind without a backward glance.

No one commented on how the darkness lifted and the sunlight shone at exactly halfway across the M-shaped Hernando de Soto Bridge. If nothing else, that oddity alone was enough to prove to some that the city had been specially marked as cursed. "The Lord done spoken!" the preachers cried and gathered their flocks with them to safety. SUVs and church buses honked and stalled on the crowded bridge, the people turning their backs on the hulking Pyramid that glowered mutely behind them. Many remained hovering in the fields, camped out in West Memphis bottom-land in their cars and tents. They didn't worry about waiting lists for trailers, FEMA had not bothered even shipping any. Still others just headed on down to the dog track and casinos, carrying their last dollars and their Emergency Preparedness bags with them. And those who once thought they lived in Germantown, and Cordova, and Collierville, soon learned the true geographical reach of East Memphis. The sun was out in their neck of the woods, too. Only the good citizens in North Mississippi sat smugly in their homes, daylight shining through their curtained windows, shaking their heads at the spectacle that had finally overcome the City.

Nelse lies in her bed in what would have been late afternoon, twilight, just before the old evening, when the first lightning bugs would come out. Her head ached, migraines, vestiges of the crazy dream. The same she'd had since she was a little girl. Had someone already figured out why a focusing mirror must be parabolic in shape? Why a flat or spherical mirror won't work? There was a logical reason, a kind of quiet grace, she knew, but none for why the sky in Memphis remained forever dark, nor why she remained, when so many others had fled, praying and crossing themselves, never looking back.

Closing her eyes, she imagines various shapes; her mind traces the trajectory of light rays, ancient messengers of stars long dead before the journey. Silvered glass curving, nothing like the shadowy glass in her grandmother's chiffarobe.

Big Mama, are you with the stars, up in the heavens shaking your head, trying to help me figure this out? Yellow and gold light rays careened at angles to the perpendiculars, reflected at equal angles, slow danced like she used to by herself with her father's quiet storm albums, her mind heading back into space. Polished glass flexed and curled, like the dark lashes of her closed eyes. She wiped a tear away, imagining glass gently sweeping through space as helicopters droned above. Glass holds memory, mirrors distort reality. There had been no mirrors in her grandmother's house.

The world buckled to its knees when the sun stopped shining in Memphis. Just as it had when Nelse took her first algebra class. The lesson began with word problems, and while the teacher droned on about state tests, Nelse had felt herself warming inside, like when she'd lean her head against the window and let the sun warm her skin. At first they thought it was a power outage, a fluke by Memphis Light, Gas & Water, but when the signals uncrossed, MLG&W had promptly released a statement that basically translated as, "We ain't got nothing to do with the sun!" Nelse remembered when a straight-line wind had come flying off the Mississippi River, cutting down hundreds of the city's oldest oak, pecan, and poplar trees, all the way from the banks to the city's limits at Stateline, how they lay piled up all over the city like corpses. But this was nothing like that. The only trauma was that building inside the people. They spent the first day trying to figure out if they'd finally lost their natural minds, but NPR and the National Guard soon told them they had not gone stone-cold crazy. Memphians were fine. The sky was not.

"How the hell can particles in the air do this?" Marva, Nelse's next door neighbor, wanted to know. Nelse usually only saw her when Marva darted across her yard in the mornings to steal her water, "My dahlias take better to the sweet water in yo' pump." Truth was, Marva didn't want her own water bill to be sky high. Today she didn't even try to hide her hustle. Marva had stood in the middle of the devil's strip, clutching the flowers to her chest. "What's gon' happen to my garden?"

That first nightday, Nelse opened her bedroom window and the wind fluttered the lace curtains as if a handkerchief waved by invisible hands. It had to be a mistake, a grave error, as if someone had taken a great cosmic clock and sprung much too far ahead into the future. It had to be a power outage in the night or the work of Nelse's diabolical pills — which dulled the migraines, felled her nightly like an ax to a tree, and turned her into a sleepwalking clock-changer — or a dark cloud sent by terrorists, terrorists who hated the South and its barbecued pulled pork. Perhaps they really *had* lost their minds.

"What is the mayor going to do about this?" Marva wanted to know. She sat now on Nelse's lumpy sofa, too frightened to look outside again. Every light in the house was on, a parody of morning, as if it were the eve of a New Year. Nelse sat bravely by the window. "They say it happened after South Africa, all those years ago," she said. "Capetown water all dried up. Fire in the sky, too. The ash was so thick that for three whole days it was utter darkness."

"But nothing's happened. Our water's fine. We aren't in a war. Well," Marva said, giving Nelse an exaggerated side eye, "those foreign ones don't count if nothing's happened *here*."

"The weatherman said it isn't dangerous. The sun just isn't out."

"Are you going to the lab?"

"I don't think so. Were you going to the gym today?"

"I don't know." Sun or no sun, 24 Hour would be open anyway.

Nelse stared out at the gloom, shivering. She could only

imagine the commotion downtown at Buckman Labs, or in the 'hood, whose footprint was getting larger with every wave of white-and-hanging-by-the-skin-of-their-teeth-black-middle-class flight. All down the street, on the other end of the city, the young people wandered beneath the still-unlit streetlights, some with flashlights or lanterns, laughing. No old people out on the street at all, not in this kind of confusion, not with the sidewalks as loud as the Memphis in May festival and the flash of police lights like *Cops* everywhere. The chargers speeding up and down the expressway, blinding everybody, menacing and panicked, sirens blaring. In the house across the street, Nelse could just make out a couple sitting down to a candlelit breakfast. And below, in front of the neighborhood eyesore, the only mango yellow-orange house in the cove, stood a Haitian woman and her daughter, hand in hand, nearly indistinguishable in headwraps, talking quietly, looking straight up at the black sky. It was ten in the morning and as dark as the inside of an eyelid.

And Nelse hated it.

"We'll be alright," Nelse said, trying to sound like she believed it. "Not time to worry yet." But she looked over at Marva rubbing an ink spot out of the sofa's upholstery, and though it was not time to worry yet, Marva began to cry. Finally Marva announced they must call family and friends. No one should be alone. Nelse, who had no friends beyond her work at the lab, pretended not to hear as Marva desperately called one adult child after the other, until there was no one left to call. And so Nelse found herself doing the unthinkable. She agreed to invite Marva's friends over for lunch and make what they could from the pantry. For some unspoken reason they dared not go outside, though the city had finally put the streetlights on. Nelse imagined that the throngs of young people downtown had lessened with the dimming novelty of it all. Perhaps they'd gone inside to make love, busily conceiving the population boom they could look forward to, if and when the darkness finally lifted. "No Show Sun Spawns Blackout Babies," the *Memphis Flyer* might announce.

Marva made Caesar salad and pasta by dropping eggs into the crater of a flour volcano. She did this in silence, flour puffing into the air as if she had burst the seeds of a milkweed. Nelse thawed and roasted a chicken with cilantro, lemon pepper, honey, and herbs.

As she worked her stomach groaned, not from hunger but from fear. The idea of strangers rambling through her kitchen, rifling through her silverware put her teeth on edge. And most importantly, she had no idea what she should wear. She had long since stopped worrying about style, or the mysteries of her hair that broke combs and spat out plastic teeth and grease, or her problems knowing when folk say what they mean or when they mean what they don't say.

At noon, she heard a rattle from the living room, Marva drawing the curtains. Nelse understood. They were not chosen, they could not bear witness to the constant night. Then she heard — like an exhalation of relief — the sound of a match. Candles. The scent of vanilla and pears filled the air. Only two neighbors came, those who had heard of Nelse's work in *"the sciences"*: an elderly colleague of Marva's who'd also retired from the college and a kindly, nervous painter Nelse had once met briefly at an artist's reception at the Brooks. They were good, intelligent small-talkers at a party; neither was suitable for the endless night. They had clearly come out of loneliness. Nelse and Marva found themselves smiling and dutifully

filling dusty wine glasses and listening for a doorbell that never rang.
What was meant as a time of solace had become one of civic duty.

"I hear they are turning to rations," said the colleague, a
professor of magical realism with a graying Afro. Nelse wanted to
know what kinds of rations. "Gas," he said. "And fresh food and meat.
Like in the war." He meant World War I. The helicopters hovered,
dropping water bottles and energy bars from the dark sky. Marva had
stumbled on some, after raiding Nelse's water hose. "Who knows?
Maybe nylons, Marva." Marva would not have it. "Ridiculous," she
said, regretting the company of this pompous man. The curtains
blew open to reveal the unearthly blackness. Nelse said she could
not remember much about the war, nor anyone who had ever been
in it. The painter spoke up, and what she said chilled them: "I think
they've done something." Nelse quickly said, "Who? Done what?"
Marva gave her a look.

The painter winced at her own thoughts, and her brass
jewelry clanked on skinny wrists. "They've done something and they
haven't told us." *They're always doing something and they don't
tell us,* but Nelse kept her peace. The professor seasoned his salad
with a practiced flick of his wrist. Nelse feigned indifference. The
chicken still sat in the kitchen, glistening and uncarved, smelling like
burnt sugar. "You mean a bomb?" "An experiment or a bomb or I
don't know. I'm sure I'm wrong, I'm sure — But you know they keep
spraying us from the skies," the painter said and tapped her temple.
"You know it's not for mosquitoes." "An experiment?" Marva said.
She looked frightened.

Just then, they heard a roar. Instinctively, they went to
the window, where in her haste to open it, Nelse knocked a little

sandstone elephant over the sill and into the afternoon air, which was as red-dark as ever, but they could not hear it breaking above the din: the streetlights had gone out and now the city was alive with cries. Nelse wanted to kick them all out and listen to her father's albums. Why did the streetlights go out? It's unclear. Perhaps a strain on the system, perhaps a wrong switch thrown at the station. Perhaps a big-bellied squirrel, scampering where it wasn't wanted. But it was a fright to people, but not quite a mighty inconvenience. That was when the blackouts began, the rolling blackouts, meant to conserve electricity. Two hours a day — on Marva's and Nelse's block it was at noontime, though it made little difference — with no lamps, no clocks, no Wi-Fi, just flashlights and candles melting to nubs. It was terrifying the first few days, but then it was something you got used to. You knew not to open the refrigerator and waste the cold. You knew not to open the window and waste the heat. You knew not to open your mouth and waste your breath.

"Temporarily," the mayor said, now composed. "Until we can determine the duration." Of the darkness, he meant, of the sunless sky. When he said this over the radio, Nelse glanced at Marva and was startled. As a child, she had noticed how sometimes, in old-fashioned books, full-color illustrations of the action would appear — through some constraint at the bindery — dozens of pages before the moments they were meant to depict. Not déjà vu, not something already seen, but something not-yet-seen, and that was what was before her: a woman in profile, immobile, her hair a wild puff like a demented dandelion, her face old-fashioned, last century's features, resigned; her eyes blazing briefly with the fire of a sunspot; her hand clutching the wine glass in a tight fist; her lips open to speak to someone not in the room. A song in reverse, played much too fast.

"Marva?" she asked. Then it was gone. Her neighbor turned to her and blinked, saying, "What on earth does he mean by 'duration'?" What she really wanted to ask was why didn't Marva's children ever come? She didn't ask because she already knew the answer. They all did. They were afraid. They all were. They were all waiting for someone or some answer to come to them, to help them figure this all out. They sat alone in the darkness, reading by candlelight, as Nelse had done as a child, panicked as pigeons, waiting for someone to come, and yet they would not stir an inch. Why, the children had asked, didn't Marva just drive in her Benz and come to them? They were closer to the authorities and could take care of her better from their homes in Harbor Town. Why wouldn't she when she'd always done so before? They were busy with their own children, trying to keep them calm, entertained. No, they weren't afraid, just ... The adult children finally decided to leave without Marva, when they'd run out of reasons not to come to her. After the riots began, about two weeks later. She'd be alright, they rationalized. She was staying with a very responsible neighbor. They couldn't quite recall her name. The nice negro who worked at the laboratory. Didn't matter that they didn't know Nelse from Booboo the Clown.

Unused to company, unused to another mind living and breathing and tidying and, goodness gracious, *commenting* on her things in *her* personal space, Nelse doubled the doses of the sleeping pills, began floating through her day in a fog. It made the time huddled in the darkness go faster.

One nightday Marva convinced Nelse to drive out with her to the farmer's market in Klondike. Surely there must be ripe tomatoes still there? It was only the second time they had gone out of the cove since that first day of the darkness, and they were still unsure if they were right to do so — if it was frivolous to be seen in a tiny market with overhead mirrors to discourage the thieves and poor people jostling against wealthier ones, all grasping at the last remnants of normalcy and good health. Marva felt everyone should be in mourning. She had taken to wearing her pearls and best black dress, just in case.

"The mirrors should be covered," she had said to the artist and the professor at that first gathering. "Mirrors are portals to the spirit world. There are enough haints here now, don't you think? Shouldn't there be wailing somewhere? Nelse, put on one of those whining, crying, hiccupping records you call 'classics,' why don't you." Nelse could hear the exaggerated sniff from the kitchen.

"If you covered the mirrors, we won't have nothing," the Graying Afro had said, anxiously glancing at a reflection of himself. As the darkness hung over the city, unmoved, he had slowly begun to lose the iron grip he held over his tongue. He was a parody of a parody, a kind of Cornel West bow-tied 300 beard brigade, gone to seed despite his fastidiousness and absolutely pristine pedigree, he seemed to be losing his diction and his battle with the belly; and each day his ability to code switch effortlessly seemed to slip and fade despite the gray in his goatee, and the lines now permanently tooled across his forehead, he appeared all the more goatish as his tongue failed him. "Don't matter no way. They still gon' blame You Know Who. I can hear them now, *black president done burnt up the sun!* Mark my words, we'll be reading about that in the paper come Sunday." The artist shook her head. Light gleamed off her gold-rimmed glasses. Light gleamed everywhere: off cutlery and plates and crystal, sequins and earrings and pearls; it was indescribably beautiful to Nelse. Perhaps like the discovery of some rare bird, the last of its kind.

"I have a blind friend," the Graying Afro said, then suddenly, hopefully, as if he'd only been waiting politely to ask. "Hey, aren't you a scientist, a physicist working with lasers? Why don't you know what's going on?" For the first time that long nightday, Nelse found herself laughing. "Oh, I just study light theory," she said. "I don't actually do any blockbuster movie-type experiments. I think ..."
As she struggled to describe her work, the group stared at her as if she'd suddenly sprouted wings. For a moment she felt panic. Did she misunderstand? Did she make a mistake? Did the professor mean for her to answer or was he just being polite? Nelse stood, pondering this, feeling once again like an imposter, a faux human being. "You mean, you don't *do* anything?" the Graying Afro asked, incredulous. "They pay you to just sit around thinking up ideas?" Nelse wasn't sure if he knew he had said *thankin'* instead. The professor's speech was shifting, like Nelse's grasp on social decorum.

They stared back at her expectantly. "Yes," she said finally. "A little like what you did at the college. You didn't actually *do* anything yourself, did you? You thought and discussed what other writers did. You didn't actually *create* anything original, did you? Commenting on what someone else did, that's not actually doing anything, is it?" While his mouth opened and shut like a fish without air, Nelse found herself thinking about his friend. She hadn't thought about the blind. Aren't they lucky, she thought, and absently drank from Marva's wine glass. Marva gave her a look. Nelse ignored it. She couldn't possibly know what it could mean. She couldn't possibly explain to them that the star they'd once loved had an iron heart and was dying, had died ages ago. The professor went on seriously. "She says she can't help it, but it's satisfying. She says she hates herself for feeling it, but it amuses her that the rest of us think the world is going to end. Because it's the same world for her. Ain't nothin' changed," he added and frowned, as if he'd only just heard himself. "Nothing has changed."

"It can't be," Marva said. "She can't tell there's no sun, and the plants ..." She thought of her dahlias. "For her, it *is* the same world, dark as it's always been." Nelse relaxed her grip on the glass and pursed her lips. "That's stupid," Nelse said. "I'm sorry, Marva, but it is."

Marva turned to Nelse. "Child?" A moment later there were splinters of glass all around them, then great shards and then what seemed as if a thousand thousand dark-robed men running down the street, filling the cove, spilling into their manicured yards, and . . . torches, and lanterns, and certainly things were already set on fire in the street before the awestruck neighbors had the sense to stand up and run to the back of the house. It happened all at once, as if in a dream, and yet took an extraordinarily long time. There was no way to remember it right. First came the shapes, then came the colors, and when they moved, Nelse had to focus all over again to comprehend it, like a kaleidoscope. Without pen or pencil, all Nelse knew was that, when she awoke, wiping sleep from her eyes, she found herself shoved against the wall with Marva and all of them, her napkin in one hand and the wine glass in the other.

They spent the night at Nelse's place on an inflatable bed and the lumpy but irresistible cobalt-blue love seat she'd found at an estate sale. Marva had sensibly found one of Nelse's throws and tossed it over the wretched thing. Alvin, the Afro-Am prof, slept on the living room couch. Nelse stayed awake, *figurin'* and *figurin'*, clutching her father's albums and running fresh equations through her head. They had always been so beautiful, now they were useless. Six billion years before they would even notice that the sun had burned out, six billion years, eight minutes, and nineteen seconds. Could the six billionth year be now? If so, why only in Memphis? Outside, the darkness seemed to deepen. They could hear the low moan of the rioting streets as if a great monster, Godzilla or Ultraman, were being tamed.

"It feels like World War III," Nelse whispered, tracing the outline of Minnie Ripperton's hair.

"World War IV," the professor corrected her.

"I've never felt so dumb before in my whole damn life, not even when I was a child."

"Enough. You too hard on yourself," Marva said, yawning. "You'll figure this out. And if you don't, somebody else will. They have to. They always do."

"Do you know any blues songs?" Nelse hoped the bars would keep the chaos and the figures from crashing through her mind.

"Get some sleep, girl. We'll see how things are tomorrow. If they ain't blocked off all the roads, we can drive out to the river, think about crossing that bridge. Get on out of here. Hell, there's still sun in West Memphis."

"Well, shit, that's *all*," the professor muttered, then laughed in hyena bursts.

This was Nelse's turn to sit in silence. Then, after the numbers stopped turning in her head, "'I had a dream,'" Nelse said quietly, "'which was not at all a dream. The bright sun was extinguish'd, and the stars ... ' I can't remember how it goes. No," she shook her head, as if to erase the poem and began to sing, "Well, all last night, I sat on the levee and moan ... "

"Hush, child. It ain't yet time for no Negro spirituals."

"'I had a dream, which was not at all a dream.' Oh, what is it?" Why couldn't the words come to her as surely as the math? The numbers were racing faster and faster now.

"Hush," Marva whispered, pulling the throw overhead. "Close your eyes, child. At this hour, even haints sleep."

Nelse turned to look at her, but in that moment, the bay window crashed and the room was filled with glass and splintered screams. In the darkness, the women reached for each other. Nelse snatched Marva's hand and dragged her into the pantry.

They spent the night, wide awake, afraid to speak.

In what should have been morning, things were no better, debris lay everywhere. The others had gone. Outside, the quiet street looked worse. Rattled, Nelse and Marva prepared to leave, too.

"Do you want me to take you to your children? I'm sure we can find them. They could not have gone too far. Just over the bridge."

Marva bit her lip, finally gave a grateful smile. "Yes, I would like that. Thank you."

Nelse had just finished packing the car, taking the last of their food and water, when Marva grew still.

"Turn back," she said.

"What is it?"

"Turn back. I can't leave ... without it."

Annoyed, but thinking Marva had forgotten yet another of

her endless bottles of medication, Nelse steered the sensible gray sedan
back into the cove, parked halfway in the drive, the engine running.

"Do you want me to go look with you?"

"No."

Nelse did not like the flatness in that word. Something in the
back of her throat, an itch like the beginning of a cold, disturbed her.
This time, Marva's voice was devoid of its music. There was no echo,
only that unspoken *hush, child, please.*

Confused, Nelse waited in the car. And waited. Then waited
some more. Finally, when the engine started to rumble, sputter
in protest, she decided to go in. She had never been invited into
her neighbor's home, never thought anything of it, but what she
saw reminded her of that last, recurring dream. *In her dream, it is
another nightmorning and Yaya has gone to park her cart, lay her
head on the steps of the church, the Church of the Holy Name of
Jesus. It is three in the morning, but the hours mean nothing here,
and the child is not tired, though circles like half-moons border her
eyes, ashen her cheeks. From the window the child watches the elder
asleep on the stone bed. Yaya is so still, so very still, like a statue.
There is so much the child wants to say. If she could, she would call
out to her. Instead, she is drawing strength from the numbers, the
mathematics pouring into her like breath, drawing strength from
the stillness inside her.*

Nelse stumbles, pushes through Marva's front door and
steps into the living room. It is dark and still and almost silent as the
dream. Forcing her mind to take control of her feet, Nelse walks up
the stairs to the second floor. In the time it takes her to reach the bed,
to grasp Marva by her thin shoulders, to hold her damp head, Nelse

is certain she has lost her ability until she hears herself speak.

"Marva, wake up. I'm here. Wake up."

On the way to the bridge, Nelse drove silently past burning ranch-style houses and bungalows, past green City of Memphis garbage cans kicked up and down the streets, lying open on their sides like split carcasses. The radio was full of static, whatever had blocked the sun, now blocked all the signals. Nelse drove, not quite sure if she would even make it downtown. As she turned off Chelsea, Nelse found herself thinking about a different kind of figurin'. Her mind filled with shifting possibilities that made her stop at Watkins to wipe away fresh tears. And in these dark memories, Nelse would always later place one more figure in the scene, collapse or fast-forward time, just like in her dream, so that Marva made it to the bridge with her, and never looked back. Ridiculous to have thought of it then, but there it was. Glowing dimly in her memory, the memory of her friend, the memory of the sun.

RIVER CLAP YOUR HANDS

Night

All night long, the weary sound of water dripped from the roof into the bucket below, eroding her dreams. Ava woke from a sleep which bore her like an ocean, her mind still filled with the raindrop drum. The moon had veiled its face so that the stars could not see her cry. She woke and saw the street alive. She remembered when the neighborhood was submerged. She remembered when she was ruined by waters, ruined and resurrected by waters that bore spent seeds, the corpses of trees, and times that would never come again. Neither born nor named, time swam lifeless inside her and the lifeless tides swam with her. Ava touched damp garments that clung to her skin, close as guilt.

Watching the early morning walkers with their dogs at their sides, Ava was reminded that she lived among a people who believed in seasons. She lived among those who believed in the story and the song, among people who believed in prayer. Yet she knew nothing but the language of loss in a landscape she no longer recognized.

Ava rubbed her palm across the empty bowl of her stomach. Now she longed for the days when she felt full, when the nausea filled her and all she could taste was the salt from the stale crackers she nibbled on. Longing gnawed at her brain, consumed her waking thoughts. She never had the chance to hold it.

Rain

Rain made her anxious. The river swelling outside beyond the bluff filled Ava with dread. The rain fell faster, harder than it had last night. Outside, the walkers had long since scattered. Only the hardcore remained, refused to retreat. All was a sheet of gray steel. Inside, her mind was pitch black, except the brief flashes of light that stung the sky of memory. The couple who came for her, flashlights in hand, the beams reflecting off the violent waters that careened outside her door. Paralyzed, her body was caught in between. Trapped between a birth and a transformation. The old house had become a ship, tossed along the siren's song. Long after, terror filled her, even on the brightest days, flashbacks of all that she had lost. She was weary, tired of losing what she'd never had.

"Maybe it's a blessing," Grandmama said. "Maybe the Lord didn't want you to have that child. Birthing in the middle of all that strife. The Lord spared him." Grandmama was convinced the child was a boy.

"You carrying that baby mighty low," she had said. But that was then, before the first gills came.

"Sometimes, I wish He had spared me."

Grandmama sucked in air, a tone to freeze eardrums. Her eyes were cool water.

Wine

She had loved him. Most nights Ava told herself she had. She missed the way his fingers traced her flesh, the way his eyes widened, marveling at her smooth palms and their missing lifelines. She remembered him tracing the curve of throat, him lingering there until she could not breathe, the simple pleasure before his tongue found the gills. He had drawn away as if her touch had stung him. She never would forget his fear staring back at her, pupils dilated in widening circles, receding like the ripples in the river, him pulling away like the tide of the sea.

That night she drank red merlot, glass after cheap glass, and listened to Aretha, feeling like everything but a natural woman. That night her mind was all rivulets and rock pools. She spent the evening ruminating, returning to the same eye of water. Ava added three teardrops of pokeroot to her glass, and felt her throat constrict and release. Grandmama's rootwork. She always had a recipe but nothing could fix this, heartbreak. The flesh had grown raw and itchy inside, a wound that would not heal. Suddenly a soul in the lost and found didn't sound so unnatural to her. She had felt more than good inside, more possible with him. Now she felt undone, in flux. She was turned inside out. It was some time after the third or fourth glass, when the wine dribbled down her chin like ruby drops of blood, that she realized it was not his absence she mourned. It was the willful blindness that his presence helped her hide. Now how would she hide from herself?

Bridges

When Ava was a child her mother recited poems to her. Fierce poems of fault lines, of rivers turned, of a great tortoise whose back was as wide as the river's hips, of ancient paths lost and regained. They would emerge from beneath the Old Bridge. Together they dried themselves on the river's shore and watched the two trains running overhead. The air stung. It would take hours for Ava to perfect the rhythm of breathing. Sometimes drifters would leave piles of driftwood, old bottles, used cans. Her mother would make a fire and with a stick she would carve old signs and symbols in the soil. On those cool, mosquito-filled nights, Ava swatted flies and was warmed by her mother's company. Comforted by her mother's voice, her gills receded into her flesh, disappeared with the wind.

Mama kept her secrets close. Tight as water skins. "The Old Bridge is not the first bridge. Another lies in the water below," Mama had said, motioning with her hand. The thin membrane of webbing had finally dried and dropped away. It lay in scaly piles in the sand. "The first bridge was the river's spine, the Great Turtle. Our people swam across it, drifting finally into these waters. The first people we met lived up there, high on the hills." The high bluffs of the quiet river city were Ava's first glimpse of what would later become her home. Mama kept her secrets close. Ava learned this when she woke and discovered that she was alone. Mama had left her sleeping on the river's bank.

Hunger

When the river came alive, it hungered. It grew teeth and rose from its banks, swallowed the parks, the bending paths, the abandoned cars, the empty lots filled with broken glass, and encircled the bone yard, and the house. Ava woke to the sound of water running, like a faucet left on, and at first she thought it was a dream. She often dreamed of the river, the banks where her mother left her all those years ago, before the tall fishing man discovered her weeping by the still smoldering fire, before he took her home where she met Grandmama. But when Ava opened her eyes she realized the water had joined her, and that if she did not rise it would cover her and all the room. Then the cramps came, thunder deep below her chest. The baby, it was coming too soon. The water had awakened it. The water called to them both. Ava felt the gills open on her neck, the skin lengthen and stretch between her fingers. She needed to get out of the water, she needed to resist its call. Trapped between the birth and her own transformation, she climbed onto the top of the desk, then took a breath, plunged into the water's oily depths, swam out the door, in search of Grandmama.

Hearts

It was the blame in their eyes that made Ava shun their company. The silent accusation made her huddle in the staging area on her own. People wanted to know why, couldn't understand how. The mayor said to go. Staying wasn't part of anyone's plan. "Why?" was the question that rested on everyone's lips. Why did Ava and so many others decide to ride out the storm? How could they not know the storm would ride them?

Grandmama once told Ava that her husband's heart had just stopped. "It knew Amp wasn't gon' never quit working, so his heart just revolted against itself." She said she found him lying on the floor he had lain down himself. "He came from a people who always used their hands. Sometimes," she said, "against themselves. But not my Amp. He built this house when we married, built it before your daddy was even born. I guess it's good he didn't know his boy wasn't gon' live long as him. In his way your daddy's heart revolted, too. Sometimes it ain't good to love so much in this world." For Ava and Grandmama, the house and its memories were all that they had left.

To keep the house when her husband died, Grandmama cleaned cracked china and porcelain bowls, shined broken mirrors and windows that stayed closed. Her hands cooked meals for dinners she was never invited to, graced tables with straightback chairs where she could not sit. Where she worked she heard haints in the halls and would return in time to make Ava's late-night dinners, telling her stories that left her amused, enthralled. She complained that there was nothing truly alive in some of those other grander houses, the walls had veins with no blood in them. Grandmama said a house has got to breathe, got to have some soul and a little laughter to make its foundation stay strong, said not every house, not every family can carry the weight. She said what Ava and she shared made their home more beautiful, more sacred than the fanciest castle. Ava believed her, too, right up until the water came and took her past and future, her home and her baby.

Loss

Long after they lost their house in the flood, after they moved to another river city, Grandmama stood in line with hollow-faced folks. Worried and weary, she waited like the others to get her pills. The churches collected toothpaste and brushes, brought clothing and prayers. The kindness made the loss less sharp. The city's humid heat made them feel less naked. "But feeling clean don't help me sleep," Grandmama said. The water haunted her dreams, too. So she waited and swallowed pills she knew by color, tried to muster up an appetite to eat. Grandmama missed her garden and her homemade cha cha. Ava missed her baby.

Pain

When Ava found Grandmama, she was upstairs still asleep in her bed. The look on her face was pure disbelief. She refused to leave the house without getting herself dressed.

"I'm not going with all my business hanging out," she cried. "If the Lord gonna take me, I am at least going to have on my good dress." The pain in Ava's face made her stop.

"What's the matter, child?"

"The baby," Ava managed. "It's coming, I can't stop it."

"Stop calling that boy 'it,' and come help me pull down this ladder." The water was rising up the steps. Framed photos, dishes, and books floated just below them. It took all Ava's strength to help her Grandmama up into the attic. The pains came so strong, she wanted to lie down in the murky water and let the flood carry her wherever it willed.

"Come on, Ava," her Grandmama said, reaching for her. They waited in the attic, darkness all around them. "We in God's hands now."

Air

While the water rose and their lone flashlight faded, Grandmama hummed and sang. She began with the stories Ava heard as a child, the ones that told of a people who came from water, who lived and breathed it, the way the others swallowed air. The infant Ava had loved and feared rested in a worn sheet between them. Its skin felt smooth and warm to Ava's touch, but she knew when Grandmama first held it, that there was something wrong. The child, a boy, never took its first breath.

It was Grandmama who heard the people screaming below. She called back, thankful already though they had not yet been delivered. Racked with pain so deep it seemed to sear her belly, Ava managed to rise from grief, the blood slick and running down her knees. She took the flashlight and knocked out a hole in the roof. With each strike, the rain came faster, her tears harder.

"We're here," Grandmama shouted. Ava did not wait for the reply below. As Grandmama stood up, widening the hole with her shoulders and waving to the couple in the boat, Ava took the silent child, caressed its little winged limbs and released it into the water and the night. It was dark, later they would need a flashlight just to see the food they ate, but then, hovering in the house that was once her shelter, all Ava wanted was to see her child's face. For a moment Ava thought she saw the tiny body shudder as the water covered it. Inside she felt her heart revolt. He came from a people who always used their hands. Sometimes against themselves. Ava turned away, her face full of tears.

"What did you do?" Grandmama cried. Her eyes were fetid floodwaters, her voice cold enough to stop a heart.

Silence

The house they loved was a waterlogged corpse, but the city was not all they left behind. Something had changed. The water between them had darkened and risen like the river and the flood. They spoke in clipped sentences. Grandmama slept as much as she could, while Ava dreamed awake. She replayed each second of memory, trying to recall if she had imagined the infant wriggling, picturing if and how the child might have lived.

Thirst

The night rain came and invaded her sleep as stealthily as the night of the hurricane, Ava woke with a hangover and one question on her mind. She flung the coverlet back, placed one bare foot on the hardwood floor. Stood in the open door, wearing her good slip, wrinkled and wine-stained. She took a deep breath, inhaled the rain and the sunshower air. Grandmama had answered her call on the first ring.

Now, after making their way to the river's bank, Ava slipped out of her shoes, stepped into the muddy water. The river whispered around her ankles and her feet.

"Listen," Grandmama said, the weeds and trees swayed behind her. "The river is trying to tell you something: move, change. If your mama hadn't gotten lost, if she had stuck to another plan, she never would have met your father." Grandmama bent and picked up the shoes, shook loose soil from the soles. "Here, at the riverside, is where they began. When she left the last time, she knew your daddy would return to the same place where he first met her. She knew he would never stop searching, never stop remembering. Sometimes it's dangerous to love that much."

Ava had peeled off her dress and stood in the open air, the wind brushing her nipples, still plump with mother's milk. Her daddy had said she had her mother's face, strong bones, wide nose, wider forehead. Moon-marked, Grandmama had said, so she kept her in the sun. The closer Ava got to the river, the less air her lungs needed to breathe. She felt dizzy, her skin tingled and writhed with thirst. "Being lost helped us find you, Ava. You always thought the river took something from you, took your mama away, broke your daddy's heart, but maybe the river gave you something more."

Skin that was once dark and burnished now took on a copper-like sheen. Scales that were barely detectible appeared more pronounced. Ava began to walk into the waters, not far from the strip of sand where her mother had once told her lies and read her poems.

"I'm not mad, Grandmama, not anymore," Ava said. She unraveled the thick French braids she wore. Her hair puffed around her shoulders in a dark, wavy cloud. "I just need to try to find him. I know what I saw, know what I felt. I think he's alive."

Grandmama waved away a witch doctor who hovered near her ear. "If you're going, you need to listen to the river when you can't hear me. She ain't going to tell you nothing wrong. Listen to her now. She is telling you that there ain't no shame in changing. Baby, you are what you are. You come from this here water, but you also are part of this land. All them years I tried to keep you safe from this," Grandmama pointed at the Mississippi, "but when I wasn't looking, the river come to take you back anyway. So find what you love most from both of those things that make you, and then you go on out in this world and make yourself."

Ava walked deeper into the shallow water, felt the river whispering, pulling all around her. Grandmama clutched the blue sandals, crushed the sundress to her chest. "You don't want to listen to me, then go ahead, listen to the river. It's been calling you since you were born. The water is wise. When you feel there ain't no other way, do like this river do and bend."

Grandmama stood away from the water, heels planted in the sandbar, as if she was afraid the river would rise and take her, too. Unwilling to leave on bad terms, but unable to stay now that they were good, Ava rushed out of the water to give her Grandmama one final hug.

And then, as if the sky had waited for this moment, the rain stopped. The only echo was Grandmama's whispered "Be good, girl. I hope to be here when you come back," and the hush of the river wind. Ava took a deep breath, inhaled the last of the sunshower air. Humidity wrapped around her ankles, pulled her closer to the bank.

Sunlight shimmered

on the brown river's surface

the gold mermaid smiled

STARS COME DOWN

That afternoon three soldiers came to the Mound. They scattered the goats and the chickens, ran the stray dogs away with their steel-toed feet. They went to Candylady's house, black-booted and stoked up, laughing as she fumbled at the screen door. "Where the good shiz at?" they said and rummaged through her cooler. They stole her flat sodas and popped the tops right in her face. Pulled her liquor from the high shelf and danced, waving the amber bottles high above their indigo-stained heads.

"I'ma need this, and this, and this."

They stumbled and swung at each other, bumbling around like strange blueblack buffalo. The floor beneath their boots sounded like broken teeth and glass, the guns on their hips thumped, silent reminders. They snatched up Candylady's nowlaters and stepped on her lemonheads, too. One grabbed a pickle from the great glass jar and sucked it lewdly. He leered as the peppermint and juice ran down his busted chin. Candylady slammed a newly empty drawer shut. Bags of skins lay scattered on the floor. Each Saturday Booker

T's soldiers got in her stash, pushed her into the back room, and got on her very last nerve. She decided this Saturday would be the end of it. The end. She took a key from the counter and went to the back. They tumbled out the front door. Drank the warm pop amidst the skeetas and the flies and saved the dark liquor for last.

Auvonnetaye watched them from his window across the street, as he waited for his Papa to slide on his shoes. They both listened to the soldiers' raucous laughter, while the television whined and whispered its warnings. Papa borrowed the flat screen from a family of Langstons who lived down the street. They had tried to escape when the Mound broke out in war. No one had seen them since. Papa had watched their front door for three whole weeks before he crept across the street. Papa took their books and their flat screen. He left the music and their rotten food. Auvonnetaye was being raised as a Langston, too, but even at ten, he knew there was more to life than poetry.

Mr. Lerner had told him so.

The boy had grown wild and wiry like autumn weeds in the three years they'd lived in the Mound. Tall for a Langston, more built like a Nat, people sometimes spoke to Auvonnetaye like he was grown. Mama said it was his height that confused them. Papa said, "Naw, when you a black child, they always think you grown." Mr. Lerner said it was because Auvonnetaye was exceptional. Auvonnetaye didn't quite believe him but he liked hearing that.

"We're all exceptional," the child said. "We're Langstons."

"Well that may be," Mr. Lerner said, "but you are special. You are something else."

"Baba Shabazz at Academy says if you are too filled with

pride, you will have no room for wisdom."

"And Baba is right, boy, but years ago, Deacon Douglass said it was easier to build strong children than to repair broken men. Back then, the people thought he was talking about education. Back when to read was a death sentence."

"They killed you if you could read?"

"Boy yeah, reading could get you blowed off."

Auvonnetaye squenched up his face. "But knowledge is power!"

"Exactly. But in those days, they didn't want everyone to have power. If you got a little, that meant they didn't have none. Then them other ones sabotaged our schools and made just being born black the death sentence. If the water hadn't claimed them, I don't know if the people, if the Booker T's or the Garveys, or anybody else would have ever truly risen up. Deacon Douglass said to build strong children, but The Leaders of Umoja did better than that. They engineered a future."

"A future where we can succeed!" Auvonnetaye said. "They planted and we are the seed."

"*Hmpf,* they planted alright," Mr. Lerner said and rubbed the stubble on the back of his head. "The Leaders of Umoja genetically engineered the future. Took the best of us and made the best of you. All the great icons of our past, reliving again, stronger, wiser, greater. But you're not like them other seeds. You, young man, are more than they know. You are something else."

Auvonnetaye tried not to listen when Mr. Lerner and Papa spoke like that. Mama never liked it either, said it was dangerous. Her eyes would get all twitchy-twitchy and she'd warn Auvonnetaye to never repeat that. "You ain't got to say everything you believe out loud. Forget that testify stuff. That's why we got thoughts. Even the grass got secrets." So Auvonnetaye moved to higher, more familiar ground. He felt safer that way.

"Determined heart," Auvonnetaye said as he placed his small fist over the center of his chest. "Convicted minds," he said and pointed his fingertips at his temples. "Joined hands." He encircled his hands perfectly. "Umoja!" Auvonnetaye cried, determination in his brow. "Together we achieve more!" He exhaled, his back relaxing into a curved "C." "We do the Pledge of Unity every day. I know it by heart."

"*Umhuh,*" Mr. Lerner said and stroked his beard. "*Same purpose, sure direction, striding toward the future together,*" they sang in unison. "*We share all, submerge egos, overcome and overstand as One.* See there, I know it, too. Let you tell it, you just now reaching double digits and already know everything. But everything ain't always what it seems. Did I tell you the story of HighJohn?"

Auvonnetaye missed the dry porch talk of old men, the begrudging approval of Mr. Lerner and his friends. Of the Old Ones who had witnessed the Uprising, after the water had poisoned most of them, the ones who had been around to hear the negotiations that would make Umoja part of the reparations, Mr. Lerner was the only Old One left in the Mound, and Mr. Lerner was the only one who still called him by his real name. The Leaders of Umoja had said it was too ghetto, fifty-eleven letters to say one simple made up name. Even Papa had erased his son's given name from his speech. Somehow remembering certain things could make others easier to forget. Now the street that Auvonnetaye had come to know had grown as empty as Candylady's store after the soldiers had gone.

"Be right back," Papa said, after he brushed his hair and

struggled into his too tight coat.

Auvonnetaye had a summer nose. He followed his father into the slow rain. In the Mound, the weather was sometimey, alternating in fits and spells between the wet cold and oppressive heat.

"I said I'll be back."

Auvonnetaye paused, then turned back around, his body half in the house, half leaning against the screen door. "Finish your homework and don't let no skeetas in."

Auvonnetaye poked his finger through a tear in the wire mesh.

"Ya hear me?"

"Yes, sir."

Outside, burned out apartment complexes crowded the skyline. Windows disappeared into mist, and the cloudy sky rained down soot and ash in slow motion. Auvonnetaye stared out at the checkered world, digging his palm flesh into the wire mesh. He was irritated with his Papa and still puzzled by his Mama's visit in last night's dream. At 4:44 am for the past seven days, a strange woman with a black veil over her head had been sauntering past the house. She went up the road by the Langstons' house, she stood by the Zoras' abandoned, burnt out bungalow, and disappeared into the strange forest that had sprung up after the siege. Auvonnetaye waited for her to reappear but she never did.

Behind him, the news had droned on about the latest civilian deaths, the uprising in the Dunbar projects, the resistance of the Garveys and the few remaining whites, and now the news shifted to the weather. The eclipse was expected that day. There hadn't been a total solar eclipse visible since '24. Auvonnetaye hoped the sky would clear up enough for him to see it. He sure would hate to miss a sight like that.

He was supposed to be working on his Extras, but right now he was busy at nothing. The words kept running together, and he couldn't get his mind to concentrate. The more Mr. Lerner told him about the way the world used to be, the more he wondered how it could be. For Auvonnetaye, the present was like one of the Mr. Lerner's great calculations, which were nothing like what they taught him in the Academy. He felt he knew what the answer was supposed to be, he just couldn't tell where everyone had gone wrong. His worries followed him to sleep. Mama visited him in dreams. Came back to charcoal embers, whispered the names of people who did not live anymore. This time she brought twigs to rekindle something he could not quite remember. He would wake to braided dust, the twigs gathered neatly in piles around his bed. Papa said he walked in his sleep. Mr. Lerner said the ancestors spoke to him. Whatever they said to Auvonnetaye, they didn't make no sense. At Academy, he performed the expected motions and answered their questions as he had been taught. At home, was a different matter. Ever since they'd buried Mama, the boy walked around most days, his mind all jumbled-tumbled, confusion and grief. But night, the stars come down and it seemed they sat among him. Darkness changed the order of energy inside him.

At night his thoughts came shimmering, like the shirt-tailed ghosts of his earliest memory, back when he went to a school and played in a yard that wasn't surrounded by a chicken wire fence. Back when his parents lived in their own house, one that they had chosen, and were not forced to live in the communes that the Leaders of

Umoja had set up. Mama said this new black freedom was too much like the old. Papa said it will work out, just wait and see.

Mama had gotten tired of waiting to see. Auvonnetaye was getting tired, too.

Auvonnetaye put away the Academy's books and dug his hand beneath the fat-bottom cushion of her favorite chair. He reached inside, his fingers grasping in the darkness. The tablets were hidden inside a bundle of fabric, ripped from an old pieced together quilt, one of the few things his Mama had brought from their first house. Auvonnetaye could hear Mr. Lerner's high whistle drifting from the back.

"Ooh chile, freight train a comin'..."

He grabbed his tablet and streaked out the back door.

"Don't even say nothing."

"I couldn't find my..."

"*Mmmhmm*, boy, how I beat you here and it's your house?"

Auvonnetaye smiled but didn't answer.

"I know things are hard now, but you got to hold fast."

"Hold fast to dreams for if dreams die..."

Mr. Lerner said to hold on to dreams, but Auvonnetaye knew that dreams were not the only things that could die.

The children had stopped singing, voices drowned beneath the gunshots and flares. Auvonnetaye watched the solders' frenzied dance. As he walked slowly by them, he could smell the soldiers' sweat from their dark uniforms.

"We settled for synthesized blues," his mother said when she visited him last. She wore a crown of twigs braided through her hair. "Unrebellious saxophones." She mimicked the notes, punctuating each with a curved finger in the air. "Even slave songs lost their refrain," she said. She stepped over the soldier's still bodies, tracking blood with her bare feet. "My people, my peoples, have we lost our souls when we got free?"

For Auvonnetaye, Mama was both storm and sun. She was the blood and the bone. Even when the soldiers finally allowed Papa to bury her body, Auvonnetaye remembered.

Mr. Lerner remembered, too. He called the first days of the war, the God-bless-the-child times, strange-fruit-you-never-eat times. "You don't know nothing 'bout that," he said, his opening for every story he ever shared with the boy. He would summon Auvonnetaye with a wave, his hands coarse and swollen. To Auvonnetaye, Mr. Lerner was a genius, a superhero in the flesh. Mr. Lerner survived wars and worry without maps.

"Back when we took Umoja, when they used to call it Memphis and West Tennessee, we had to fight then. Wasn't no time for half-stepping. Mother Nature took care of half of it, we took care of the rest. All these soldiers do today is hum and spit," he said.

"And take people's shiz," Auvonnetaye said, grinning like a cricket.

"Don't talk like that, boy."

"That's what Candylady say."

"Candylady grown, you ain't."

"I'm the tallest Langston in my line," Auvonnetaye said, tugging at the "L" on the stiff collar of his shirt.

"Then your line is very short." They laughed as they walked to the outdoor shed Mr. Lerner used for Auvonnetaye's lessons. Papa called them his Extras. When Mama was alive, she hadn't approved. "You gon' get us all killed," she'd said, when Mr. Lerner would come for him, after the family's dinner. Now she quoted revolutionaries and sang their names in his sleep.

"Watch out!" Auvonnetaye said and kicked two fat yellow mushrooms that had popped up overnight. "Candylady calls them fairy rings. Say if you step inside, *bammm!*, you gone."

"*Bam* you gone?"

"*Mmmhmm*. Step inside, you come out in another place," Auvonnetaye said as Mr. Lerner opened the shed's green door. "Stay out the forest and stay away from fairy rings." Auvonnetaye kicked another for emphasis, grounding the lurid fat blossom into the wet earth.

Later, Auvonnetaye wondered if it had been his fault.

Mr. Lerner was telling him a story, trying to keep his mind off of his Papa and the soldiers at Candylady's house. Papa had been over there a long time. *Did I ever tell you about the time HighJohn tricked Ole Massa into locking up his own fool self? Naw, I didn't. Listen,*

HighJohn de Conqueror, high john never conquered, the smartest man on the whole plantation. He was the master of etch and stone, the trickster god of those who ain't got no home, the teller and the tale. And the tale I'm finna tell you is tried and true.

Mr. Lerner always started his storytelling by asking for permission. Since Mr. Lerner was always the oldest and usually the only elder there, he always granted himself the right to the story. And since Auvonnetaye was always the youngest and the only child there in the little garden shed, he always granted himself permission to hear the story. But that time, Auvonnetaye couldn't focus on Mr. Lerner's voice. He could hear the worry behind each word. All Auvonnetaye could think about was where his Papa was and why he was taking so long to just visit across the street.

Now the boy felt guilty that his father had been cross with him before he'd gone. The last time Auvonnetaye saw his mother and father together, they had been cross with one another, too.

"Ain't nothing wrong with what they did." Papa had said. He waved the spinach leaf on his fork at Mama before popping it in his mouth. "They did what needed to be done. What should've been done a long time ago. Why can't you be satisfied? Ain't you glad we free?"

"Is this free? I mean, you're the word man, are we and is we?" Mama pointed at Auvonnetaye, at the tower of books that covered every wall in the room. "Is any of this free? We're here, all together, but we can't think for ourselves. There is still somebody else trying to tell us how and what and who we should be." She turned to stare at Papa, who stood up to clear the plates. Papa hated emotion. He said unnecessary tears made his whole neck and back itch, and for Papa, all tears were unnecessary.

"They said we would hitch a wagon to our own black stars," Mama said, the water running down her face. "Why can't we choose our own destinies, if we are so black and so free?"

Now see, Mr. Lerner had said. *Massa didn't know ole HighJohn was sitting up under the window sill, listening to him and Missus tell all they natural business. By the time Massa come down the row to give HighJohn another order, looked like ole John done already finished it. That made ole Massa think HighJohn was a wonder, a marvel and a magician. Of course, we already know he was! He was a High God from the Africa Land. But to Ole Massa, he was just another brownskin black body twisting in the dust. He'd slapped his side and say, I got the smartest nigra in all of Tennessee. And ole HighJohn just smile, grinning from ear to ear, talking about, 'from river to river, bank to bank, that I is!' And that give ole Massa another idea. He decide he gon' start striking a wager with his friends from around the bend. If he bet on black, on ole HighJohn, he knew he could make some pretty coin off all of them highwaisted fools. So HighJohn played his part and played it well, waiting until ole Massa was walking round there with his pockets full and his head a little too puffed up.*

Ole Massa, HighJohn say, you is the winningest, sportingest man I know.

That I is, the man replied, jangling his coins in his pocket. Betcha can't out sport me.

Now that lip get Ole Massa's attention. He irritated, his nose all twitchy-twitchy, but he listening good, 'cuz one thing he do know is that HighJohn do deliver.

What you talkin' bout, John?

Ole HighJohn smiling hard now, nothing but teeth 'cuz he know he got Ole Massa now.

I tell you what we gon' do, he say, and he lean back and point to Ole Massa's walking stick...

Auvonnetaye never got to hear the end of Mr. Lerner's tale. He had fidgeted so that the elder got irritated.

"I see you're not gon' be no good until I see about your daddy."

"No sir," Auvonnetaye said and he lowered his head, his little fist squooshed up under his chin. It didn't take nothing to see that the little boy was a fidgety ball of anxious nerves. He was doing all he could just to stay in his seat.

"You wait here and I will be right back."

That was the last thing Mr. Lerner said to him.

One moment, Mr. Lerner was laughing and telling lies and the next moment, the boy heard a sonic boom, a monstrous fiery sound and pieces of life floated in the air all around him like some kind of strange confetti.

That day Auvonnetaye walked and walked, calling for his Papa and Mr. Lerner, but more soldiers ran past him and shoved him aside. He fell onto what at first he thought was a wet heap, until he saw the dead soldier's eyes. He screamed but no one paid any attention to the lone Langston. That day Auvonnetaye learned a lot more could die besides dreams. He walked in circles until his belly was in his back. Then he walked back to what was left of his home and fixed himself some dry cereal to eat.

That night Auvonnetaye shut his eyes and tried to sleep. His ears still rang and the confetti still floated in the air around him. He lit a candle by himself. There was no longer anyone left to light it for him. It took him three times to get the match to catch the wick, then the candle flame kept twisting in the darkness. Skeetas whined and moaned in his ears. With his eyes shut he saw the candle's flame take shape. It was the eyes of his Mama. It was the back of his father. It was the face of the dead soldier, oily with sweat.

He lay in bed, flattened by the weight of what he had seen, senses dulled by the persistence of heat. Inside he felt as lifeless as ashes. They fluttered around him, spilling from the hole in the sky above his head. Occasionally a dark figure would shuttle past the hole in the ceiling, then the night sky would clear again. He felt as if a great hand had washed clean the darkness huddling in the pit of his belly, so he gave up his bed and fell asleep on the floor.

While he slept he dreamed his Mama stepped through a mirror. There was an aura around her head, red golden light that blinded him for a moment. She sang his bedtime song to him, the one that would slow his mind and send him to another land.

Stars come down
Come and walk with me
Stars come down
Come talk with

Tell me a secret
only the darkness knows
inside me, a sun grows
Show me the mysteries
only the darkness knows
inside me, a universe flows

She sang so sweetly, he wanted to hold her but when he saw her face again it frightened him that it dripped like hot wax, that her features ran like rain. The dark water roiled and recoiled, and there standing before him was Mr. Lerner. His eyes were dark holes. His teeth fell out of his mouth, one by one, as he gazed at him. Auvonnetaye woke with a start, the sadness like lead in his belly.

"Follow me," Mr. Lerner said.

Auvonnetaye stood still. He didn't know if he should obey or run.

"You wanna hear the end of the story, you got to follow me."

Auvonnetaye pushed open the screen door and stepped off his porch. He looked around, rubbing sleep-crusted eyes with his knuckles. Ash and embers were smeared across his face. His hands were black, as if he had snuffed out a candle wick with his fingertips.

Down the street he could hear the rumble of great machines and the muffled shouts of soldiers. A group of scavengers sat in the yard of Candylady's still smoldering house across the road. Two women sat underneath what was left of her tree with bored eyes, fanning themselves with box tops. One or two chewed on pecans, mandibles crunch-crunching, pausing only to spit out the wet husks, the brown shells peppering Candylady's yard like dead cicadas. A man inside worked quickly, sifting through the splinters of wood and furniture melted like caramel on what used to be Candylady's living room floor.

No one paid Auvonnetaye no mind. He scanned the street, stomach grumbling, saw a stray dog posted up outside the house that used to belong to three Zoras. Auvonnetaye remembered the little girls with their neatly plaited hair, their bright ribbons and loud jump rope rhymes. He loved to watch them turn and sing the songs his Mama said don't nobody sing anymore. Mama said they would grow up to be the memories of the people. Auvonnetaye wondered who would remember him now. Everyone he had known or loved, Mama, Papa, even the Candylady was gone, but somehow Mr. Lerner had found a way to come back.

Mr. Lerner poked his head around as if he could hear the boy's thoughts. The golden hairs on his long, wiry Malcolm X beard twirled and writhed, as if each hair moved of its own volition. Auvonnetaye wasn't sure if he liked this version of Mr. Lerner, but his old tutor's voice remained the same, so the child did what he was told.

He followed.

Fear followed him, past the theater on Lamar with the gold and green marquee, past the crossroads where three black stray dogs chased him up 240, the busted highway cut off from itself, down the dark alleys and dead end streets, through the scraggly stumps, across the tired backs of upturned trees, over a brown battered N SHO A sign, into a clearing where it seemed, incredibly he found himself.

One minute he was scrabbling up a concrete block outside the abandoned casino, the next he was running from shadows, looking up into his own face.

They stood mirroring each other, one in the stark uniform of the Mound, the other in grass-stained blue jeans, a drab gray T-shirt, and a black hoodie. The boy held a gnarled, crooked stick, almost as tall as him. The handle was a bulbous tree root.

Auvonnetaye, dirty and weary, stood shivering, the fear finally taking hold of his mind. Silently he sang his bedtime song, willing his mother to protect him.

> *Stars come down*
> *walk by my side*
> *Stars come down*
> *come let me ride*

Auvonnetaye sang but she did not come. His whole body shook like a tambourine. His wide eyes darted back and forth like a cornered animal. Mr. Lerner was nowhere to be found. Maybe he had run too fast and left the old man with his ghostly beard behind. Now Auvonnetaye was in the woods on his own, the woods Candylady said don't walk in. He looked around for a place to hide, but then looked down and stumbled over the last thing he wanted to see.

The clearing was flanked by a wide, nearly perfect circle of yellow mushrooms, fat juicy ones, like the mushroom he had kicked when he had warned Mr. Lerner about messing with fairy rings.

Guilt filled his heart and tears stung his eyes, but Auvonnetaye didn't want to cry in front of his mirror.

The mirrored one stood and watched him closely. He seemed to know that Auvonnetaye was working hard to make a hard decision. The other child stepped back, as if to give him space. When he moved, the hoodie fell down on his shoulders, and Auvonnetaye saw a hollow-cheeked, pale-faced boy with red-brown hair. His eyes looked familiar, like his own, but he was no Langston. He had never seen such a child before. The boy was not like the people in the books the teachers talked about in the Academy. His eyes looked like he had seen the red confetti, too.

The wind brought the sound of running water. The chattering of birds hidden high in the treetops calmed the quaking until Auvonnetaye's body had settled on stillness. He waited to hear the high pitch whistle but only silence met his ears. Where had Mr. Lerner gone, when he needed him most? The red-haired boy turned and paused, as if an invitation. Was he there, beyond the forest, in the place where no one was to go?

Fear rooted Auvonnetaye to the spot where the first plump mushrooms sprung from the earth like bright yellow umbrellas. Tears stung his eyes. He remembered Mama's hot wax face, her features that ran like rain-stained tears. He wanted to kick the mushrooms, to crush their wide-brimmed heads, bury them beneath his feet. Why had they left him all alone? He couldn't be a Langston by himself.

"What's your name?" he asked the boy but he could not will the tears away. His Papa would want him to be brave but Mr. Lerner would want him to just be.

The boy tilted his head, the hoodie bunched around his shoulders. "John."

"HighJohn?"

The hoodied-boy offered a gap-toothed smiled. "Hi. What's yours?"

Auvonnetaye wasn't sure how to answer. Grief held his

tongue. Even the sun was sad for him now. Mr. Lerner would say, just enough light to drown in. With Mama and Papa gone, Mr. Lerner, too, he was no longer sure he was a Langston anymore. Would HighJohn laugh at the sound of his name? At fifty-eleven letters for three-syllables?

Auvonnetaye looked up and saw the sun hide its face. Shame warmed his own. Sunlight flares, then fades. The moon glided past, darkening the whole sky.

"My name is—"

Suddenly the scent of smoke and candle wax filled the air. Out of the corner of his eye, the woman in the dark veil danced past him.

"Wait!" he called. Her hands circled the black blur of her veil, still in motion. She was carrying something, large and heavy.

Auvonnetaye stepped through the ring in the forest. He crushed a fat mushroom underfoot. The veiled woman had left a trail of paperback books and canned tomatoes. They were strewn along the path like breadcrumbs. When he climbed the top of the hill, Auvonnetaye heard the soft tinkle of bells and saw a new world unfold beneath the passing moon. The red-haired boy followed him. A halo of light shimmered overhead.

"HighJohn," Auvonnetaye said, not looking at him, staring up at the sky. "Can you tell me the story? Can you tell me how HighJohn tricked Ole Massa?"

"Yes," the boy said and held out his hand. Auvonnetaye carried the stick.

Fireflies flickered, lit up the night as the two boys disappeared in the distance.

CHILD'S PLAY

She put the gloves on each hand and let the clear plastic snap back around her wide, brown wrists. It startled Her, popped and hummed, like when the first star blew nova. These were long-fingered, big boned hands, wide in the center, strong, generous. God found that She liked them, and it was good. She let the dry, smooth powdery sensation of the gloves sink into this new skin. Funny, She always forgot what it was like to slip into the cells and membranes, the blood and bone of these Living. It too was a humming, a hymn really, a kind of cellular symphony that reminded Her of why She'd made these Living most like kin.

She listened through Willie Mae's inner ear, Willie Mae who lived in a treeless shotgun house on Randle Street in North Memphis, Willie Mae who worked as a lunch lady in a charter school shoehorned into another school. God listened and heard the curious contralto of the women's voices. Their laughter tickled the inside of Her, made her want to add this one's voice to the song. God wondered what its key was.

"They think they the only ones run things. Don't they know we got power, too? Try to put some tired, gray, mushy broccoli on them trays, and let them take one bite. *One.* That child will never eat broccoli again. *Ever.* Not for their whole life," Ira Lee, the other Living one said, her eyes wide as a 12-quart pot. "Not one piece, long as they live, and breathe, and walk God's green earth."

"Child, I told you that one was crazy," Willie Mae said, nodding at a young woman's retreating back. "Always pushing through the line. Can't wait her turn, knocking the poor children over, and can't even speak."

"How they s'posed to learn about manners if they own teacher ain't got none?"

"That's what I'm saying. Children learn what you show them, not that foolishness grown folks say but never do."

"Amen," God said, and it was good. *Amen, Amen, Amen.* This one's voice! It reminded her of that other Living, the one that lived not so long ago. She had been singing since she was...what would this one say? God stretched and yawned, reached into wet, webbed electric lines of the Living's memory. What was that word, how would she say it here? Yes! She had been singing since she was a *little bitty baby, not even knee high to a duck.* A duck! God chuckled, and it was good. She liked how this one spoke, how all the Living in this part of the great, wide world turned the Word on its head and made others listen with another ear. Willie Mae was no Mahalia, nor no Bessie neither, but God could hear some of the same genius genes *hymnsinging* in the woman's blood. God wondered if the lunch lady knew she could sing, *sang* as they said around these parts. God wondered if she wanted to. God wasn't sure if Willie Mae, who had

stood in size ten, padded Hush Puppy shoes for fifteen years in the
kitchen of Scenic Hills Elementary, *Bobcats, go!*, this lunch lady who
fed a whole generation of Memphis City Schools students, but had no
children of her own, God wondered if she even wanted to sing. Did
Willie Mae enjoy music? God shifted inside the Living's skin and sent
a tiny, electric pulse in through the backdoor of this one's memory
rooms. Later, much later, perhaps a new cell would form and grow,
multiplying and dividing until a new thought was had. Maybe. God
wasn't sure, and see, that's the part some of the Living got wrong.

She wasn't omnipotent, all knowing. At least not anymore.
Over millennia upon millennia, Her memory had begun to fail. Or
more specifically, She'd loosened her grip, let the rope and its myriad
threads hang lax in Her great, gifting hands. The details, all the
many-layered membranes, the labyrinth electric lines of possibility
had stretched and yawned over the pulse of time. She'd let them
wander in and out of Her thoughts, let them twist and turn upon
themselves until sometimes She was as addled and unsure as the
eldest elder, navigating between the Past, the Present, and the Part to
Be, the Part that Could Be—if.

Like now. One temple faced the faded "Milk Does the Body
Good" sign and the other was turned against the "Power of the
Pyramid" poster on her right, but this *dang, Dang!* mandatory
plastic cap dug into her crown and her forehead, made her whole
brain ache. And it did not take God to know that a migraine headache
was no good. The ill-fitting cap made her head ache so that she could
not remember the parts of the recipe. Neither God nor Willie Mae
could remember if the recipe called for two parts relish and one-part
celery, or if it was two parts celery and one-part relish. God relaxed

and let the Living take a moment to sort it out. She liked how this one's mind moved through its problems, a most unusual thinker. This one took the parts of her problems and lifted them up like different colored squares in a great, big ole crazy quilt. She turned the thoughts around in her mind, thirty degrees to the left, forty-five degrees to the right, *indigo, cobalt,* no, *haint* blue fabric flipped this way, and *Red Banks, Mississippi* red that other way. God floated inside a cool, shady corner of the lunch lady's mind, sat and rocked a while in a great, comfy chair. The woman's thoughts blew past Her, welcoming as a river breeze. Willie Mae's thoughts shimmered and swayed as if to say, *"Come on in and rock a while. I have so much I must tell You."*

Willie Mae took the great glass bowl in her left hand, a giant silver spoon in her right. She mixed the tuna in brisk, bold, deliberate circles, *whomp.* The flesh on the woman's great arms shook and swayed, *whomp,* like a lazy comet's tail or an eight-year-old's snake hips in a hand-me-down hula hoop, *whomp, whomp.* The lunch lady's underarm flab jerked and hooked in a slow, elliptical motion. God relished this and rippled pleasure, the great eye of a hurricane. And it was good, so very good. Problem solved, haint blue and red banks now blended into a prayerful purple. The rocking stopped. God sat still, wrapped in a patch quilt of thought, humbled by this Living one and even a little afraid.

In the stillness, She remembered why She came here. Why she rocked inside a woman who was more at home in this school cafeteria kitchen than she ever was in her empty house with its mesh screen doors and storm glass windows mosquitoes still managed to get through on Randle Street. God remembered why She returned to the Living that She had made, why She explored the playgrounds of their unusual minds. It was always this *unpredictableness*, this universal element of surprise. She liked how the wise ones followed their first instincts. The recipe! It was indeed two parts relish and one-part celery. The children would love it, but something was missing. The lunch lady and God sent out tiny tendrils of thought. Of all God's gifts, She coveted nothing more than onions. *Hmmmm,* these She could not resist. What recipe for tuna fish salad could be complete without some relish—sweet if you could get it—some celery, some juicy boiled eggs, garlic salt, a dash of mustard, real mayonnaise—none of that "whip" stuff, God liked real mayo, God didn't like ugly—and a healthy dose of the sweetest, crispest white onions? The lunch lady's full lips smiled. *And since She was up South, in the land of the tastiest, why not indulge in a bit of pecans. Wouldn't sprinkling in a few make the tuna salad quite perfect, even more irresistible, delightful, beyond special?*

Pecans?

Willie Mae frowned, her great, gifting, skilled hand poised above the kitchen knife. It hovered above the neat pile of pecans, as if they were the wrong key on a grand piano. *Pecans? Nuts? In her mama's tuna fish salad? Might as well put raisins in chicken salad!* God felt the lunch lady's thoughts ripple, rumble even, the first thundered warning of a summer storm, resistance.

No one put nuts in tuna salad, and if one did, if one was odd enough, walnuts might do. But pecans? Pecans belonged in pie. Everybody on God's green earth knew that. Great, sticky slices of pecan pie with golden honey and maple syrup, sweet and pure. God settled back in the rocking chair, chuckled and waited. She let

Willie Mae's thoughts jump and tumble. Resistance whacked the pine floorboards of the woman's mind. An infinite hum buzzed between the turning ropes, like the old General Electric fan that whirred lazily on the canned goods shelf. The sound alternated between the consequences and the possibilities; a Double Dutch rhythm beat inside God's inner ear. She waited and listened, while the woman wrestled within herself, then Willie Mae dropped the doubled ropes. Her resolve rang out loud and clear.

And that was another thing the Living got wrong. God was neither the turner of the jump ropes, nor the jumper. She was the turner, and the jumper, and the doubled ropes that hit the pavement and the rhythm in between. She was all this and nothing. She could change the time, call out for a new rhyme, but in the end, She was the ripple of air that sang and hummed beneath the Living's jumping feet. Sometimes the spirit soared, flawless, formless in the air, and sometimes the spirit faltered, stumbled, and tripped over the twin ropes—and missed a beat. It was not God's place to choose the rhythm of the game, but only to maintain the music. She set the heart in motion, but it was not She who chose its lifelong rhythm or how it pumped and if or how the Living danced to the beat.

Willie Mae shook and nodded her head, while God sat in the corner of her mind and rocked quietly, tapped a restless foot. Finally the seesaw settled with a loud *thud*. The merry-go-round ceased its endless squeaking and spinning. Haint blue blended with Mississippi red. Willie Mae scooped the pile of pecans in her great brown hand, scooped them like a handful of jacks or the newborn, dying stars God had scattered across the universe.

"Willie Mae, what you doin'?" Ira Lee asked. God heard the

name and the tentative, nameless tune that escaped from Willie Mae's lips, and it was good. God clapped Her hands like a small child, rested them in Her billowy lap.

"Nothing." Willie Mae the lunch lady took the knife and *chopped, chopped, chopped* and diced the pecans into tiny bits of brown dust, so small an eye could barely see it. She then scooped them in the palm of her hand and sprinkled them in the great glass bowl of tuna. She took a finger, wrapped in plastic, and spooned out a taste. *Hmmmm.* God sighed inside her. The tuna salad now complete, she covered it. The aluminum foil crinkled and crackled beneath her heavy hands. The lunch lady hummed a lilting little tune to herself, quiet and shy at first, then her voice rang out bold and joyful as a rising sun. Willie Mae rested the bowl on a shelf. She gently closed the refrigerator. Her padded size tens seemed to glide and dance across the checkered linoleum floor. God rocked and waited inside, silent as a womb.

The next day, Willie Mae adjusted the plastic cap that covered the white, spirally curls atop her head. She would have preferred a hair net, but don't get her started talking about how they run down the public schools. The elastic snapped and popped her temples, etched a groove in her forehead. She adjusted it again. The tight band was giving her one hell of a headache.

"You a'ight?" Ira Lee asked and tied her Memphis City Schools apron twice around her wide, lumpy waist.

"Yeah," Willie Mae said and placed a few more empty trays

on the counter.

"Girl, you put yo' foot in that tuna salad."

"Thank you." Willie Mae let the compliment ease the crick in her neck and whistled a few more notes from her strange, new tune.

Comfortable now, she watched the first classroom of children clamor into line. They shouted and poked each other. They tried to skip, and when caught, scurried back and giggled into place. They traded insults and tossed jokes and dented cartons of chocolate milk as they did each day. The teacher, *Ms. Thang*, as Ira Lee called her, sashayed in line in a bright and beautiful, tight-fitting floral. This dress was new. All of Ms. Thang's dresses were new. Ms. Thang never wore the same dress on any given day. She tossed shiny, brown hair over thin, stooped shoulders and elbowed one or two of the third graders, as she bulldozed her way through the line. She carried her tray high above her head, stiff-armed like a University of Memphis running back or that cross-bearing Statue of Liberty over on Mendenhall and Mt. Moriah.

Ms. Thang did not speak.

Ira Lee shot her an evil eye and Willa Mae's apron shook as she laughed. When the child Sabra came, pony tail turned lopsided, the great black, wiry afro puff leaning in the heat and the humid air, Willie Mae felt sorrow in the back of her belly. This one had great round eyes, big and shiny as the cat eye marbles Willie Mae collected when *she* was a little girl. And a way about her, a tremble and a shake that made Willie Mae think of a frightened bird, like the ones long ago, cornered by that mangy stray cat in her Uncle Juicy's old orchards that became shotgun houses, and the shotgun houses that became high-end condos. Willie Mae grabbed the silver spoon and gave the great glass bowl a big dip.

"Here, child," she said. "Something extra for somebody special."

Sabra gave her a quick, dimpled smile, polite and furtive. To Willie Mae, the smile was like the sun that peeked from behind a cloud and hid again. The girl moved slowly, head bowed, through the line. Sabra did not tell the nice lunch lady that she did not like tuna. She did not tell the nice lunch lady that she never ate it. But something, a little tickle in the temple above her right ear, made the child take a scoop with her chubby finger. Something made her scoop it up, made her *pop* it right in her snaggle-toothed mouth. *Hmmm,* the tuna was good. Real good. What had the nice lunch lady said? *Something special for somebody extra?* No. *Something extra for somebody special.* Yes. That was right. Gold star for Sabra! The nice lunch lady had called her *special.* Sabra was special. Sabra liked how the lunch lady looked at her. Like she really was special. A real good girl and not somebody nasty. Not like Ms. Whittle looked at her, like she was somebody poor, like she was somebody *everybody* should feel sorry for.

There were three Jaylens spelled three different ways in Ms. Whittle's third grade class. Sabra waited in line behind Jaylen Number Three when the first hiccup hit her. Sabra's belly bounced and lurched, leapt up and down like a basketball before the tuna bounced from her belly and raced through her neck, tumbled past her tongue and slid over her teeth. Sabra shook and her cat marble eyes spun in her head as the plastic tray with the tuna and sweet green peas and the carton of chocolate milk and her spork spilled onto the linoleum floor. She was falling when she heard Ms. Whittle scream and the lunch ladies cry.

"Somebody get her! She's fallen!"

Two, four, six, eight warm, strong hands grabbed and held her up. Sabra heard Jaylen Number Three call her name, heard the children's high-pitched screams, like Ms. Whittle's loud whistle at recess when it was time to line up, time to go back in. Sabra felt dizzy, couldn't feel her toes. Her throat seized up on her, like when she sucked chocolate milk through a straw. Her skin felt hot and swollen. She could not breathe and for a moment Sabra felt like one of those red balloons that swell and blow up, the ones UniverSoul circus clowns twisted into puppies and princesses for the kids who had spending money on that third grade field trip. Then Sabra didn't hear anymore, then Sabra didn't think anymore, at least not for a second. Another wretch tumbled and shook inside. Her body quaked, tectonic shocks of tuna spilled down her crimson and navy blue plaid dress, ruined her, down, down to the shiny tips of her patent leather Mary Jane shoes.

Inside Sabra, God rocked and waited. She swung back and forth on a tiny wooden plank held by two great ropes. She listened for the *hum-hum-hymning* sound of the child's fretful breathing. She waited and wondered if this Living one would be alright, *a'ight*. She waited and wondered until She heard the E.M.T. grunt and snort. He muttered a curse, held the child in his arms, gentle, real gentle like a limp, black Barbie baby doll. God rocked and waited as the tearful teacher mumbled something about "an allergy to nuts." God rocked and waited as the school nurse cried, "anaphylactic shock." God waited until She felt the sharp needle's sting, quick as a cottonmouth's bite.

God tucked in Her knees, swung back real wide then jumped

inside the E.M.T. and listened as he muttered his litany of prayers. The siren blasted as the bus sped down Scenic Highway, turned on two wheels off Walnut Road, hopscotched through traffic. God waited and wandered as the E.M.T. called on Elegbá. He wiped his smooth, hairless head and held the little girl's hand. Bright blue and gold bead necklaces swung on his neck, tangled in a heavy black rope dangling with keys. The young man's prayers alternated between Cuban Spanish and English, sprinkled with the seeds of an ancient language God recognized as one of Her many names. God listened to the man's prayer and it was good. *God bless the child, God save and protect the child, God don't let this little girl die on my shift, shit, God, please.* She waited inside him and swung Her legs until, prayer ended, the child delivered, they both heard the doctor's gasp when she examined the child in the Emergency Room.

God pumped Her legs, threw back Her great lolling head, until the doctor waved at a weary nurse in violet scrubs and brand new shoes, until the weary nurse called for the social worker and the social worker stroked the child's wiry, curls that sprouted, thick and puffy around her temples, stroked her as she cried and snotted, whispered then sang a song of unbroken blues, until the social worker closed the door behind her, let out a heavy sigh, plopped down in a warped wheeled chair, and picked at the dirt beneath purple painted nails as she whispered in the phone, *hush, hush, hush,* to the school principal.

God waited and rocked, rocked and waited until She heard the school principal slowly, punch out the rhythm of 9-1-1, rocked and waited for the beep that would bring the police out to the elementary school on the hill. And God waited until She heard the mother's sharp cry as she collapsed, a broken pile upon the hospital's shiny floor. God waited until the father fell, in slow motion, like a great building imploding, in disbelief, waited as he wailed the name of the family friend who broke sacred trust, the name of the man who ground a small girl's innocence in the dust. God kicked Her feet, *pumped, pumped* Her square knees and took a great deep breath. Waited until She could hear no more, until She could feel no more, until She was certain the child would be in harm's way no more. God closed Her eyes, threw back Her great head, gave Her legs one last big *pump*, then released the swing's heavy ropes, and leapt back into the universe.

HEAD STATIC

Drums split skulls at breakneck speed. DJ Animosity amped up the bass, wrist spinning wicked circles of black wax as Claire ET whispered the evening's mantra in a voice full of rum and coke, delicately rolled fragrant cigarettes, inhaled Beyrooty blunt style. The crowd pulsed before them, one heartbeat pumping fists not blood, arms thrown up in the air, barely space to breathe, let alone dance. Claire ET sent her voice out, spitting rage, a gumbo stew: tongue splicing American English, Kreyole, and Lebanese French she'd picked up on the roads.

"Hold up!"

"Wait a minute!"

"Hold up—"

Behind the wheels, Animus heard the call, didn't wait for the response they both knew too well. He tore through the prayer with another soaring vocal from Lebanon's own strain of oud strings and traditional Nay, breathy as any blues harp, programmatic beats

raining down souls of Arabic fire, scattered and remixed. Claire didn't
have to look back to know his hands were a writhing blur above faded
keypads, hummingbirds flying backward across an indigo screen, legs
planted strong as cedar trees amidst a snake's nest of wires and plugs.
The music flowed through him—riddim memory—churning up choruses
and hooks from music's past, her words propelling him and the crowd
forward, rage turned to sweaty seduction.

Uhm, me so hungry... me love you long time...

She let her flow bend into a mindless curve, let the crowd's
body swell lift her mind up and out of the music's moment, beyond
the hunger's reach. Claire was somewhere above and beyond the
relentless beat at the pit of her stomach, her temple twitching. Her lips
automatically spun rhymes through time—ripe with plum lipstick, some
homemade gloss, a sista back in Little Senegal had made her with shea
butter, pressed oil from baobab tree. A hundred years before that, Claire
harvested the chadique fruit in the mountains of Haiti, extracting its
calming, regenerative powers from the citrus peel. Back then everyone
was some kind of ancient mystic, peddling mojos and homegrown spells,
warding off ailments not yet witnessed.

And how could they have known?

Then, despite the hype, the music was as simple as disease.
You either lived it or died it, wasn't no in between. Old heads
wore their rhymes like war wounds, wanga pakets, blessed badges
of honor, picked at the rhymes and discussed the pus they called
mainstream culture, the gentrification of hip hop, while the new
skool bumrushed the ivory towers, collected doctorates and dj
degrees from European uni-vers-ities.

Animus called it blasphemy, but that didn't stop him from

downloading his soul like everyone else. Used to be, heads carried their music in milk crates, the blue kinds tossed back from high-ass corner stores and around the way bodegas smelling like sour milk and spice. They used to tie bandannas through the gaps, makeshift straps, clever ones snapped guitar straps to them and slung them over their shoulders. DJ'ing was strictly for the strongboned, you had to put your back into it. They carried personal libraries of wax, held them in their arms like newborn babies, the album covers frayed around the corners passed down generations, but when they pulled the LPs out, the vinyl was so shiny you could see yourself in it. Black liquid mirrors, spit shine, correct, calling old spirits home.

And that's how Claire felt now. An old spirit, pinned under the black needle of earth, feenin' for a music that didn't yet exist. Hungry to feed on a sound that had not yet been invented. Waiting and listening, always listening, feeding but growing weaker. Listening still for a frequency, a series of notes that could send her up and out, through space, through time, but to where the first sound began.

Spit shine correct, Claire had spent decades foraging through black vinyl, seeking black gold, the sound, the taste of freedom.

And this before the arrival of synthetic knapsacks zipped and decked out with secret pouches, metal mouths to hold new tech. Now days, heads carried their music in their skin. Claire ET and Animus seduced them with old school flava, peddling salves in carefully remixed soundbytes, oiling the young flesh primed for limbo. Clare grew lightheaded, her temple pulsing to the beat of strobe lights. She had to calm herself, meditate on the delicious herb. She could almost taste the sound of their songs singing beneath their slick-stained skin.

"But hold up—"

"Wait a minute!"

It was time for another remix. This one jumped to the throwback house music days, no Detroit basement electronic grooves but Chocolate City heatwaves in tight biker shorts, doing the bump.

Sexy sexy... Ain't nothin' wrong with doin' Da Butt all night long...

E yeh E yay, E yeh E yay E yay Eh!

Ow, sexy sexy...

Claire liked the way they flowed here, no need for random mic checks or translations. They carried the latest speeds in sonar text beneath membranes. But weak as she was, Claire still refused to feed fully. She knew her refusal would set her boy off, and with Animus, the complaints were always in heavy rotation. He guarded his turntables, like some kinda Black Cerberus, badtalkin' the new folkways with his left hand, while feeling up the new tech with his right, sampling all music but loving only the blues. Animus said the youngbloods were too young to see with their inner ear, an easy criticism from one who had always been double-sighted. He had been traveling with her for one hundred and thirty years, had seen the changes before they'd come, even when Claire picked him up from the crossroads on the backside of Mississippi back in 1922, and rode him two counties past Clarksdale. Past Beale all the way up to Chicago, he had seen the changes. He had been her right side man, the background singer always at her side. Anthony Moses Turner had put down wood for 'lectric, and with Claire's help, managed to record a side with Memphis Minnie. They moved on after that, label wasn't paying negroes much of nothing no way. And by then Claire had been traveling long enough to know, wasn't nothing in rambling, nothing at all.

2

As usual, traffic was a mutha. Claire planted her left arm firmly on the windowsill, kohl-rimmed eyes blinking back dust, trying to will a cool breeze through the heat and noise.

"You a'ight?"

A nod, slow head shake. She drove with no pleasure. Last night's performance had left her energy low. She knew she had to move the crowd literally—every rhyme she made, the flow she played, had to connect in the heart of them. She fed off the music and their energy. When she first arrived on earth, she had not understood the music and the energy, the heart and the sound, was one and the same.

Now she was rolling strictly in conservation mode. *We wicked we wicked we wicked* was the ticker tape in her head, red neon lights flashing in her conscience's display. She wanted to turn it off but couldn't. She was losing control, a little more each day. Nothing would come clear until she had her feed. And they were still eighty-one miles from the desert.

"You sure you know where you going?" Animus asked.

"Yeah, why you keep worrying me?"

"'cause if you'd fed last night like I told you, you wouldn't be sitting here looking crazy. There was absolutely nothing wrong with that flow, nothing at all. That set could have held you for a while."

"How many times do I have to tell you? I don't have a while..."

Claire bit back the old impulse. She and Animus had traded enough wounds to last them a dozen more lifetimes. She didn't have the energy to try to explain to him again. He never understood, took her refusal to feed as personal rejection. Because he'd lived so long, he thought that what they had together was infinite. It was hard enough for her to concentrate, to stay in the moment, keeping her mind on his voice, no matter how irritating his words, her eyes trained on the war-ravaged road ahead of them. He didn't understand just how easy it was for her, these days, to let her inner ear wander off into the music he could neither hear nor understand— and never could. She stifled the impulse to scan for outlaw stations. They still weren't close enough, though no matter how long she'd been journeying, she always was surprised by what could be found in even the remotest, most barren of places.

No land was without music.

Even the most devastated landscapes yielded songs, of sorrow and joy. The last thing Claire needed, so close to the end of her journey, was to get picked up in traffic. Better to just let it ride. She sucked her teeth and listened as rocks crumbled beneath her tires. Better let the devil play on his own.

She slowed down as they passed a lone man leading a camel. His head was covered in a fading cloth, his djellabah and sherwal coated in a layer of sand, the color of the desert around them. The blue of his camel's bags had stayed with her long after his slow-moving silhouette had disappeared behind a cloud of dust and wind. Michel had told them to follow the ancient road past the city, beyond the Roman ruins, to a place where the last cedars remained, untouched in a Lebanese desert. There, he promised Claire would find what she had been looking for. The music that had begun haunting her past sleep. She let the window pane bite into her arm, the baskets of embroidered scarves and traditional brass and copper jangled in the back seat.

"Did you pay Michel?" she asked.

Silence on the other side of the car, silence for eleven more miles, then, without a word about whether or not he'd taken care of their informant, Animus reached over to stroke her thigh. His warm, rhythmic motions nearly beat back time and worry, nearly erased the years she'd been lingering in doubt about him. She had fed Animus in the way the music fed her, extending his life to a fraction of her own. But she knew, no matter his skill, he could not travel to where she must go.

She glanced over at him, her eyes a question. Still no words, just his rhythmic stroking, as if the skin's music was an acceptable apology.

Claire drove on in silence, then stopped just short of the pass leading to the mountain. From here, the Mediterranean Sea and Africa seemed a stone's throw away. She hadn't dared return in so long. Collecting the world's rhythms only to bring them back home. Animus had been a beautiful and fierce companion, rising up to every improvisation she had come to master, and even adding his own strange poison to the brew, but she could feel the pull of a music even he could not hear, a pull his inner ear was never trained to.

3

She whispered the first blues in a young slave's ear back in a Tennessee cotton field, offering the blue note like a blessing. The child's tongue had struggled for the notes, his face streaked with sweat. There, among the wild oaks and pecans, the n'goni and the kora were no longer even myth. They had to bend the flat fifth from catgut, made the body from pine. She'd shown the child where to tap the wood and how to make it whine like the great wolf's river. A flagrant violation of her mission, the choice was the only natural one she could see. She was sent to observe the creators, not to collaborate, instruct, or direct. But she couldn't resist because she remembered hearing that rhythm in Mali, the power it held and the hope it contained. So much had been taken from these people, flung across the waters in waves of sound that would bring even her elders to tears. Language and lore, their song and their spice, even their own mother's memory. She had wanted to give them a gift, a song of themselves, for themselves. A new music, perhaps the Great Going music, to serve as their sword and shield. A music she hoped would free not just them but her as well. A song to rend the world apart and sing it back again.

4

She had never seen a tree such as this. Its limbs curved and bent upward as if outstretched to touch the sky. Claire wanted to crawl beneath its branches, lay her head down and call her journey to an end. It had been so long. So long since she had first arrived on the planet, gathering songs with the others. So long since they had been scattered, Claire forced out, exiled and abandoned. She had broken the first covenants. *Start low, go slow, catch fire, rise higher.* Instead of taking notes, she had added her own. Fascinated by the diversity of sound, the life stories behind the music, unlike her sisters, she had chosen collective creation over collecting creations.

For years she wandered alone, until she found Animus, whose laughter and sheer hunger for music and life made her forget the judgment of sistren. But the song changed, as they often do. Words rewritten, notes rearranged, whole verses forgotten. She found herself seeking her sisters, curious about what they had made of the journey. Then one day she woke and discovered that she could barely hear their distinct signatures humming in the back of her mind. And when the last ones faded, she called out with her own, but no one answered.

Claire had to rely on instinct, on the faint trail of her sisters' old signatures. Feeding was like a whole-body vibration. Music transmitted energy to her body, forced her muscles to contract and relax hundreds of times per second. In this state she could absorb the flow from other moving bodies, dancers whose rhythms echoed and flowed with or against the rhythms of sound. It was while feeding that she had felt closest to her sisters. Now rattled by their silence, Claire desperately followed what remained of the others' trail. She collected pieces, tiny fragments of sound but she still had not completed the song's last sequence. *The Great Going Song*, the one that captured the true spirit of a world, its story, its many stories, the call that would bring their journey to its end and return them back beyond the stars. Fuller, richer, finally ready to hear their own world anew.

In the waning light, above the glittering dust of the desert, the burnished sky looked as if it too bent to the tree's will. Its roots rose out of the pink soil, entwined like a nest of snakes, then sank below. Claire and Animus stared at it, wondered how far the roots reached beneath the desert's embrace.

"What do you think? Fifty, sixty feet?"

Claire shrugged. "I'm not sure what this is. Maybe further." She placed her hand on the tree's smooth trunk and listened.

"Underground is underground because it must be."

Travelers had to negotiate sound in relationship to emotions, people, their stories. The way dancers negotiate space through choreography. She and Animus were caught in an old dance of their own making.

"You, me, we are rhythm. Moments in time," she said.

"It's been a long time, girl. We're good together."

Claire wasn't sure whether it was her or Animus who needed to be convinced.

She raked her nail across the trunk of the tree, pressed her palms into the bark, listened to the sounds hidden beneath wood.

"Why did we come here?" he asked, stared at the opening sky.

"To reveal the marvelous," she said, her voice far off, as if she was chanting.

"*We* are marvelous. I thought we were happy."

She wasn't sure how to answer that, the question he had not asked.

"A journey proceeds in all directions," she said quietly. Her hands still gripped the tree. "It's time I go home."

Animus sighed, hemmed between the mountains and the sea. "What did that brother say?"

"Which brother?" she asked, her ears, her eyes, the skin on her palms straining. It had taken her a while to get used to the man's sense of humor, how he would enter a conversation sideways, then lead you to a serious realm. Animus was trying to throw her off. She wouldn't let him. She had to concentrate. She was certain the music she sought was somewhere out here.

"The one with the big eyes," Animus was saying.

Claire frowned. "Do you know how many big-eyed brothers there are in this world?"

Animus laughed. "The fiery one you liked to read. Wrote a book about Beale Street that didn't have nothing to do with Beale Street."

"Jimmie."

"Yeah, Baldwin. Your *Hallelujah Chorus* man. What did he say about home? '...home is not a place...' "

"It's an irrevocable condition."

"Yes," Animus said. "It's irrevocable, I love you. So you already home. Ain't nowhere else to return to. You're here."

"No, not here," Claire said sadly and shook her head. She pulled away from the tree, wiped her palms on her pants leg. "It's out there, near the sea. Where I began." She walked toward the open car door. "Stay or follow," she said, leaving Animus to stare after her. It was the same choice she had always given him, right from the start.

5

In the beginning there was Jack and Jack had a groove and from this groove came the groove of all grooves. And while one day viciously throwing down on his box, Jack boldly declared, "Let there be House!" and House music was born.

Music was more than a reflection of culture. It was the sound of souls moved to their core. There were some clubs Claire and Animus would go to where the sound was so pure, the music made the dancers levitate. Of all the music he had seen born, House music was Animus's favorite. You could enter a club, the Warehouse, the Loft, the Music Box, Powerhouse, and hear Philly, New York, Chicago, Detroit, DC all on one floor. All textures, all styles. If the music fit in a set, it was the set. And after a while, the set was not complete unless Claire and Animus was there.

Ron Hardy, Traxman, legend after legend. Claire remembered them well. There were no seats, no chairs, no signs, just one green light and pulsing sound. Back then, Animus purchased two copies of every record. Original version of sampling. If he had a new record that no one else knew about, he'd black marker the whole label, so none of the other DJs could bite his shit. They were all traveling, incognegro, deep underground, especially after the backlash to Disco. Whole screaming crowds of youth throwing black music in piles, a bonfire of souls, compressed memory.

But House emerged from melted wax, rose like a phoenix from Disco's ashes.

It was one of those things that when you heard it, you knew something special was going to happen. When Animus's signature first made its way across the waters, Claire knew she had to be there. She was in Aux Cayes, cooling her heels in the whispering sea, despondent, long after the trail of kin had gone cold. She had thought she was so close that time, but she hadn't been physically near one of her sisters in nearly four hundred years. The absence pained her now more than ever. She was having a harder time rejuvenating the cells in this body, and the time between her feeds were growing longer and longer.

Claire was losing her appetite, her grip on this world's sound. The old curiosity that once propelled her through concrete jungles, sand-colored villages, and mountains was waning. More than ever she was aware of just how alone she was, cut off from those who truly knew her. Or at least knew what she had once been. She was alone and very possibly dying in this form. At some point, soon, she would have to return to the source, but without the others, without the full song, Claire was not certain she could do it. And without her sisters, the only one who could claim to know Claire was the man she'd cut loose, the one she'd let go, she told herself, to pursue other songs, higher music.

She was waist-high in the island's cool, turquoise waters, reflecting on what she had seen in this strange, nomadic life, when a wave hit her. Claire could feel something reaching for her on the other side of the ocean. Something new, something expansive, something perhaps even a little dangerous.

She followed the sound signatures, the vibrations in the water, sank so deep into the sea that she had to remember to come up for air. She needed air yet. She listened with her whole body, then eventually traveled back up the dark road to Antoine-Simone, on to Port-au-Prince, up into the sky. The new sound had led right back to the sidekick she had wandered away from years ago. She had not expected to see him. He was posed behind a table covered in equipment and wires, dressed in a white robe like a mad scientist or a priest. She pretended not to notice the sliver of gray in his hair.

After Claire had split that first time, Animus found himself immersed in the world of a new kind of DJ with a new audience, house kids. The early innovators used turntables and mixers to piece together one long track taken from the best parts of their favorite songs, looping only the parts that moved the crowd. Computer controlled, rhythm composed, their technique reminded Claire of her own. Secondhand stores and thrift shops is where they copped equipment. No access to recording studios didn't stop them from creation. Newborn music pressed on old, melted down vinyl, remixed to be reborn again. The DJs lived for the house kids, their energy. When Claire arrived, so did she. All of them did records, some of them did entire genres. It changed the whole game. High hats, claps, and drum beats, acid trax phuture shock. It was a sound, born in the underground, but it could not be contained. The groove spread. In London, house music had soared to the top of the charts faster than anything since the Beatles.

Claire found Animus, perched high up in a dim lit club, surrounded by his beloved crates, the albums she thought he loved more than her. He said it was the purest sound and Claire had to agree. He leaned over a pile of disco classics and Eurobeats. Dub effects and dropouts, tweaked tempos and layers and layers of percussion beats, he had an impressive arsenal of techniques at his disposal. He was DJ Animus, the architect of sound.

"So, you're jacking bodies now," she said.

He pushed the microphone away, a smile curving his full lips. "Better bodies than souls."

And like that, they were united again, the years apart forgotten like a dream half-remembered after sleep. Together Claire and Animus made sure the new rhythms spread across the world, one body, one club at a time.

For Claire, house music was revelatory because it showed the non-musician that they could make music, too. The creation was both intensely personal, externally expressive. It was a skill humans expressed around the world, a gift that had never changed, one she would always admire no matter how many times she witnessed it.

The movement on the dance floor was a release for people, the need primal. Claire watched the dancers in the darkness. Their bodies moved as if each existed within its own time. Her eyes were drawn to two men who seemed to meld into one another. They moved like liquid fire, as if they emerged from a single flame. The music called to Claire, poured through her, so she danced. She danced until her body erupted into invisible flames of its own, until her skin was so hot that when a denim-clad man reached for her, he drew back his hand as if he'd been burnt. She danced as she did on arrival that first night long ago, when she found herself moving toward a fire circled by hard hands beating drums. The ochre-faced people she met there told her ancestors spoke to them in the curve of animal skin. Standing shoulder to shoulder with her sisters, she had listened, nameless, in awe, struck by the wisdom contained in the space between palm flesh and the ear. Claire danced to drive trouble from her body's every pore, to plunge her fingertips into the club's pulsing light. Like everyone else in the crowded, shadowed room, she danced to forget. She danced to remember, danced on heels that lifted the night.

6

The hush of darkness on a battered road was all that Animus could hear, but beyond the first drops of rain, Claire could sense more than weather. Descending from the mountain's wet desert, a sound drew her, called across the water. In all directions the lights in the city twinkled. The rain made them look like falling stars.

As he drove, Animus watched her with eyes full of worry. Was it for her or for them both? He had to have noticed that she was fading, her appetite to feed grew less and less. When she fed, Claire tapped into the energy that flowed from the bodies in motion around her. Absorbing the music and the dancer's flow was the one time she could be completely present and completely absent all at once. But now she was less interested in being present at all. She hungered for something that music could no longer feed.

When they reached Beirut, Animus wanted to stop and do a set at Club 808 but Claire asked him to drive on. He kept trying to engage her in conversation during the flight to Cairo, but she only mumbled and stared out the window. "It takes two Niles to make a melody." Finally, he let her sleep. When she woke, she traveled in a fugue-like state. They crossed the water on a burst of sound and after a brief layover, the sound led her down to Sudan. Here she sensed a powerful presence, something ancient but new, a place where she could meet her true self.

"I've heard of underwater temples," Animus said and adjusted his shades. "Whole cities even, but what kind of music do you expect way out here?"

Claire shrugged. His oversized goggles reflecting the bronze light made her smile for the first time that day.

Up ahead the pyramids looked like grand termite mounds rising from the sand dunes. Some had been layered with old art, the kind most often relegated to rooftops and railyards. The scrawled graffiti could have been at least a hundred years old. Humans had the same impulses no matter what era. Claire walked past seven of the crumbling structures, their tops removed, until she stood before a stony stairway that led to a murky pool. Animus dug his boot into the sand. "I'm not going down there and if you got any good sense, neither would you."

"I may not have to," Claire said. It was the most she had

spoken all day. She descended the stairs, one step at a time. "When have you known me to have good sense?"

"Heh! It doesn't look like anyone has walked down there in ages. Why can't we just find the local spot and hit it up? You know they jukin' somewhere."

"Because I just want to feel it, if I can." She walked until the water rose up around her. "If I am not mistaken, there are three chambers here. Buried worlds of forgotten gods. If I can just touch it..." She sat down on the lowest step and raised her palm above the muddy pool. She heard Animus's boots on the upper steps. "Don't," she said. "Give me a minute."

With her palm resting on the top of the waters, she waited.

The water had been an excellent guard against the ravages of grave robbers and of time. No one had walked in the buried tombs for many years. The second burial began with the rise of groundwater from the nearby Nile. The third came from the increase in agriculture and the fourth from climate change. Claire was uncertain if the final resting places of the people she had known long ago would survive a fifth burial.

Claire stared into the waters, her palm shifting. The only sound that rose was the eddying of gold flakes rising to the surface, the last of the shabtis, engraved figurines said to serve the dead within. For a long time Claire listened with her palms, but when nothing answered back, she emerged from the tombs cut in bedrock, disappointment etched on her face.

"No one in their right mind would be playing out here. We need to move before the sun sets." Animus folded his arms, awaited her protest. To his surprise she only nodded.

"Hotel?" he asked.

She shook her head. "I'm in the wrong place."

"Yeah, no shit."

"No, I mean, these are the wrong pyramids." She pointed. "I've got to go there." It had been ages since she had been in that part of the world, the point of their first arrival. But the wind sang change.

Everything had shifted. The sands, the pyramids, the nations and their boundaries, even the people and the very air itself. Nothing remained the same.

"The pyramids I seek are completely underwater."

"Where?"

"New Sudan."

"Where the hell is that?"

7

In the late morning they headed east and arrived at a sand-swept town near a desolate stretch of desert. The sand-colored buildings leaned and swayed. "Stop Destroying Nubian Lands" was scrawled across one of them. Animus ate a crust of kisra bread and spicy stew offered by a family whose eyes shone pity when they watched them drive up, the car sputtering its own refusal to accept what Claire was beginning to think of as a personal exodus. The spice in the air, the scent of onions made Claire want to linger, but her collecting days were coming to an end.

They drove on until they finally passed lush alfalfa fields that rose from the desert like great green mirages. They were officially entering New Sudan, the ever hopeful bread basket of Africa once it unyoked itself from a legion of foreign leases. Powers rise and fall, but in this part of the world, all fates were linked by one ancient river. They snaked through the road along the great walls that formed the river's manmade reservoir. As Animus drove, Claire heard the lake waters weep. They gurgled tales of forced displacement, tales of families lost, of the water wars that came in the grand dam's wake. The water's song of woe, of missing loved ones and separated clans, reminded Claire of her own.

When they reached the crest of the hill, the great lake stretched out before them, Animus insisted they run down together.

"Here," he said, his open palm an invitation. "It takes two of yours to make one of mine. Your hands are so little."

"You've been saying that forever and a day," Claire said.

"It's still true."

Claire entwined her fingers into his and held on. If she got to the bottom of that hill and nothing was there, no one to meet her, if all the journeys she had made in this blue-green world derailed, she could think of no one better to witness her exile than him. His name had long been stitched inside the crinoline lace of her soul. But companionship, Claire knew, was not the question. How to survive another trip gone wrong, that would be the challenge. And how long would Animus survive without her? A bluesman who dared to knock at the door of the cosmos, he should have been buried in a pine box ages ago.

When Claire first fled the safety of her world with her sisters, she did not know what was out beyond the deaths of stars, beyond what they knew, the familiar. Bound for whatever world that waited, they traveled in search of the new neaux, the music that fed souls, the music that contained whole worlds of its own, extended lives. Now the sun was setting behind her and she was beginning to feel the weight of years. To her surprise, more than anything, she began to crave silence. Despite her body's old hungers, it was the silence between notes that made her inner ear twitch, made her whole spirit lean in.

Is that where they had gone? Into the silence? Her sisters who no longer called for her? The only ones who knew her true name? Whose trace she could no longer find in this world's constant din?

In that moment Claire longed for them. To lay her head upon their knees, her fingers entwined with that of her sisters. To share the notes and the music that had separated them all those years. Anticipation hummed through the air. It would hurt to leave Animus, her faithful friend who marked the changes with her. But as each day passed, her body slowly failed, resisting the music that had once sustained it so completely. She didn't need to hear another song to know that she could no longer bear to travel the world, wondering if she was alone, the last of her kind. Had her sisters returned home without her knowing?

So she would leave or try to. The music she carried inside, her tome of memory, was what she hoped would remain with him. The music and the memory. She was supposed to take it all back to their world, new rhythms to feed her people's old hungers. But what she had come to know and love of humans is that they needed it more than any of them ever knew. She squeezed Animus's hand, then released him, running toward the waters that cried out below.

I'm going to meet my sister
Going on home
Going to meet my sister
She said she'd meet me when I come
Only going over to Jordan
Only going on home

Wading in the water, she remembered the dirt roads she had left behind, the film of red dust around her ankles, the blue chipped paint around the window shutters, the whisper of wind in the floorboards, the creak and splinter, whisper and hush of the shotgun, the great wooden bed she and Animus had made love in, the cool kiss of the cotton sheets, the scent of his warm, brown skin in the Mississippi sun. She would miss him. She would miss them. But this longing for home, the pull of waves from a force none of this land might ever see, was stronger than love, than the sum of all of her centuries on earth and all its memories.

"Claire...Claire, where you going?" He walked carefully through the water, across the craggy rock face, then caught up with her, fear in his voice. The name sounded foreign to her ear. She had been calling herself that since that first landing.

Knee-high in the water, he stared at her, his eyes like light bending through glass. His voice a whisper, raspy and treacherous from the journey from Lebanon, across the water into the deserts, down into the most hidden parts of New Sudan. He could not hear the water's cry, the pull of something hidden within. She rubbed her fingertip over the callous at his wrist. He was rough beauty in her hands.

8

They say that the skin is the largest organ of the body. For Claire what had once been like a great, open door was now a small, brutish wall. What once poured through her and from her now climbed out of her reach. In the twenties and forties, scientists who formed the *Journal of Acoustical Studies* conducted experiments to measure how much sound the human body and fur-bearing animals could absorb. Claire's body absorbed ohms and omens, her flesh heating up to temperatures so high that had she been an actual human, she may have died. For Animus, she filtered the effects, lending his body some of her own restorative powers through her song, touch, and kiss. But with increasing frequency, Claire's ability to do so had been slowly fading. She didn't need an omen to know that she couldn't sustain them for long.

And if she could admit it, she'd had enough of chasing sounds, listening for miracles. The differences between her and Animus were more than just a matter of biomedical acoustics, of bone and flesh. The mechanical and fluid properties of coupling, of living numerous lives together, of trying to grow without growing infinitely apart. Familiarity had taken its toll. Over time they had traded places. At first he tried to make her settle down, Chicago, New York, Istanbul, a nameless town high up in Pakistani mountains. But the gift of time she had given him, changed him, too. He now wanted to move steadily ahead, to keep gathering and searching, and it was Claire who wanted to be still. She had reached her upper frequency limit. Weary in a world she no longer had any language for.

Set against stone, Animus's body language was unmistakable. Head flung back, fingers covering his eyes, his back

and his jaw a study in grief. She had become an expert in the gestures
of disapproval, distaste. His face tilted up, mouth fallen open,
eyes narrowed, what he wanted was something she couldn't name,
something ever climbing out of her reach. A storm that drove them
inside for days, his desire to live, another space emptied by loss.

"You were asleep while I was dying."

"Naw, never," he said, balancing in the blue-green water. He
could see the drop up ahead.

"Yeah, you were."

Over his shoulder, a constellation of nightflies flickered in
the light. She could remain or swim into the circle of sound, sink into
luminous possibility. Like the moment when a river changes course,
as if turning away from the past, forgetting. She too could turn away,
forgetting, but from which past? The human or the other?

In the water she could feel them more than hear them, like
the tongues of dark bells, a chorus of prayers, singing her back home.
She could tell, one by one, her sisters had come here before her. The
water seeping into her pores practically hummed with the weight
of them. The great dam with its dark waters all around, the sunken
tops of the pyramids invisible beneath their feet. Like space, the
world of sound was vast but not unknowable. Music opened doors of
possibility, pathways that led to greater understanding.

"Listen and absorb the best of the best, then place our
signatures in the universe. That was the task. Collect the story, save
it, pass it on. Making meaning from meaning. But what we do, it's a
kind of spiritual graffiti."

"What you do is theft," Animus said with bitterness. He stood
shivering in the water. "So here we are, a different crossroad, same

shit. You want me to stay or follow. I choose to follow."

"You know you can't do that," she said.

"Then stay."

Claire walked forward, her clothes growing heavy with water.

"You're like any other colonizer," he said. "You take and take while you pretend to give. But what you give is nothing we can keep. You took my life, promised me another, and now you just want to leave?"

Claire's body was adapted to hear many things, her lover's pain not the least of them. Like a great tuning fork, the sorrow and anger in Animus's voice echoed the back and forth of her own pain, disturbed the air in her spirit.

"I extended your life. This music your species makes, it's meant to be expansive, shared."

"Oh, so I'm a species now? After all these years, it's like that?" The hurt coming off him hit Claire in big waves. "This music is just food for you. You're a bloodsucker. There ain't no art behind your hunger."

"How can you say that?"

"The same way you can say goodbye." He turned from her, as if to leave, his boots full of water. "I've been right here with you. Been about as dead as somebody can be without being dead," he said. "At this point, I'm just trying to keep my head up. That's all I can do, while you vamp out."

"It's not what you think," she said. "It's not that I'm leaving you, it's *what* I'm leaving you. All the years, all the music, it's somewhere out here, I can feel it. My sisters, I think they are..."

She removed the bracelets that looped around her wrists, then began to push the water and kick, heading deeper into the lake.

The bracelets glittered briefly in the sun then sank, disappearing into the darkness below. Claire could hear Animus's outcry and the desperate splashing as he swam after her. With each stroke, the rock face disappeared beneath him. She turned.

"No, Animus. You can't follow me here," she said, her face wet. Animus could not tell if it was from the reservoir water or from tears. "I know this is hard, but whether you believe it or not, I have prepared you. You are the only one who can do what needs to be done. And I do need you, Animus. This world needs you. Because whatever happens here, I am leaving it all to you."

Animus threw his arms out, swam toward her. "Leaving what?"

The water rose around them, howled in answer.

"This." She took her wet palms and placed them on his temples. Animus stared into her eyes and screamed.

A symphony of discord unfolded inside him at an unnatural pace. Furious noises, nimble chording, harmonics and melodic hooks from across the ages ricocheted off the inside of his skull. He held his head to still the sounds, fixed his lips to scream out 'stop' but the music spliced his thoughts and filled him with songs of life across continents, across time. Some he recognized, most he did not. But underneath the pain and his struggle to hold it all in his head, he heard a velvety throughline, a copper tone that reminded him of Claire. As much as he had witnessed, Claire had collected sounds Animus could never dream.

He stood shivering in the water, though his skin was hot. His brain felt as if it had been set afire; his soul felt shredded—and reborn. Steam billowed around him, around Claire. His cheeks burned where she held, then released him.

"What I've given you is...everything," she said, her voice was starting to warp, as if she were speaking from inside a tunnel. She caught him by the shoulder, held his body up before he collapsed. "I was supposed to take it with me, but it doesn't feel right, not anymore. I think it's supposed to stay here, with you."

"And what am I supposed to do with it?"

She laughed. "You know, I'm really not sure. Whatever you decide, Animus, it's going to do good."

"Claire, there's got to be..."

"Another way is not only 'possible,' another way is happening. It's already here."

Animus stood at the water's edge, pleading with her, but Claire could not hear him. She imagined her sisters flowing in from the manmade sea. The pyramids sunken below, their eyes streaming with tears as she clasped their hands in her own. She imagined their true names, whispered them like prayer, *The Great Going Song* calling them back to the place they were born, back beyond where the stars gathered.

Suddenly the wind rose, the sound was like thunder breaking the sky.

A cyclone of water spun, emitting a low hum that grew louder, pulsing through the air.

"Animus!" Claire cried over the rush of wind. "Your life, love, it's the instrument. Your life is your instrument."

He reached for her but giant waves encircled her. She raised her hand, as if to wave at him before disappearing under the dark waves.

9

He could feel it before he could hear it. Something strong enough to take his breath. Animus tried to keep afloat, calling out to Claire. He dove deeper into the water. His eyes searched for her but he couldn't see. The water heated up. His head broke the surface and he flailed, gasping.

"Claire!"

He thought he saw her and swam toward the shadowy figure, but she slipped through a rift. Animus came up for air, then he heard it. A low-pitched keening, a sound only an animal might hear. They had traveled so far together. This force who, like an answered prayer, had rescued him from a mud-dark path carved in Mississippi. He had fled a plague of winged beasts and boll weevils who devoured the great balls of cotton risen from the earth. He took the devastation as a sign. But hunger found him standing on the blood-red crossroads, ax in hand, trying to figure out which way to go. Unlike the legends, Claire had made no promises, but she delivered him something he learned over time not to fear. How to make a guitar weep and sing, how to trick the sands of time. This force who had traveled from beyond the named stars. This force who had honored him as his friend and lover. Floating in the water, he was trying hard not to think of the great manmade lake as her grave. If he could, he would save her as she had saved him. He swam toward the direction of the sound, wringing every bit of strength he could from his muscles, but he hit a wall of sound. He could not break through it. Great chunks of stones rose from the water, a giant swell, a wave of buried history.

It was as if the lake was hollowing out, swallowing itself whole. The water rising, revealed what had been hidden. The

Nubian pyramids Claire had spoken of. They dotted the valley
and surrounded Animus. He swam to hold onto the top of one.
Something metallic was rising up. It glittered in the sun. Animus's
eyes widened in shock. An unnaturally long, golden arm clutched
something his mind could only register as some kind of strange
instrument. Was it a trumpet?

Animus counted eight valves, the bell size, monstrous. The arm
lifted it as if it was light as air. Another arm shot up from the spinning
water, balanced the instrument, and the wind blew stronger, making
a deep rich sound, much lower in pitch than any trumpet Animus had
ever heard. He felt the blast of sound deep in his chest and stomach.
Then the fingers began to play. Animus marveled at the dizzying finger
work. The notes moved between chaos and beauty, sliding out and in
again. The only time Animus had heard anything close to that was at
his grandfather's church all those years ago. He remembered when the
women spoke in tongues and his father used the bottom of his foot and
the wood plank floors for percussion. After back-breaking, soul-crushing
work in the fields, how they drummed themselves back to wholeness.
How they sang in strange tongues that renewed strength and helped
them dream a future.

A tempestuous sound shrieked through the air, notes that
transformed the horn into something close to human. Then a great
column of sound bore the instrument *up, up, up*. Another hand was
rising. Coppery in the light. *Claire.* Animus felt her warm presence,
heard her unique melody whisper through his head. Her tone was
brighter, more intimate, as if it was reaching out for something,
leaning forward. It had to be Claire, no one else sounded like her.
His Claire ET, finally united with her sisters. The wind roared as the

sisters' fingers raced across the valves, pure joy ringing through the bell. At first, Animus thought the strange horn played itself, but he was wrong. The horn was played by love, by joy.

Your life is the instrument.

He was thinking of Claire's last words when the horn changed tones. The three hands melded into one, gold, silver, and copper entwined. *Follow the beat 'cross the light,* he heard. *Shadows light the day.* Animus strained to hear more as the horn rose higher into the air. He tried to watch it as it climbed higher and higher, its tone growing impossibly purer, but the glare stung his eyes. He hurt. Like staring at the sun. The water around him hummed, an electric, iron scent filled the air. *I am,* he heard the horn cry as it cut through the sky, *the black gold of the sun.* The wind trilled its goodbye. *Let the light set you free. Go where you want to be. Be* was the last of the horn before it disappeared into the sky.

He rode on the back of the swollen reservoir. Grief was his passage back onto land. Animus watched the lake so long that he could no longer tell where the water stopped and he began, but Claire never came up. When he finally stood, his legs felt like iron, his heart and head dumb flesh. He staggered toward the broken road where they had parked the car. He knew she had gone, but still he had waited, hoping. As he left, Animus passed a group of children playing in a field amongst the majestic, crumbling temples. Little sprigs of grass, defiant, sprung up around the remains of fallen statues and what was left of the pyramids. The children's laughter followed him as he walked, his head still ringing, his clothes no longer wet. The sound of the strange instrument haunted him. He could still see it rise, golden from the blueblack waters, held by Claire's sisters. He could still see Claire staring back at him before she disappeared under the waves, could hear the song she played to remind him that through the music she gathered, she would always be there.

The car was smaller, dustier than before. Animus wiped his eye and put on the goggles. He remembered the great burst of light that pierced the sky when Claire soared homeward with her sisters.

Now scorched flat earth, sable sandstone stretched as far as he could see. He was alone. Inside Animus felt the fire that brings round the sun. On the way to this place, Claire had said that it took two Niles to make a melody. Now he knew it took more than that. It took the whole world, many hands. He would do as she asked. Or he would try. He would take the music she had gathered, the music she seared into his flesh and press it into the form that they had loved best. Black vinyl. Whatever she had given him, these nine bar blues, he knew it would be good

> *Light from comet's tail,*
>   *the future shining bright*
> *music from the earth's womb heals*
>   *reveals the gods' afterlife*

THE PARTS THAT MAKE US MONSTERS

We didn't want your nail clippings or your blood. Your laughter, or tears, would do. That strange light you saw drifting where a shadow should be, was the promise mother made when she bore us. Where we lived, there would always be sun. Where we go, there would always be light. That star never scarred or scared us. Even in the face of our father, the sun's blistering gaze, we were the daughters of night.

On that first journey across the waters, we held each other close. When we shut our eyes we floated on azure sleep, lifted by wave upon wave, until the darkness behind our golden lids became lonelier still. Before they trapped us, we bathed in leaves, bark, stones, and spice. We sang no fear. We knew. Ancestors descend when needed. Spirits rise when called. It was the way of the world, the way day follows night and moon, mother said, it was moon who follows ocean's call. For it was the water that carried us in the womb and water that reigns supreme.

When they chased us from the village into the forest, when we fell into the arms of ghosts, we knew we would have to feed, our worries and our appetites, replanted in strange, disordered lands. With lowered eyes we watched the traders, whose skin was the color of clay, the wet earth that came from waters, the moon clay our mother and her sisters used to mark their territory. From the way the ghosts moved, the way they stared through us, barking out words that sounded like insanity falling, we knew. The clay moon ghosts believed wherever they walked, wherever their square toes landed, was their territory. We sang the song of our mother, sang the songs that came before. Force marched through a door of no return, we wore our chains like an elder's gold, carried our song inside, still waters flecked with shards of moonlight. Three days later we entered the dark maw of what the ghosts called ship. We lay in the bottom of the belly with the others. We lay in the noise and the filth with the mothers, and the sisters, and the daughters, listened to their dirge song of shrieks, moans, the twisting of tongues, the deaths of worlds yet born. We did not speak with words but with feelings. Ours was the language of survival, flight.

Mistress Godwin was a laughing girl, a mere child, barely a woman when we joined her. Her cheeks and eyes still flushed with the sounds of mirth. Disappointment had not yet clawed its way into her heart. Her breasts were hard blossoms yet to break earth. *Mistress*, we sang, *Mistress Godwin*, but she did not speak or smile. In this strange land, dead tongues no longer answered us. *God wins*, we laughed, *god wins*, we cried. The sound of our pleasure frightened the blackbirds in the trees.

When they found her, her skin had grown pale, her temples the color of sour milk. We only meant to take a little, but the hunger had long since overtaken us. We wanted to taste the sound of her laughter, to let the womanchild's joy fill the hollows that hid deep inside. Like the ghosts, we took too much, and just like them, we were not ashamed. Thirst is thirst.

When the good mistress grew still and joined whatever cold ancestors that claimed her, we dropped the slop bucket in the field, left the dough rising in the wooden bowl, abandoned our chores. We drained the others and fled, taking their laughter with us. Into the wild forest, we ran, cousin to the bush that once betrayed us. We hid in wildness. We hid in plain sight. In hickory and peepaw and loblolly pine, in the light that has always claimed us.

We waited. Sparkling light where shadows should be. The blackbirds visited, kept us company in the silent years when even the first ones marked our hunting ground in the language of their fear. *Croatoan*, they later said, *croatoan* carved into the heart of a tree. But no tongue has found the right tones to name us. Twenty years later, finally, the blackbirds crowed good news. When the new beast arrived, it bore one hundred and twenty souls, but none like us were in its belly. We took what sustenance we could from the joyless ones who struggled to make the dry-bone land home. In time, their parched throats would rival our own, for the old gods of this land refused to send rain. And thirst is thirst.

Leaf, ghosts, earth, light. We suffered together. Finally, when we had grown so weak, our light only the spark of fireflies, twenty and odd men joined the colony. A few suns later, a woman appeared. *Angelo. Angela.* Their ebon skin and eyes stirred memory, the ghost of their laughter refracted light of our own. The sound, infrequent as it was, reminded us of home. And because we are our mother's daughters, we left the men and the lone woman who could be kin. After the journey across the big water, their bodies held such little joy, we were ashamed to drain them. We knew. Even in strange lands, old seeds release fresh roots. Eyes stinging with memory, we fled again, taking the silver shards of light with us.

We left temptation and the shadows and something close to sorrow. We buried thirst and the seed of ourselves deep within the forests. And the years passed through us. Past the cypress and the oaks. The memory of laughter floating around, dust motes in sunlight. With time, memory became our only home. The old home was a memory time would not let us forget.

Some night-days we dream. Our thoughts are upside down.
We hang from our feet in the limbs of thick-boned trees.
The blackbirds come and sing to us. They say we have become the language of fear, the hushed gasps and breath around open fires. But the stories they teach are wrong. Darkness is not the only thing to fear. Sometimes the dark is hidden in light. Once girls, we have grown old here. Once girls, our hearts have become hard like the mottled bark of the strange trees that grow here. There are layers to this loneliness. We feel its bite. Its teeth are sharp. Hard things hold beauty, too. The world we live in is a fire. The people we love all burn. Ever hungry, our

red gum smiles hide the empty pit within. We know. Legends rise from all the broken places, emerge from the stories and the memories, the half-remembered and the ill-formed, all melded together, united in one. In this land we are like moons who have lost their water. We no longer hear the ocean's call. If water no longer speaks to us, are we still our mother's daughters?

The parts that make us monsters are not the teeth or the heart but the mind.

The part that makes us monsters is bone and sinew, spirit and flesh.

We have not been ourselves here. We will not be ourselves here.
We are always ourselves here.
We are always
here.

THE DRAGON CAN'T DANCE

The first time I danced, I hated it. Six years old, skinny as a string bean, shy, observant, the last thing I wanted was to be pulled into my nana's long, strong arms, and swept onto the makeshift dance floor at her birthday party. My hair was tightly braided, laced with the new gold and white beads Mama bought just for the occasion. My freshly oiled temples smelled like heaven, hurt like hell. Coconut and mango braids throbbed with the beat that thumped from wood veneer speakers sprawled across two wobbly card tables in a corner of the garden. Nana threw back her head and pranced, that's right, pranced past my two uncles, my sisters, Papa and Mama, past all her old neighbors and church friends, and rolled her ample hips like a much younger woman. I was scandalized! Everyone clap clapped and howled at the vision, bellies full of roti and spicy jerk chicken. Nana wore red. And she looked amazing, a juicy hibiscus blossom in her hair.

"Four score! Four score!" she cried, channeling Lincoln or the Bible. The sparkly eight and zero bobbed and weaved on her rainbow crown. In her birthday hat, she looked like a goddess or a ten-year-old. I could not tell which, before she reached for me, and I was swept into the swirl of sweat and laughter, the deep pulsing music, the mass of warm brown arms and legs, fiercely dancing in her herb garden behind her brownstone in Brooklyn. As she tugged and jerked my freshly cocoa-buttered arms back and forth, a wicked puppeteer, I was mortified. Not like the time I spilled soda on my white skirt at school, and the big girls pointed and teased me, shouting "Sanaa started her period! Sanaa started her peer-ree-odd!" It seemed as if everyone in Crown Heights had gathered to see my humiliation. They say the dragon can't dance. At six, neither could I.

Thinking about it now, I cannot believe how much love I took for granted. I'm talking about real love, the kind you can touch with your own hands and feel its arms around you and breathe in. When Nana made me dance at her eightieth birthday party, I was so embarrassed, so afraid I'd make a fool of myself, that her joyful, public love of me felt more like a slap than a celebration. While other kids tap danced and moonwalked over the old *children should be seen and not heard thing*, bucked and clamored for adult attention, *any* attention, I preferred back then to recede into darkness, to be the silent night that cloaked the bright lone star. Nana wasn't having none of that. When she pulled me into her arms that smelled like cinnamon, sweet milk and lime, I was angry. I felt exposed, naked. Dancing exposes you. In dancing, your body, traitor flesh that it is, reveals all the things your spirit tries to hide. Drawn from the margins into the center of my big family's love and laughter, all the vulnerabilities, all the hopes and questions, all the fire spark of early, tentative temptations flowed through me, flowed out of me—and I hated it.

Then. Then the drumbeats in my feet, the longing to fly that flamed through my limbs, possessed me. The sensation singed skin, engulfed my anxiety, burnt away my invisible cloak. After that night, dancing became addictive.

Me and my girls, we used to turn up, shut it down right there in Goat Park. While the boys were out on the asphalt, sweating and cursing, checking bricks and trying to dunk in their throwback Jordans, we would be over by the raggedy ass slide, far away from crying babies and fussing nannies cussing in their mother tongues, but close enough for the fine boys to see us, making moves, moving in time, and imitating our favorites. Chanel could fract better than anybody. Her arms and hands flying in precise, quick fast patterns. Her sharp elbows were arrows that pierced the air, even her long spiraling locs swung in time to her rhythm. Bijou's neck and thighs were like that old school silly putty. She could stretch and slide, whine and grind like she was all water, not bones and flesh. Me, I was the choreographer, always been, always will be. Sanaa, Queen of the Stans. I could do all my girls ' moves and then some I never shared. Even back then, I dreamed new steps and stans in my sleep, woke up counting beats and wrecking rhythms, even when I brushed my teeth.

To dance was to live.

Other younger girls and little children sometimes watched us from the sidelines, tried to mimic our moves. None of them had enough booty yet, the extra bounce for the ounce that added that special polyrhythm. But I wasn't stingy. I taught anyone who wanted to learn and have fun, and some of them were really very good.

Back then, I gave my moves away for free.

"Might as well," Bijou used to say. "They gon' steal it anyway."

Chanel disapproved, flinging her locs back to underline the point. "You can't give away everything, Sanaa. Some stuff you got to keep for yourself."

It was when they asked us to perform at the Rucker Park Streetball Fest, an annual fundraiser against police brutality, for the families of the latest victims, that it all changed. That's when Isis first saw me. We couldn't believe that Ice came to Manigault. Her appearance was completely unannounced, otherwise she and the Goat would have been swamped by fans and paparazzi. She was promoting her upcoming release and would be the celebrity judge for the tournament. Everyone and their mama, folk who know damn well they couldn't ball or stan, was trying to get up in that competition. It was chaos. Harlem was out of control. There was no way they were going to be able to hold the people back, but we weren't ordinary people. I had been waiting for a chance like this since beyond forever, and now here it was. I had no idea just how jacked up it would be.

While the seconds counted down before curtains, my stomach filled with a hundred steely butterflies. Their wings shredded my confidence, then my doubts. After collaborating with Isis for so long, I still felt anxious, still felt the nervousness before I was tasked to move the crowd—her crowd. But just like the times when I battled street crews with Chanel in Goat Park on the West Side and with Bijou on the drummer's hill in Harlem, my nervousness was quickly replaced with extreme focus. When green zeros filled the air above me, I watched our splendid bodies explode into action. As I moved I almost forgot that the force behind Isis's explosion was my own.

Under my stage lights, my skin glistened like blue-black diamonds. I did the counts in my head, allowing Isis's music to flow through me, flow with me. Inside my crystal cave, as I called the room designed for my unseen solo performances, I danced with only the barest of clothing. Dark brown threads designed to wick sweat, designed to match my skin, monitored and transmitted my every movement to Isis without hindering my movement. I was the behind-the-scenes choreographer and the spotlit superstar—all at once. As a child, like many girls, I used to dance in the middle of my room, until one of my sisters would walk in. Then I would stop for a moment and giggle, then begin the dance again as if no one was there. As I danced alone, I was the brightest star, the only star in my imagination. In the crystal cave, whose walls sparkled with light and data and pulsed with the music's rhythm, the illusion was the same. In the cave, I was the puppet and the puppeteer, a tamed dragon.

Instead of breathing fire, I was the flame.

Management wanted to install climate control, to reduce the possibility of my sweat damaging the software and equipment. Under our special contract, "unprecedented" my agent had said, there was a severe gag order—proprietary tech and cloak-and-dagger secrecy—and clause after clause after clause. So many fine points and legalese that I finally signed it when my agent emphasized the number of unprecedented zeros that would grace my first check. Management was worried about me damaging the equipment, but no one was worried about the equipment damaging me. Climate control for their suit. *Ksst!* I laughed at this, said I preferred to sweat. Surely they had insurance for cosmic funk. They pushed back. I pushed harder then. It would make the dance more authentic, and Isis, despite her meteoric rise, needed all the help she could get. My dance was born in New York's streets, channeled fractals from across the nation, adopted traditions from around the world, reimagined Ailey and Dunham, Jamison and Jackson reborn as starship troopers, flinging their black bodies through space. Isis was born in the city of a thousand suns, her voice quickly becoming the anthem of a legion. To deliver, I needed to feel the saltwater beading on my skin, to feel the fire coursing through me.

I needed it far more than Isis and her backup dancers, gifted girls who twirled and stamped in perfect synchronized steps. I watched as the dancers performed my choreography, as Isis, the blazing star, performed my steps mere nanoseconds after my own movements, the delay an unavoidable consequence of the ocean between us.

Mistress of my crystal cave with its vital signs monitors and cords, its wall-to-floor screens reflected the sold-out concert stage and the audience that screamed four thousand miles away in Freetown. I could see the stadium reflected all around me. Each set for Isis was a variation of an ancient Egyptian or other pseudo-African theme. Over the last of our forty city tour, the world had seen Nubians and Pharaonic Pyramids, Dogon masks and references to alien close encounters with the inhabitants of the Dog Star, Sirius. The last show in Paris had Isis lounging on Napoleon's tomb, surrounded by obelisks and giant replicas of herself. Tonight's show in Sierra Leone, diamond capital of the world for centuries, was an ahistorical remix of surrounding nations. Our biggest number— my biggest number—would find Isis rising up from a rolling pink lake like the one in Senegal, its waves carrying her up to the base of a skyscraper-sized baobab tree that held her throne. *All praise Isis, Queen of Life.* For her finale she would appear to break into a hundred pieces, then resurrect herself for the last song.

Even though Isis could not create her own dance, I knew better than anyone how good she was at creating her own myth. Friendships, family, and fans, she hustled them as deftly as a goddess. All were ripe for sacrifice.

"We sisters," she had said when I had mustered the courage enough to tell her I was gone. Even her voice had taken on my cadence. She could code-switch with the best. "You need me, I need you. Sanaa, Na-Na, they can't do this without us. I can't do this without you."

I guess Management had told her I was serious this time, so Isis made a special live-in-the-flesh personal visit to me. It had been a long time. It caught me by surprise, and I was angry that she could still flatter me, that I still cared so much about her opinion.

I was suited up, the brown fabric covering me like a second skin. She stared me down, watching me hungrily. Like my hips, my skin, my blood she wanted more than food, than air itself. For what it's worth, Isis had plenty game. I didn't want to play anymore.

I no longer welcomed her visits.

"Na-Na."

I didn't answer. Walked off the set, manually raised the lights in the cave. No illusions now. Just the truth. My heart rate skyrocketed. Management monitoring me could tell I was about to bust a gut. The cave suddenly filled with the hiss of fresh oxygen.

"Sanaa?"

I turned from my wet bar, nothing fancy, just aloe juice and wheatgrass shots and whatever "proprietary" ingredients they stashed in the energy blasts. The nasty taste, like much of my life in the cave, I had long gotten used to.

Isis had completely shaved her head. Only little blond stubble, her new growth, was visible, and the tell-tale tiny cuts on her scalp where Management had implanted nanitic sensors. The old scars still looked like angry red ants. Unlike the dark ones that dotted my spine and every limb. I realized I had never seen the real Isis or her natural hair. When we first met in Goat Park she was rocking a red Afro and Bootsy shades. She looked like Little Orphan Annie and the Mack. I must have looked at her like I was crazy, but how could I not be? I had wanted to be a dancer, but now nearly all of my flesh sang the body electric. Mite-sized robots, nanites translated my thoughts to movements. Management's processing banks instantly transferred this data to satellites that downloaded it to Isis, wherever she was in the empire star. My dance became Isis's own. An interstellar duet, imperceptible to the media or her global fans, we were captives of the flame.

And zeros or not, I was losing, had lost nearly everything. When my nana died, Management would not let me go to the funeral. I was furious. Trapped in the crystal cave, I raged for days until my body was spent. Isis was scheduled to perform at a major, international awards show. I could not be spared. The satellites watched over both of us, no matter how far apart we were, no matter how much I grieved. Despair filled my crystal cave.

"Oh, this," she said and raked freshly manicured pointed nails across her crown. Her fingertips looked like daggers. Manicurists and stylists were sent to me each week, but I kept my nails, my hair simple. Who would ever see me?

"Management wanted me to cut it," she said. "They won't tell me yet what they're going to do to my hair. You know them. Always got some next level plan for me to take over. First music, then the world." She laughed carefree, the way only white girls could, and walked over to me. She smelled like roses or was it that flower my nana used to wear, the one in her garden. I had to work harder and concentrate to remember, to hold on to where my family and I used to live. To remember their faces, and the foods we used to eat, my friends, Bijou, Chanel, even the fine boys in the park, everyone that Management paid off long ago so they would forget me. I was losing parts of my memory, losing parts of myself.

I couldn't believe I used to love her.

"We are like this," Isis said. She grasped my hands, formed a knot. "Sacred. Nothing is more sacred than sisters, than the bond we have."

I wanted to cry, but I was too exhausted. Did she even care that I no longer remembered my sisters' names?

"I love the new choreography, love it! Girl, you're brilliant! With it, there is *no way* we can't make history. Not this time. We're selling out everywhere, and I mean everywhere. So you can't leave now. You can retire later but not now, Sanaa. And you know I love you."

Why it got to be like this, I wanted to know. Why can't nobody want me, all of me, just as I am? I used to have that, didn't I? I couldn't remember. I let go. Her hands felt clammy, cold, inhuman. I didn't want to be near her anymore. We were close enough.

If she noticed my distaste, Isis was too professional to let on. I'm sure management had given her a script. Isis was good at memorizing her lines. She lip-synced better than anyone who ever lived.

"Got somethin' for ya." She handed me a box.

Ksst. I didn't want any more payoffs from her, no more expensive trinkets and souvenirs. What's the use when I no longer had a life?

"Go 'head, open it," she commanded. There was the Isis I knew. I snatched it from her open palm.

"I don't need your toys, Ice, I need my freedom."

I tossed the velvet ribbon and opened the latch. A gold and diamond encrusted ankh decorated with a scarab beetle rested on a white satin lotus flower.

"Thanks." I walked away. I needed to shower, to sleep before the next rehearsal. It was obvious that neither Isis nor Management cared about me. Something about geese and golden eggs.

As I turned the lights back off, I could see Ice's face before she slipped out the door. If I didn't know better I would have sworn she was crying.

"Keep it," she said before the cave sealed me in. "I have one, too. Just like it. You might need it one day."

Something about the way she said that, no hustle, no hype, made me shiver. I walked back from the sauna room and into the main set, raised the lights. The crystal cave hummed quietly. The big screens were turned to saver mode. Pictures of the past tour dates flickered by. Barcelona, Rome, Munich, Istanbul, Amsterdam, places I might never live to see. So why would I need a gaudy necklace, even if it was worth two mints?

I picked the box off the floor and examined it. A typical jewelry gift box, plush, expensive looking. I flipped it open, pulled out the cross-like ankh. I was offended because it was like something Isis's press crew would hand out in swag bags. Besides the crap ton of diamonds, nothing special. Or was it?

"Music: Ndegeocello, 'Dance of the Infidel,'" I said. Light trumpets and jazz drifted through the air. I set the box down on a coffee table and sank into the couch in the rear of the cage. The seat cushions molded themselves around my body, enveloping me like a cozy cocoon. The amulet was expertly made, heavily encrusted with jewels. But it wasn't the jewels Isis wanted me to see. There was something beyond them. Something extra that she hadn't wanted Management to know.

I traced my fingertips along the curves of the ankh, then noticed that the largest diamond was in the center, below the scarab. I stroked it with my thumb, then pressed down hard. To my surprise, the amulet broke apart. My left hand held the bottom of the cross, in my right was the top of the golden bow with the scarab beetle. I held the dagger in my trembling hand and sank deeper into the couch. The blade was sharp, lethal enough to pierce skin, slash arteries. Ice said she had one of these, too. Was that her retirement plan all along?

I rejoined the ankh, held it by its glittering bow, placed it carefully on the table. They said the dragon can't dance. I always thought that wasn't true. Looking in the mirror that was my crystal cave, I didn't know anymore.

WHO NEEDS THE STARS IF
THE FULL MOON LOVES YOU?

Sister was detangling her hair when she heard Faith scream. She put the bottle of rosemary and lemon oil down on the edge of the sink. Scented water dripped down her neck, wetting the back of her shirt and her shoulders. Sister stared in the mirror, her eyes weary half-moons, as if she'd woken from troubled dreams. She stepped over the fluffy blue towel and walked out of the bathroom, a black, wide-tooth comb stuck in her hair, an upturned fist.

Faith lay on the floor on her belly. Her wiry, grasshopper legs were stretched out so far, Sister had to hopscotch so she would not trip over them.

"What you done did now?" she asked, but Faith didn't answer. Instead, she scrolled down the bright screen, her finger a dark blur casting shadows in the living room.

"*Faa-ith*, I don't want to see any more of your crazy videos," Sister said. "All that foolishness makes my head hurt." She paused and waited but Faith kept scrolling. "I don't see how you can stay on there so long."

Faith only nodded. Sister frowned. It was the silence that worried her. It wasn't like Faith not to laugh or speak. Faith and Sister were *two scars on a dead woman's belly.*[1] Of the two, Faith was the more sociable of their mother's daughters. Faith always had something to say. Now she lay there like a bump on a log. Sister decided that maybe she should investigate, so she dug the big black comb deeper into her halo of hair and peered over Faith's shoulder.

"Who is she?"

"Her name was Sandra."

Faith put the black sharpie down and held up two signs. "Justice for _____ (fill in the blank)" covered one sign, with "AM I NEXT?" scrawled in Faith's wobbly handwriting beneath it. The other sign was more plaintive. "END RACIST POLICE BRUTALITY NOW" it said simply.

"Which one?" Faith asked, flashing each sign beneath her chin. Her eyes were night-black lace, dark, defiant. "Which?"

Sister studied the signs, the words in her mind stuck in her throat. She raised her hand to point but could not move her limbs fast enough. The name, Sandra, spun inside her, and she couldn't keep the young woman's eyes out from her own lids. Sister could see her, the parked car, the concrete sidewalk, and hear her screams muffled in the darkness past seeing. Then the names came. The others her mind had kept in a locked box until this moment.

Latasha Hallins, shot in a Korean corner store in LA. Keara Crowder shot by her husband in Memphis. Bettie Jones gunned down in Chicago. Asleep in her bed, Aiyana Stanley-Jones was only seven. Yvette Smith. Miriam Carey. Mya Hall. Tanisha Anderson. Malissa Williams. Rekia Boyd. Tarika Wilson. Eleanor Bumpus. Kathryn Johnston was shot when policed burst into her home, and Pearlie Golden was shot multiple times in her front yard. Unlike the other young women, Pearlie had been ninety-three and Kathryn, ninety-two, but the litany didn't stop there. Sharmel Edwards. Tyisha Miller. Shereese Francis... No woman or girl child was safe. The names kept coming.

I do not even know all their names / my sisters deaths are not even noteworthy...[2]

"Sister? Are you listening to me? Don't you ever get tired? Spending your life in the front yard?"[3] Sister could feel Faith's sharp words cutting into her, but she could not hear. Her ears were filled with names. "You need to come *too* this time," Faith said. "You can't ride the movement out in your living room forever." Disgust, a shadow, covered Faith's face.

Sister tried to look away, but now her hands and her feet were frozen. How to tell her, *I dream of your freedom...*[4] that I wished you'd never learn that *black is not beloved,*[5] that the words are pressed up in my throat like a fist, that the tears boil in the pit of my belly, like some kind of strange bitter brew? How to tell her that when I try to drink or eat, all my stomach and tongue desires is poison, hunger, a food for assassins, dirges for deacons of defense?

Her nails raked the dry, patchy skin along her arm. Sister looked down. Inside she was changing.

The whole world was watching, but what did it see?

Sister turned her eyes away from Faith, her fingers covering the black bristles erupting all along her arms, her shoulders, and her spine like ebony spikes.

"Well I'm going to leave without you, if you're just going to stand there looking crazy." Faith opened the door and stared up at the sky. "It's dark out here. I can't see a single star. Oh, wait," she said. "There's the moon." She waited, then sucked her teeth. "At some point, Sis, you gonna have to *do* something. We can't keep going on like this."

"But...I..." Sister began, but the names kept coming. They hung in her throat, dangled in her belly like a long endless rope. *At first they used a noose, now all they do is shoot...*[6] She gasped, unable to breathe. All the water seemed to evaporate from the air. She stumbled and reached for Faith, at least she thought she did. She reached, but suddenly a hundred Faiths swirled in the air around her. They all frowned and recoiled from her touch.

"*Ff-ai—*" she gasped, her wet hair resting limply on her shoulders. "*Ff—ai...*" But Faith had gone.

When Faith returned from the protest, weary but hopeful, at least some of her anger spent, she tossed her bent sign onto the dinner table and called for Sister.

"Where you at, girl? You missed it," she said, kicking off her shoes at the door. She placed her boots neatly next to Sister's sandals and pulled her earrings off. A brass hoop got caught in her curls. "So many people showed up. Beautiful people, we spilled all into the streets. You would have loved them. One group had these giant puppets— You hear me? Marionettes."

But Sister didn't answer. The TV was still on and all the lights. Faith ducked into the bathroom and stared at all the hair products scattered across the counter. Sister's bottle of homemade detangler still sat on the sink, untouched. Faith picked up the damp blue towel and hung it up.

"Sis, what's up? You sleep?"

She pushed open the bedroom, their mother's old room but Sister wasn't there. Her black comb lay in the middle of the floor.

Faith shuddered. She heard someone calling her. She turned, but no one was there, nothing but the ghostly blue TV light from the hall and the full moon in the window. Faith saw Sister's clothes tossed in a corner of the room. A sense of dread filled the air. Then she heard it again, faint and quiet, soft as a breath.

"*Ffaa-ith.*"

The sound vibrated against her skin, tickling the fine hairs along the nape of her neck, inside her ear. She knew that voice. Her old woman's name, the one mother had gifted her, had two whole syllables—but only in one person's mouth.

She turned and then she saw it.

Just below the bed, in a corner of moonlight, the crazy quilt pattern just barely touched the floor. Faith kneeled, her eyes wide, searching.

It skittered once, then rolled over. The size of a newborn kitten.

She raised her finger slowly in the air, then gently brushed its little silver back. It flinched and the ball tightened. She touched it again.

It shivered, laughing or afraid, Faith could not tell which. All she knew is that her sister had once reached for her, and she had turned away. Now her sister held herself.

Faith picked up the tiny ball, careful not to crush its curved back or its tiny antennae. She held it in the palm of her hand, brushing her fingertips across its silver-coppery shields, until it slowly uncurled itself, one plate at a time, its tiny legs tickling her palm. Faith held it, the disappointment she felt earlier now a dull ache in her heart. It crawled across her palm, its little pill-shaped body resting on her lifeline. Faith stroked its shiny back, knowing she would

always remember her face

always say her name

"Sister."

Notes on *Who Needs the Stars If the Full Moon Loves You?*

[1] After Lucille Clifton's *two-headed woman* (University of Massachusetts, Amherst, 1980)

[2] In 1979 after twelve black women were murdered in Boston over a span of a few weeks, Audre Lorde wrote "Need: A Chorale for Black Women Voices."

[3] From Gwendolyn Brooks's poem "A Song in the Front Yard" (*Selected Poems*, Harper and Row, New York, 1963). Revisit the little girl, "Pepita" in Brooks's title poem, *In the Mecca,* conceived in 1954 as a young adult novel, then published as verse in 1968.

[4] Lorde wrote "Need: A Chorale for Black Women Voices" for Patricia Cowan and Bobbie Jean Graham and the hundreds of other mangled Black Women whose nightmares inform these words (*Undersong: Chosen Poems, Old and New,* Norton, New York, 1992)

[5] Lamentation from Gwendolyn Brooks's title poem, "In the Mecca" (*In the Mecca,* Harper, New York, 1968)

[6] Sandra Bland (@a_sandybeach) of Chicago tweeted this at 9:43 am on April 8, 2015 with the hashtags #BlackLivesMatter and #SandySpeaks, three months before she was found hung in a jail cell in Waller, Texas on July 13, 2015.

310 LUCY

t's kind of scary to me. Kind of lonesome. I see people go in but I never see them come out. You know how a house can take on the spirit of a place? Well, that's how the house at 310 Lucy looks—defeated—vacant and neglected the way we all feel living here.

Any day of the week I come out and sit on my porch. I see the same boarded up windows and broke down handrails that's been over there for the better part of ten years. Used to be a tree in that yard, a big pecan tree, but lightning struck it down, then the white fungus erupted on its bark and branches, great big old canker sores. After the lightning and the leprosy, then come the city. They chopped it up until the poor thang wasn't a tree no more but a body that's been mutilated. No arms, no legs, not even a neck. But the little bit of stump they left got sprigs of green.

Wouldn't it be something if people were like trees? You could take your finger and scrape the branches, see if the tissue underneath is green. If it is, you know they alive. If it ain't, you know their spirit is dead.

On these streets they let the liquor dance. Spirits dance in their veins. I see them with their pants sagging low. With their titties all out for everybody under the sky to see. They like to laugh loud, open-mouthed, the kind of laughter where it's all tongue and teeth. I don't judge no more, just witness. I know now it's a kind of silent, coded language, one you won't know how to speak unless you know what it feels like to want and need to be seen.

Like that old yellow house across the street. I see it everyday but it might as well be invisible. The woman who owned it years ago, long dead. Buried over at Calvary. The slumlord who call hisself "investing," rent it out to some young folks. Poor baby looked older than the mama. Four weeks later he evicts them, then he rent it out again. I see that sign go up in the yard over and over. I watched them set folks' furniture right out there on the street. The sheriff left and then the rain come. By the time the rain stop falling, all they have left is waterlogged memories.

It go on like that for a while, and then one day I notice the sign don't go up. No one moved in. No one put out. So I got used to watching the house watch me. Then one night, when the last dope boy's car drag races down the street, I see people going in there.

They didn't have no furniture. They didn't have no clothes. Look like all they had was theyself. It's common for folks to move in the middle of the night—don't want no roguish neighbors scoping your stuff and plotting to steal it from you. But who move in without a plate or a stitch the first? Especially when MLG&W ain't turned on a bit of utilities?

When I see whoever they is sitting up in the dark, not even a flicker of candlelight, I put my cigarette out and go back in my own house. I figure that can't be but one or two things, crackhead or flophouse. And I lived too long to be sitting cross the street staring at all that mess.

But the police say wasn't nobody there when they stopped by, and the city say ain't nothing they can do. Probably another one of those out of town investors. They buying up parcels of cheap land and don't give a damn what nobody here do. So I wait. Like the investors and the city waiting us out. Hoping we'll hurry up and die so they can snatch up our little piece of land and do what they been planning to do anyway.

Then one day, two more people walk down the sidewalk and up the stone steps. They looking straight ahead, don't even speak. That's fine by me, because I don't like nobody in my business, but just like before, they go in what was supposed to be a boarded-up door. This time, I wait all day and all night, but they never come out again.

"Something going on," I tell them but by now, I'm already on the police's take-your-time-she-crazy list. They can't find anyone in there, and to make it stranger, they say there isn't a stick of furniture. It doesn't look like anyone has been there in several years. Just dust and dirt, and ain't no footprints either. But I know what I saw. People going in but they never coming out.

After that last visit, I watched on different days at least a dozen pair of folks I had never seen before. They walk down the sidewalk and up the stairs, and I couldn't get a single one to answer me or speak.

Who they are and where they're going, I didn't have a clue. They looked like regular folks. Grown people, got-good-jobs people and some with children, dressed nice, like they just got off work or were walking home from school. Normal folks, quiet mostly, but a few times, I catch them whispering, excited.

Then one night, I'm watching the evening news and a face flashes across the screen. A missing man. My throat catches 'cuz I've seen that face before. He smiled right at me, refused to speak, as he walked right through the yellow house's door. The news says it took a while for his family to realize he was gone. Said he was the kind of person who could sit in an empty room and you would never know he was ever there. I sit in the eerie blue light a long time after that. Thinking back on all I have seen, the visible but invisible faces that come down our forgotten street and disappear inside that falling-down-empty house, to arrive at a new place that no one sees. Where do they go, I wonder? How? But I never ask why. A mystery whose answer gnaws at the insides of me. Maybe when I get tired, too, I'll get on off this porch, walk up them crumbling stairs and find out.

I know this. If you don't look closely, you will make the mistake and think all we got here is empty lots with cinder blocks, stone staircases that lead up to empty dreams.

But this is the place where the end-of-the-road go. This is the place where the on-my-last rope flow. This is where you come to find yourself. The place where the black sheep disappear in the wild forest. You see a dead tree stump. I see a sprig of green. You see an abandoned, empty house. I see a tent of miracles, a house of dreams. Much has disappeared among the abandoned houses, the blighted streets.

Among the lost things, find yourself whole again.

SHANEQUA'S BLUES— OR ANOTHER SHOTGUN LULLABY

She never told nobody, but Shanequa knew before anyone else did, how big it was, this thing that was wrong with her. She was only seven, but seven is a holy number, and she was only a girl, but a child is a sacred thing, and she was already dying, but she knew even so, all the same: even back before they come to bury her, she knew about the tree and the great navelstring, the many-limbed, dark-barked tree that grew on the bellybutton of a place some called *Guinee*, *Abyssinia*, and others just called Africa, great garden of life.

Partly she knew from sleep, the part of night they call dream, and it was this dream that Shanequa had the night her spirit rise, the night they say her heart stop and her body grew still. On that night, Osiris held her tiny heart-soul and weighed it in the balance against Maat's plumed feather of truth. Together the god and the goddess weighed her soul that night in the place Between, the place between dead and alive, and it was he who whispered to Shanequa, and *touched* her, and it was because of his touch that she remembered his instructions now.

Shanequa knew Mama wouldn't like what the god had told her. She knew she'd tell her to close her eyes and forget, to draw a picture and turn the god's words into a story, call the story a dream. And that is what Mama had told her, *if you can name your fear, then it don't have no power on you.* Mama had said it, smiling, like she'd read it in one of her books, but Shanequa didn't know if she believed her. Didn't know if Mama believed herself. She'd told Mama that hard secret, had whispered his name, even when she could still smell his stank breath and hear his scary voice telling her not to, but Mama didn't act like she heard her then, never even mentioned it again. Shanequa had struggled hard to name her fear but saying the words didn't do nothing. At least not then. It wasn't until she got sick, real sick, did the man she named stop, and the time before last, when Shanequa had come home from the hospital, he was gone. Maybe that's what Mama had meant. Maybe Shanequa's words, even half whispered when Mama's back was turned, had made her mama's ole nasty boyfriend go away. Maybe there *was* power in the words, but if there was, Shanequa didn't really see it, not until the god had shown her.

No, Shanequa knew that Mama wouldn't like the god or what he had said at all. That Shanequa would have to die first in order to live. But even more than the certainty that she could never tell Mama *that* truth, Shanequa knew something about magic because its dance lived inside her heart, lived for seven years in her bones. She breathed and drank the dance, long before the disease had blown through her blood, strangling each cell, finally overtaking her life.

It was the dance she performed, when they thought a seizure had captured her. It was the music she heard, instead of her mama's sharp screams, her mama's wailing, *somebody calling her name* in notes she'd never heard before. And that was the thing about Shanequa: the magic was inside her, and so was the dance, and so when she died she lived again, just like the dogfaced god had said, and when she crossed on over to the other side, the god touched her, and the goddess that looked like a great winged bird or a black angel or one of those black butterflies her mama used to sing about, stroked her face gently with her great feather called Truth, and they laughed and danced, holding Shanequa's tiny heart-soul up high, and then he touched her *there* and told her she would have to live, only to die yet again.

Shanequa was a little boney thing, not a hair on her head, just a smooth spark, weak but holding on to life. When the god had touched her, in that quivering spot on the side of her head, the part folk call temple, Shanequa's eyes had rolled back, her head lolling on her neck, heavy, so full of the music and the magic, her body couldn't do nothing but dance, and so she had. Shanequa danced all the way back from the god's hand. She danced all the way under, like limbo, like skip-the-loo under the black angel's wings, and the magic pulsed through her, making her jerk and throw up her arms, eyes blinking hard, blinking back tears. And when she jerked and grew still, the doctors and the nurses commanded her mama to leave the tiny hospital room, as they lay the machine's cold electric hands on Shanequa's quivering brown body, wracked in sweat, believing its fire could wring her from the dance's mad beat. But all she heard was hoodoo harps and a whole lot of bass, sound like black noise, broke down beatboxing, like the radio dial got crossed, like when Mama tried to find that old gospel station, lost between K97 and the blues.

And as she lay there, her eyes would open every now and then, and somewhere in the distance, she'd hear a shout, look up, but only see stern faces, the fear running slick down their foreheads and cheeks. She'd lay there and wonder why, no one else was dancing, could they not hear the music, didn't their own bones want to join the dance?

But anyone with half an ear for magic, half a toe for dance, can hear the river melody deep inside the blues, feel its pull on their blood, driving them to throw up each hand, palm kissing sky, and dance. Shanequa's mother, Brenda Wells, heard it every time she listened, but she only listened when she was afraid.

Brenda's Blues

Twelve.

That's how long she had before the street caught up with her. Twelve short years of Double Dutch and red rubber ball bliss before Donnell Peterson in Widow's Wyck had snatched her rope and stole her cherry in the woods by the creek. She was mad before she even heard him whistling at her heels, mad because Melody Walker had lost not one but two of her prized jacks. Melody called herself being mad because Brenda and her best friend Krystal were beating her and would have beat her again if she hadn't have turned tail and snatched up two jacks while she was running. Now Brenda had to go all the way back home to get her 'mergency set, and these were just the plain gunmetal kind, not the pretty, shiny rainbow-colored ones Brenda had carefully kept in a mesh bag long as she could remember.

So when Donnell call himself sneaking up on her, big as he was, snapping every twig and branch from the low side of the land bridge to the high side, back where Brenda and her mama and daddy lived, she didn't even turn around to look at him, just cussed him over her shoulder.

"Leave me 'lone, Donnell, ain't nobody stuttin' you."

When she was sure he had gone, when she was sure she couldn't hear his ragged breathing anymore, Brenda curled herself up into a little ball and let the tears spill out of her eyes and onto the earth, let them spill out until all she could feel was the cool grass and the twigs brushing up against her cheeks. When he first grabbed her, she had tried to snatch away, but he pinned her down, slamming her really, like a move that she and Daddy used to laugh about when they watched Sputnik and Mr. Tojo Yamamoto wrasslin' on TV.

Brenda didn't want to even think about seeing Daddy, let alone what he might say, so instead, she lay in the weeds and the little river stones, with the dandelion seedlings floating above her head and tried to rock her pain away. The first song that came to her mind was one of her mama's favorites. The last time Brenda saw her mother, she was trying to get her father to go with her to see Elvis at Colored Night at the fairgrounds. She had heard B.B. King might be there, and Rufus Thomas, too, and she didn't want to miss not n'am one of them.

But Daddy had stayed home, saying he wasn't interested in a bunch of white folk playing at nigger. "Why they can't sing nothing new? Niggas can't have shit. Next they'll be telling us they invented the blues."

"Why they can't sing 'cause they like it? Why everything got to be new with you? New car, and we can't afford it. New pussy, knowing you can't do nothing with it."

"Woman, don't start no shit with me today—"

"Don't start none, won't be none."

Brenda knew to keep the door closed, the blankie 'round her head tight, but she could still hear them yelling. But even the memory of them yelling didn't drown out the sound of Donnell's ragged breathing in her ear. She wanted to reach for something else, not another memory that only brought pain, so she tried to remember her mama singing. A nonsense song came to mind, a song ancient and familiar. She didn't know where the song came from, hadn't remembered her mother singing it, but there it was all the same. Mama's smile, Mama's voice, then not-Mama's smile, not-Mama's voice, but a creature she couldn't quite place. The sound in her ear was like a low breathing, rushing water, like someone was trying to hum her to sleep, saying words that didn't make sense no matter how hard she thought on it.

Later, the fireflies came, flitting over her head and worry hit her deep down in her belly. Daylight was turning slowly into twilight, and she didn't know how long she'd lain there, listening to the song of the strange presence. A lawn mower buzzed far off in the background. With the scent of fresh cut grass and Donnell's stale, musky scent still around her, all Brenda could focus on now was the sound of her father's anger, the sadness he carried in the back of his throat when he said Brenda's name, and the hole her mother had left when she'd gone away.

No, she wouldn't tell Daddy, not now, not ever if she could help it. Knowing what happened to her would just make the hole in their lives even deeper. Instead, Brenda held her breath. She pressed her body into the warm stillness of the earth beneath her and prayed that the silence and the soil would take her in.

When her baby's life was reduced to that flickering blue flat line, the only sound Brenda Wells heard was the strange song that she heard humming in her ear that day a fool tried to steal her spirit.

From Senegal to Senatobia
"The more you do it, the more perfect it come to you."
That's what Uncle Oumar wrote in his last letter. Mopti had read the line again and again, trying to make sense of his uncle's perfect penmanship.

> *Well, the blues am a achin' old heart disease,*
> *Well, the blues am a low down achin'*
> *heart disease,*
> *Like consumption, killin' me by degrees.*
> —Robert Johnson

He could read the words distinctly. The message behind their meaning, well that was a mystery his uncle had left unclear. Mopti had traveled all the way from his orderly desk job in Dakar, Senegal to pay his respects and bury his father's dead. Mopti had consulted his maps, read several blogs and travel features, and noted the tourist advisories. He packed one case of disposable clothing, just a few simple, sufficiently solemn bits he would not terribly mind losing. He had his hair cut extra low and his shoes shined. He doublechecked his papers, just in case.

Mopti traveled with a few token gifts, some old family photos his mother had pressed into his hand and some fragrant cooking spice. But the older brother Mopti's father had spoken so crudely of, had turned out to be far more than anyone had ever suspected. Now he knew why the money sent across the waters for his education had dwindled over the years. Uncle Oumar had lived a double, perhaps even a triple life. He'd long since abandoned his medical studies in New York, before Mopti was born. The shotgun house in Senatobia, the bull's eye heart of Mississippi, had been just one of his uncle's properties. And from what he could tell, none of them had been worth more than the land they leaned on. The lawyer said two more besides his house in Senatobia remained intact, one near Clarksdale, and the other somewhere in another small town called Mound Bayou.

In all his days, Mopti never thought he would find himself in Mississippi, but that was the path his uncle, prodigy turned pariah, had finally led him. Mopti had crossed the water to see his Uncle Oumar properly laid to rest, but his father had refused. The ocean was not wide enough to contain the gulf between the two men.

And even if Mopti understood his Uncle Oumar's words, it was the art that he couldn't make out. Oumar had drawn what first appeared to be a series of concentric circles, then morphed into what looked like pinwheels, then changed again to a jagged lightning bolt, or a zig-zaggy cross. Strange signs and symbols. Hastily drawn images whose meaning wasn't clear. The words appeared to be more blues lyrics or perhaps the ravings of a backroom madman, someone who abandoned his family, his bloodline, his future, to chase the trail of a Howlin' Wolf. Mopti imagined the sound of the bluesman's freight train voice and tried to read between the lines of the words his uncle had carefully written down. There was no one left willing to do so. No one left really who could.

Brother, I knew someday you would come for me, but you are looking in the wrong place. I had hoped that you would forgive me. Despite what you think, my love for our sister knows no bounds. I tried to save her. Was forced to search elsewhere for the knowledge Western medicine could not provide. Please forgive me. I was so very close but not swift enough to save dear Aminata. Brother, since you did not like my path in life, I am sending you on a journey in my death.

Everybody say they don't like the blues, but you wrong.
See the blues come from way back. And I'm gon' tell you something again.
The things that's going on today is not the blues.
It's just a good beat that people just carrying.
But now when it come down to the blues,
see I'm gonna show you how to be the blues.
I'm going to show you how to travel the blues
to the places the old ones don't want you to go.
You just sit back and listen. Watch. Brother.
I'm gonna show you.

- Howlin' Wolf

The letter with the strange song had left Mopti puzzled. The rooms in the small, two-bedroom, one bath house, were covered with photocopied excerpts of oral histories and interviews of musicians, stories about midnight pacts made at legendary crossroads, of artists who sold their souls to the Devil. Mopti knew very well how his father would have responded to such things. He would have tossed it all, the articles, the grainy photographs and portraits of sad-eyed, weary looking men clutching their guitars, the cryptic lyrics, and the bizarre drawings, everything would have been crumpled up and placed in the trash. What did it all mean and why had Uncle Oumar left this?

Mopti rubbed his face. Smoky circles ringed his eyes like dark moon craters. He was tired from his long travels and frustrated. His father would not approve, but Mopti felt he owed it to Uncle Oumar to at least try to decipher the puzzle he had left. Whatever it was, it what was so important that his uncle pursued it rather than travel home to see his beloved sister buried, the one he said he cherished and missed.

A large arrow pointed to an old stereo system with speakers Mopti had only seen in vintage magazines. When Mopti pushed play, a husky shout filled the room. Startled him so bad, he dropped the letter and nearly fell out of his chair.

III ... am, a back door man! I am a back door man.
What men don't know, little girls understand.
Early morning when the rooster call.
Something telling you, you better get up and go.
I am .... I am ... a back door man.

6✼9

Mopti calmed his breathing and stared at the drawing of a great tall, wide tree with a door. They didn't have trees like that in his father's old village, not anymore, and Mopti doubted such trees existed in the land where his uncle had chosen to bury his future seed. Mopti did not know why Uncle Oumar had betrayed his promise to the family, or why his obsession had led him to leave his home and disappear into the heart of Mississippi, but Mopti knew one thing for certain. The letter with the lyrics and the drawings were a map. Where it led, he was not sure. Mopti had to listen to the whole song three times before he realized, with some trepidation, the blues was the key.

Now he was driving down Main street, looking for an old dusty record shop that probably wasn't even open anymore. After he circled the block a few times, squinting at addresses, he decided to gas up and ask someone local who would know.

Mopti had just parked in front of pump two, when he saw her and heard the laughter.

"Girl, you popped that tire off so fast, you need to come and fix mine." The elder in the Cowboys hat held two bottles of water, handed one to the young boy sitting in his truck. "Started to ask if you needed some help, then I said, 'naw, this sister got it handled."

The woman chuckled, tightening the lugs. "If you don't know, better ask somebody!"

"Need to teach this one. Can't hardly get him off his phone."

"That your grandson?" she asked.

Cowboy nodded, opening the door. "Yeah, he rolls with me while his mama and n'em at work. If I let him, he'd spend half the day on that thang." They shared a laugh.

"My daughter, too. She used to..." her voice trailed off.

"Well, you have a nice day."

"You, too, sir."

Mopti watched the Ford pull off as he pumped his gas. Sadness replaced the air where laughter had been. The woman looked like she was wiping tears from her eyes. An embarrassed witness, Mopti turned away, watched the black numbers spin.

When he returned from getting a coke, he saw her sitting in her front seat, head bowed, hood up. Any other day Mopti would have driven on and "minded his," as his cousins in New York would say, but the sadness came off her in waves. He'd had bad days like this, when everything but the right thing was going on.

He bit his lip, then asked quietly, so quietly, he could convince himself that he had never spoken. "Miss, do you need some help?" She didn't answer. "Miss?"

Relieved, Mopti started to walk back when he heard her sigh. "Naw, I need a new car," she said. "Short of that, a boost. You got some jumper cables?"

"No, ma'am, I'm sorry," he stammered. "This is a rental. But maybe I could look at it?" Mopti didn't know anything about cars, how they ran or how they didn't, but he was so embarrassed, he'd try.

"No need," she said. "I know how to fix it, just can't afford to right now." There was that sadness again. To Mopti, it felt familiar, like grief. He stepped back, instinctively, before it caught him, too. He'd been pulled under his own waves before.

The woman frowned. "Don't worry, I'm not tryna hustle you. Thank you," she said. She emphasized the last words so pointedly, he knew he had been dismissed.

Mopti felt terrible. The cold drink sweated in his hands. "I'm so sorry. I didn't mean to..." He stumbled and tried again. "The idea that I've just made your bad day worse, is unacceptable. How can I help?" Part of Mopti wished he had never spoken. The other part felt he needed to. Reaching out was hard. When his father had asked him to see after his late uncle's arrangements, part of Mopti wanted to refuse. Traveling so far from Senegal to New York, all the way to Mississippi was more reaching out than Mopti was used to. He preferred the comfort of his desk.

To his surprise her dark eyes lightened, just a bit. "How do you know I'm having a bad day?"

Mopti smiled. "A flat tire, car not running, and..." he paused, then pointed at the bouquet of flowers resting in the passenger seat. "And someone you care about needs cheering?"

"You got a good eye," she said, impressed. "You sure you not tryna hustle *me*?"

The grin on Mopti's round face spread from ear to ear. The woman's easy humor comforted him. He liked her accent, the way she made the question sound like a song.

The roots reached back to Africa, but the blues were born here. In his notes, Mopti's uncle had asked a series of questions. *Why were there no blues in Cuba? In Sao Paolo, in Port-au-Prince?* In his neat, looping handwriting, Uncle Oumar answered his own queries. *Because the blues burst up from the Delta's fertile earth. The blues burst from the will to overcome sadness, to overcome anger, bad luck, exploitation, pain.* Underlined were two words, "personal" and "systemic."

Flipping through the sheath of papers, Mopti had come to understand that for his uncle, the blues were not only part of some personal quest of his, but the music also represented an ancient path to healing. Mopti was still trying to make heads and tails of it, and still wasn't sure how he would explain it all—if he dared try—to his father.

The journals were not dated. Mopti could only tell when one passage began and the other ended based on the quality of the handwriting, the color of the ink, the series of drawings. It looked like a madman had written it all, but Uncle Oumar had an order to his chaos. From what Mopti could tell, it was in New York, Harlem maybe or somewhere in Brooklyn at an old record shop, Resurrection Records, where Uncle Oumar had first heard of *The Great Going Song.*

Mopti laughed. "I'm not so sure you *can* be hustled. I wouldn't try anyhow. But maybe you could help me? I'm trying to find Sound Advice."

"Sound advice? First, you might want to finish that drink and get on in your nice car where it's nice and cool, instead of standing up out here, burning up with me."

When she spoke, colors seemed to leap out of her hands, encircle her face. Mopti watched her, shaking her head.

"Friend, you could make iron laugh."

"Thank you, I think." She squinted at him.

He chattered on, awkward but endearing. Mopti wasn't one of those men, fascinated by their own dark places. He seemed to shrink away from the shadows within himself. Instead, he walked in light, directed conversations to the day. He avoided negative holes in conversation, as if he was afraid he might fall into them. Brenda thought she liked this funny man with the big moonpie forehead and the Kermit the Frog smile, but Brenda no longer had absolute faith in her own judgment. The sound of her daughter's worst memory, one that nearly echoed her own, was woven into the sound of her dreams. Each night, she played it back, how she had tried to stop up her own ears. Pretending as if a truth was a lie. She had hoped there might be a time, some day far off in the future, when the daughter grown older might forgive. Brenda had not yet forgiven herself. She felt she had no right to forgiveness, not yet. Maybe not ever. She only wanted to make amends—or try to. She knew from her own life, you live, you may even forgive but you never forget.

So she watched Mopti out of the corners of her eye, listened with the inside of her heart.

"If you are looking for the record shop, it's not far from here. Just a few streets down, over on Main."

"That's where I was."

"Well how did you miss it? Nevermind." She grew quiet, staring at tulips and daisies in the seat of her car.

Mopti noticed a small white and red teddy bear peering up from the bouquet.

"They're for my daughter. She's at Delta County."

"Sorry to hear that," Mopti said. "I hope she will be well soon." He opened his car door and placed his drink in the cup holder. An empty potato chip bag floated past Mopti as he scanned the street and pumped gas, trying to ignore the woman sitting in the broken-down car beside him. He listened as she queried each new driver for jumper cables. It seemed with the newer cars, they weren't as necessary as before. Mopti felt discomfort sit in his belly, a heavy stone, as he sat in his rental and watched each new shopper shake their head 'no'. He wanted to help but didn't want to intrude. Good Samaritans could come off worse. But after the last person drove away and he found himself waiting at a light behind them, he turned the car around and rolled down the window. He coughed.

"Miss, miss?"

She looked up. "Yeah?"

"Excuse me. I didn't know your name." He struggled for words. "I am Mopti. I am visiting here to help put my uncle to rest. He died."

Brenda frowned. "Sorry, Mopti. Were you close?"

Mopti swallowed, the discomfort now a stone in his throat. "No but he...he is family." He looked down then released his words in a rush. "I don't mean to disturb you, Miss."

"Brenda."

"Miss Brenda, but I am new here and I don't know anyone.

I need to run some errands. It would be good to have help." Mopti bit his lip. He worried she might think he was a creep. She already hinted that he might be hustling her. "I mean directions. If you like, I could drop you off at the hospital, if you let me know where to go. Maybe you could tell me where Sound Advice is, since my GPS and I keep missing it?"

"It's right on Main Street," Brenda said, squinting at him. "But you know, ole boy is kind of weird. It's not like he's *trying* to be found."

"Oh, so you know it?"

She shrugged. "Not my thing, but yeah, it's been there a while. Has odd hours though. You'll be lucky if it's even open."

"I feel like I will be lucky if I find it."

Brenda laughed. "And it would just be my luck if you turn out to be some kind of serial killer."

Mopti looked stricken.

"Relax, I'm just kidding. It's been a long day and to be honest, I don't know how many more days I'm going to get..." her voice trailed off.

"Your daughter?"

Brenda nodded. "Since birth she was a bit of a miracle but she's not doing well. It's been tough. I need her to know that I'm there. I need to be there." Her eyes glistened, reflected sadness. "Look, I can show you the record store and you can drop me off on Main. I can take a bus."

Mopti started to protest.

"That's alright, I appreciate the offer," Brenda said, "but it's a bit out of the way for you. I'd call my cousin but she's not off yet. If we just head over to Main, I can show you Sound Advice and I'll be on my way."

"It's no problem," Mopti said. "I thank you." He unlocked the passenger door as Brenda took out the flowers and the teddy bear, then locked her car.

"Not that anyone would try to steal this hoopty."

"Hoopty," Mopti said smiling. "Everyone has colorful language here."

"In Mississippi?" Brenda asked.

"Here and New York, everywhere."

"Is that where you're from?" she asked as she slid into the seat. "I was finna say. Thought you were frontin' from Memphis. That's where my family's from. You know we got some of everybody there, 'colorful language' and all." She wrapped the paper tightly around the bouquet and balanced it in her lap. Her purse was looped around her shoulder, as if she was prepared to jump out at any moment if necessary.

"No, I'm from Senegal. Dakar. My family's from very small towns, like this, Dahra and Linguère."

"Can't say I know it—but Africa? I always wanted to visit one day. Maybe Ghana or Nigeria." Brenda's face brightened, her smile only showing a hint of sadness. "Somewhere they speak English. You know, make it easier on myself. Was hoping Shanequa and I could see the motherland."

Mopti smiled at that. He found it amusing but understood the sentiment. He couldn't imagine what it would feel like not to know where he was from. He grew up knowing his father's family was from the little rural town at the back door of the desert as his mother would say, and his mother's was near the train station, both dreaming of life in the big city, Dakar. His father said life in America was not anyone's dream until their little sister grew sick. Then a young Uncle Oumar had traveled in search of a medical education that somehow took him on an inexplicable detour. After his death, Mopti's father had discovered that his brother left a string of small properties in Mississippi. Mostly small houses with little value, certainly not worth more than the land. No one could explain why he had left New York to reside in towns no one in the family had ever heard of. They weren't sound investments and he didn't appear to have any close relationships there. Mopti had been trying to retrace his uncle's wayward steps, but he was worried. He wasn't sure where Uncle Oumar might lead him next.

"Shanequa, that's a beautiful name."

Brenda cut her eyes at him. Was he making fun of her? Satisfied, she thanked him. "It means, 'Belonging to God.'"

"Beautiful."

"She is."

"How old?" Mopti asked. He turned down the radio.

"Seven. Turn down here."

Mopti was just about to say he had driven that same street three times already when Brenda suddenly shouted, "Bingo!"

He wasn't sure how he missed it. A few doors from the Benjamin Franklin, pressed between a hardware store and dry cleaners was a narrow building with a zipper-like staircase.

"Unbelievable," he said.

"And with that, I'll bid you good day and thank you, Mister..."

"Mopti. Mopti Cissé."

"Yes. Brenda Wells. Pleased to meet you. Be good and I hope you find what you're looking for," Brenda said, opening the door.

"Thank you, Ms. Wells. I hope your daughter will be well soon," Mopti said. He felt that familiar wave of sadness again. He started to pull off when one of the waves softly brushed his spirit. He grabbed the receipt from his gas station bag and jotted down his number. "Ms. Wells, I hope this does not offend you. I mean no harm, but it would be good to have a friend in town. I am not certain how long I must be here, but if it is okay, I will pray for you and for your dear Shanequa."

His eyes were earnest but Brenda also could see the embarrassment glisten on his wide forehead.

He wavered. "Of course no need to call," he stammered. "I leave that entirely to you. But it doesn't hurt to have someone else pray for you."

Brenda stared at him, her head slightly tilted, as if listening to a song he could not hear. Finally she took the receipt and folded it in her hand.

"Thank you. Prayer is appreciated."

Sound Advice

Faded vintage posters plastered the walls. Burgundy velvet covered the steps. Mopti walked up each one, careful not to brush against anything. Flyers and event postcards dangled along the sides, stroked him like fingers as he passed. Mopti shuddered.

Now he knew why he had the devil of a time finding the place. *Must be a law against putting addresses on the buildings,* Mopti thought. He passed the near-invisible Sound Advice sign many times on his own before Brenda had pointed and he finally saw "Vital Vinyl" in tiny letters beneath it. The run-down building was designed as if it was meant to fold up and disappear, accordion-style. Steep stairs led up to a blackhole door.

When Mopti finished huffing and puffing, he looked around. Records filled the space, stacked in rows of teal blue wooden shelves and orange plastic crates, spilled across wide tables. Vintage toys, stuffed animals, old 45s and 78s, and Christmas lights hung from the ceiling. Album covers and occult signs and symbols decked the walls. Mopti saw at least three different kinds of ouija boards. No one was in sight.

"So what are you looking for?"

Mopti nearly jumped out of his skin. The voice was right behind him. A thin older man wearing a "Don't Hate the Player" shirt stood, hand on his hip, waiting. Castle Grayskull hovered over his head. He didn't look like an occultist just a hoarder.

"Something rare—" Mopti managed to say.

"Rare? Listen, you ain't seen rare 'til you've seen my X-ray collection. Straight from the Cold War." His mouth approximated a smile. "Now we thought we had bootleggers. You got to see what they made over in Russia. I mean *bone* music."

He waved and didn't wait to see if Mopti followed him.

"They had to do everything in secret. Most of the good music was banned. See this?" He held it out so Mopti could note the illuminated ribcage. "They'd etch a copy right on an X-ray they stole from the hospitals, cut a circle with some kitchen scissors, and burn a hole right in the middle with a cigarette. Could play that sucker on anything, just as good as you please. Don't tell me what people can't do when they're pressed."

"I see," Mopti said, scanning the room.

"Okey dokey," Old Player said and placed the album back in its protective sleeve. "Bone music don't float your boat, so what is it?"

Mopti paused, sorting what he should say from what he wanted to say. The store looked as if a truckload of albums had exploded inside. Vinyl was everywhere he looked. Not a single CD in sight.

Old Player shrugged. "If you're into vinyl, you're into vinyl. It's not something you can explain. It's just in you."

"I don't think much of it's in me," Mopti said, "but my uncle, he definitely was...a collector."

"And what did he collect?" Old Player asked.

Mopti tried to answer. The house on Shands Bottom Road had piles of albums stored throughout every room, even the bathroom. Most, from what Mopti could tell, were blues, some jazz but the collection spanned music from around the world.

"A single record, pressed by unknown hands, never widely released. Something called *The Great Going Song*? I think that's the name of it."

Old Player frowned. "Well good luck with that."

"What do you mean?"

"Haven't heard that name in a long time. Most folks hunting for that good and crazy."

Mopti raised a brow. "Well, I try to be good. Not sure if I'm crazy yet..."

The shop owner laughed. "No disrespect, son, I'm just saying. Don't know if they start off that way, but seem like by the time they come through, they've lost it." Old Player squinted at him. "The last somebody call hisself looking for *The Great Going Song* looked a bit like you. Old Oumar. Y'all related?"

Mopti nodded and lowered his eyes. Shame made his cheeks feel hot and flushed.

Old Player turned around and picked up one of the faced out albums. "Listen, you want some psychedelic acid jazz? Might as well listen to some of this." He handed the album to Mopti. "This is a rare one." He leaned his elbows on the counter as he moved the needle. Suddenly the air erupted into the sound of blue crystals. Mopti felt as if he'd been rained on. "What's your name?"

"Mopti Cissé."

"I'm sorry for your loss. Your uncle was a nice man. A little strange," Old Player said, "a bit obsessed, like most vinyl hounds, but ain't no sense in chasing after fairy tales." He stared at Mopti. "Especially tales that can get you killed."

If the *tick-ticking* of the overhead fan had been a record player, the needle would have skipped and scratched. Mopti's eyes and lips formed a series of questions.

"All I'm saying is that folks been looking for that album a good, long time. Nobody's found it yet, but a whole lot of folks found some shit they wished they hadn't."

"Like what?" Mopti shivered.

Old Player shrugged. "Bad luck. Misfortune. Death. The usual stuff. Which is kinda funny, since the whole point of *The Great Going Song* is to overcome death in the first place."

Mopti picked through a box of 45s on the counter. A James Brown bobblehead nodded at him.

"I've been trying to understand why my uncle wanted the album so much. It looks like he spent a considerable amount of time and resources trying to track it down. And there isn't a lot about it out there."

Old Player looked thoughtful, rested his arms on the cluttered counter.

"Some hobbies have a way of taking over you. Collecting can be like that, like a drug. You never know if and when you'll grow addicted. Sometimes it's hard to figure out when you should stop—if you can stop." He stared at Mopti, his eyes like pennies. "But *The Great Going Song* is different. It's not your ordinary record."

Mopti didn't like how he was looking at him. He turned and dug through a crate, flipped through familiar names and images. He paused at one, *Otha Turner and the Afrossippi Allstars*. "My uncle has a lot of these artists. Some he has multiple copies of. Is that *Going Song* album really valuable?"

A pinwheel spun over Old Player's shoulder. His eyes took on a waxy sheen.

"Why? You looking to get into collecting?"

"No. I was just curious." Mopti slid the *Allstars* back into the crate. "My uncle wrote a lot about different albums. This one seemed to stand out for him. But I can't figure out who the artist is."

"Nobody knows. Part of the mystery. And yeah, rare vinyl can get up to crazy amounts. I know a previously unknown blues 45, from Sun, that went for $10,000. A 78 went for $30,000. That was online and the collector didn't even blink 'cuz that was a steal. But the record you're talking about is super rare, more rare than hen's teeth. Only three copies were made."

"Just three?"

"Yep. They say the album is made of the perfect sound, full of all the colors of our world. It's a miraculous key, said to open doors that only a god can."

"A god?" Mopti didn't like this kind of talk, and the more the man spoke, the more he sounded like Uncle Oumar's strange, manic notes.

"Only one number in our universal spectrum is the same color and sound, the core frequency of creation, nature, life. The original musical scale has only six notes, but they say that there are actually nine."

"Nine? Now you're speaking my language," Mopti said. "I'm an accountant. I speak numbers fluently."

"Ah," Old Player said. "But these are the kind of numbers that can change a world, a kind of sacred geometry."

"I'm familiar with this in my country," Mopti said. "It is a science of creating space, yes? Art, what have you, that reflects faith. You build architecture, music, writings that exhalt the Greatness, the Oneness..."

Old Player's eyes sparkled, his mouth settling into a tight grin. "You *are* your uncle's nephew."

"Did he come here often?" Mopti asked, unsure if he should be pleased or offended.

"At first. He would buy me out of my blues and some of the rarer, off the beaten path jazz. Place special orders every now and then. He had an eclectic taste. Started off with Hip Hop, classics, and fresher takes. Iron Mic Coalition, Nicole Mitchell's Black Earth Ensemble, Kamasi Washington, Ekpe Abioto and the African Jazz Ensemble, big pure, free sound like that. But I didn't see him much before," he paused. "Before he died."

"Yes. I am not as versed on this as he was," Mopti said. "He certainly had a love of music that must have comforted him. I don't understand it but somehow it drove him. My family had not seen him for many years. I, myself, have no memories of my uncle, though I am told we do share a likeness."

Old Player didn't look convinced.

"But I don't share his music hobby, the collecting as you call it. What is it about this *Going Great* music? If there were six notes in the original music scale, how do you get nine?"

"It's called *The Great. Going. Song,*" Old Player said, emphasizing each word to reveal tiny, sharp teeth. To Mopti he looked irritated. "It is made up of the original six, solfeggio." He sang the notes, apologizing. "Forgive me. I'm no Maria von Trapp but you get the idea."

Mopti nodded. "I...I think so."

"Okay, well, you start with the original six that these old Benedictine monks created to sing their Gregorian chants but it's older than that, dates back to biblical days," he said. He took a sharpie from a red "Tighten It Up" cup and started drawing. "396, 417, 528, 639, 741, and 852," he said. "Plus three additional notes, 963, 174, 285. Together they form a perfect circle of sound, and that circle of sound can heal all things, make what is dark, light, what is broken whole. The nine sacred notes of healing. The basis for a song that can heal this broken planet."

Not sure how to respond, Mopti pursed his lips and nodded affirmatively. "We do need healing," he said awkwardly. He realized he would not be getting much help from here. The record store owner, who by the way, had not offered his name, may very well have helped to fuel his uncle's bizarre theories. Mopti began searching for a graceful exit.

"I've seen those eyes before," Old Player said. "The face of a skeptic. Fine. It's better that you don't believe. Because whether we do or not, there is no denying. We must find another way. And what is more universal than music? Every culture has a song."

"It's not that I don't believe, it's that I am struggling to understand."

"What's there to understand, Moby?" Mopti smiled. "It's clear that we're all off center. The planet is imbalanced. We're not connected to that oneness you spoke of. Out of sync, probably running out of time. We are in dissonance to another note. But there are nine core creative frequencies to the universe. Nine, Moby. Everything in our universe is made from nine notes. *The Great Going Song* is what the coldest musicians have been striving for. They reach and they reach and some even get real close, but none have recaptured the legendary sound that's said to open God's front door."

"This talk of music and healing, that I can follow. But this other, it sounds..." Mopti did not want to offend the man, so he held his tongue.

"Dangerous? Yes. Remember what I told you when you walked in here. Folks have been searching, a long time, and they get caught out there. Sometimes when you search for gods you find the devil."

Old Player's penny eyes flickered into slits. Mopti saw an opening for escape.

"You spoke about jazz but my uncle has a lot of blues musicians in his collection. Delta blues. The early ones. With the crossroads talk and all of that, how does this music connect with *The Great Going Song*?"

"A lot of blues and jazz got plenty of tritones, this space between notes that just don't sound right. And of course, wouldn't have no blues without that blue note. Church folks used to call it the Devil's music. It's what gives the music that restless, rambling along feeling. What made it dangerous."

Old Player pointed to a black and white poster on the wall. "So you get Tommy and Robert Johnson, no relation, talking about the devil at the crossroads. Now, Robert took this photo right at Hooks Brothers on Beale Street up in Memphis around 1935. It's the only known studio portrait of him. Look at that smile. Look in his eyes. You think that young man knew he'd be dead three years later? Some thangs you don't play with."

Mopti found himself inching toward the door.

"So you take that 741 and 528 I told you about. Play them together and it creates a sense of dis-ease. Your body's trained to hear harmony but instead you hear that weird sound, like something's off, trouble gonna come. A sound strange as that folks thought it could harm you, physically, emotionally, spiritually, so they called it 'The Devil's Interval,' the Tritone." Old Player thrust three fingers out, like throwing a curse.

"But others know of it as just a key part of *The Great Going Song*. African polyrhythms, tonal notes, throat singing, all that heal."

"Like cats purring, healing their bones?"

Old Player looked at Mopti as if he suddenly grew two heads. "Yeah, well, I guess." An air of boredom deflated his words. "Browse all you want. Let me know if you see something you like."

Mopti turned to watch Old Player disappear behind a backroom door. He was gone as quickly as he had appeared. After an awkward silence, when it was clear the owner wasn't planning to come back, Mopti stopped his half-hearted crate digging. He placed the copy of Sun Ra's *Angels and Demons At Play* atop the counter on his way out.

That night Mopti unrolled his mat and prayed for his uncle. For his mother and his father who mourned him, even in anger. For the beloved aunt his uncle could not save. For the kind, sad woman he met who grieved for her child. He wasn't sure if he understood it, but he felt certain a great sense of loss united them all. Alone in the quiet solitude of his uncle's lonely house, Mopti felt the reach of greater hands moving them. Something besides death had called him across the waters, something that made Mopti reflect on what he may have loss in his own life.

The next day Mopti headed over to the library on Ward but was surprised to receive a phone call.

"Mopti, this is Brenda. How you doing?"

"I'm well, friend. Good to hear you."

She had just left the hospital and invited him to join her for lunch. Eager to leave his window seat, Mopti tucked his papers and books in his backpack, waved goodbye to the friendly staff and met her at Coleman's.

She was sitting at a table, nibbling on some fries. "Sorry, my stomach's in my back."

"Indeed," Mopti said, laughing.

"If I eat anymore hospital food, they will probably have to check me in, too."

"How is she, your Shanequa?"

"Resting." She passed him a menu. "If you don't like pork, they have real good cheeseburgers."

They ordered burgers and gulped down soda as they talked, chatting about the rhythms that had shaped their lives. Brenda had Shanequa late in life, but the father left. *Everybody like miracles but don't nobody want to raise one.* Brenda had fled the city for the small town, in search of a quieter peace for her daughter, closer to family ties she'd long wanted to know. Mopti had remained in the city, where he could disappear in plain sight. The anonymity and routine of his work gave him comfort. The tiny hometowns of his parents, small stops between the desert and the river, would have made the pressure of constant social engagement and familiarity too much for him.

Brenda spoke with an openness that made him feel like she was one of his best friends, not that he had many. Over the next few days, they met for lunch or chatted, sharing more about their worries and their fears. Mopti now knew the child's condition was serious. She was in an induced coma, awaiting to see if her brain and her lungs could re-learn how to breathe on their own. Mopti shared some of Brenda's grief. He prayed for the child too young to have such a burdened heart.

One day Mopti told Brenda about his uncle's collection, his search for *The Great Going Song,* and his mysterious clues. When he mentioned all of the Robert Johnson lyrics and research, she delivered Mopti his most promising lead.

"It's either the crossroads or the cemetery, Mopti."

"What do you mean?"

"We got a whole Mississippi Blues Trail that goes all through the state. If tourists come looking for Robert Johnson, they going to one of the crossroads or to visit one of his graves."

Mopti nearly spit out his water. "One of his graves? How

many graves does the man have?"

"Mane, three. Can you believe it? But if you think about his life, short as it was—he was a certified member of the 27 Club—then it makes sense." She saw Mopti's puzzled face. "There are a lot of famous folks, mostly musicians, who all died tragically at age twenty-seven. Robert's mama traveled a lot when he and his family was young. They went from Central Mississippi to here in the Delta, then she married about three-four times, or something. And he was between her new husband's in Memphis and folks near here. By the time he ran off, he had already been on the road anyway."

"Where are these graves?"

"Right around each other. One not too far from where he died. You know the story is that he was a bit of a catdaddy and got poisoned near Greenwood at the Three Forks Store by somebody's jealous husband. So he's got a small grave marker out there in Quito, the middle of the boondocks. Another one at Mt. Zion Missionary Baptist Church in Morgan City, that looks like a big ole Egyptian obelisk. And the other one out on Money Road at *Little* Zion Missionary Baptist Church, also near Greenwood. A woman from the Luther Wade Plantation told somebody that her husband was the one that dug the grave. And it's near where he died, so there's that. But even so, knowing how tricky all this is, I wouldn't be surprised if he wasn't buried in none of them grounds."

"So you think I should check out the graves first or the crossroads?"

"I'm not sure you should be doing any of this. All the sites are about an hour and half away, some at some pretty obscure locations. The Little Zion is where some of my kin are buried. I haven't been there in years. You know we don't like to visit old graves."

"I understand. There are so many different traditions. I covered all the mirrors in my uncle's houses, even though it was clear he didn't live in some of them."

"Y'all do that, too?"

Mopti nodded. "There are some traditions where they will not remove the deceased through the front door, but will cut a hole in the wall and carry them out feet first."

"That ain't the kind of hole in the wall you want to be in," Brenda said. "So, you're planning a creepy road trip. How are you going to get there?"

"Drive."

She laughed. "You can drive all you want, but you ain't gon' find that burying ground."

Mopti's smooth, moon-like forehead knotted up. "And why not?"

"The folk from out there, good people but private. They take care of each other and mind their business. Don't welcome strangers stomping all over their burial grounds. They come from a long line of runners. Restless souls. Even the land can't be still. Ground always changing." She snatched his uncle's scribbled map right out of his hand. "I'm just kidding. But you got to know there, to go there."

"Why can't I just use GPS?" Mopti said, taking the map back.

Brenda sighed. "If you couldn't get down Main Street with GPS, what makes you think you're going to make it through these backwoods?"

Mopti shrugged, laughing. "Brenda! You're right, you're right."

"I'm just sayin'." She took a sip from her water bottle. "You could try it, but trust me, the roads are tricky if you don't know where you're going." She pointed at his map. "It's not too far away. If you wait until Friday, I can ask my cousin to stay with Shanequa for me. We've got great uncles and aunts out that way. Haven't been to Mound Bayou in years, not since I was a kid."

"Why not?"

Brenda shrugged. "Most of that part of my family has passed on. The rest moved to Memphis or got on down. I don't really have no reason to go back that much."

"Well, okay," Mopti said. "Let's roll."

"Oh, we rollin' now?" Brenda said and shook her head.

They started off early that Friday. Packed like mules, armed with shovels, flashlights, snacks, water, and the hand-drawn maps and notes from Mopti's uncle.

Everything started off well, but two hours later the laughter had drained out of them.

"I thought you said you knew where we were going?"

For the first time Mopti could recall, Brenda seemed at a loss for words. "It should've been over here," she said, pointing at his wrinkled up map.

"Well, it's not."

"I don't know what to tell ya. You got to go there to know there," she said.

Mopti frowned and watched her pick through her salad, then drove a fork into his own.

"How many crossroads are in Mississippi? I mean, we

have driven through five or six of them and haven't found that old church yet."

"You really think something's out there?" Brenda asked.

He shrugged. "I don't know but my uncle seemed to think so. That house back in town is full of all of his sketches and drawings. He believed the album was magic."

"Like magic *magic?*"

"Yes, healing magic."

Brenda looked up, stopped chewing. "What kind of healing?"

"That I don't know. The record shop guy said it could heal the world."

"I told you he wasn't right. And you say he just dipped on you after all that? Weird as all get out."

"What I could find in the library was just more of the same stuff Uncle Oumar had. Snippets of references in musician interviews. He kept a whole file on Robert Johnson. Most of it was just different versions on how he sold his soul to the devil."

"Lies," Brenda said. "They wrong for talking on that man's spirit like that."

"So you don't believe it?" Mopti asked.

"Hell naw," Brenda said, laughing. "It's a good ass story though. I'll give you that. But the truth probably is he went to the woodshed or found somebody who knew what they were doing, sat himself down somewhere and did his work. But naw! Got to be the devil. Got to be magic. Can't be that a negro actually worked his ass off. Sound like hatas hatin' to me."

"So you don't believe in the crossroads and all that?"

"I believe, just don't believe Robert took that route. Think about it. If it was that easy, wouldn't be no souls left in none of these counties! Mississippi gon' straight to hell."

Mopti bit into a tomato. "Brenda, you're something else."

"But I'm right though. What if all this crossroads talk was just his way of talking about something he already know?"

"Like what?" Mopti asked.

"Like the heartbreak you get when you give all you got and end up with nothing. Keep in mind, we talking about folks chopping cotton on rented land—sharecroppers, landless farmers. Ain't no question he ran away from home young. You'd run away, too. Ran away from that backbreaking no-paying work in the fields. Ran away from his parents. He was a traveling musician, hoboing on trains and such. Playing on street corners for coins and dollar bills. You think he didn't have dreams? I know the biggest one—to escape."

They sat in silence, remembering their own gambits, disappearance acts, then got back on the weary road. They headed down 55, the blur of green and brown zig-zagging, as one by one the mile markers ticked off each minute of their lives. They hurtled forward to what they hoped would not be another dead end, onward under the clouds and the scatter of wings, loose stitches of black in a sky threatening heavy rain.

Up Jumped the Devil

They took turns holding the shovel as they passed the houses where no one lived. Cobwebs and dust guarded the windows. Mopti ducked under branches. Brenda swatted clouds of gnats that rose from the ground. Together they stepped over the flat faces of rock that watched them from the earth. Out in the woods, everything was bound together, the living and the dead. They walked among the carved names, passed soil-stained tea cups, broken remnants of past lives, the black vertebrae of trees. They had found the cemetery, the place where everything comes to rest.

Brenda shuddered, skeeta-bit and full of regret. She wanted to help Mopti, but this was a road she wished she hadn't traveled. They would not catch her at sundown peering into amber bottles, a candle lit at the end. Souls were meant to be glimpsed only by their maker.

"Promise me we're not going to be out here graverobbing, right?"

"Of course not, Brenda."

"How you supposed to know where to dig?"

Mopti pulled out one of his uncle's drawings. "This looks like a big tree. I think from these notes, he was guessing the album would be buried under the Tree of Life. In my country, we call those baobab trees. Some of them are 6,000 years old, so wide, you could drive a car through them. They look upside down, like their roots touch the sky."

"Nope," Brenda said pointing. "That looks like *two* trees to me."

Mopti followed her line of vision and realized she was right. Two giant pecan trees stood like great sentinels in the back of the cemetery. Entwined, their gnarled, outstretched branches did look like great roots against the darkening Mississippi sky.

"Let's hurry up, mane," Brenda said swatting at something, "because walking back in the dark is not the move."

"Right," Mopti said and bowed his head at the tombstone. "I brought my torch," he said, then saw her expression. "Nevermind."

Mopti dropped his backpack on the ground and put on his gloves while Brenda walked back and forth between the two trees, inspecting them.

"Did your uncle have any idea which of these trees we are supposed to be digging under?"

Mopti's eyes said it all.

"*Mmmpf, mmmpf, mmmpf.*"

Mopti opened and closed his mouth three times without saying a word.

"Guess you better meeny-miny-mo it then."

"And what exactly is that, Brenda?"

She walked to the clearing in the center of the two trees and began to sing.

"Eeny, meeny, miny mo. Catch a tiger by it's toe. If it hollers, let'em go. Eeny meeny, miny mo. My mama told me to pick this one right over *here*." She bowed. "To the left, it is. And if it ain't, you can try the other one and then we're out."

"Deal," Mopti said and he began to dig in the hard earth. It wasn't as easy as they make it look on TV.

Brenda watched silently, shifting her weight from foot to foot, a silent observer until it was her turn.

"We out here diggin' for treasure like Pirate Jenny. Better be some money in this hole."

They were on the second tree just about to give up when Mopti let out a cry. Brenda turned the flashlight on it as the sun sank deeper in the sky.

"It looks like a bag."

Mopti brushed away the loose dirt and rocks. The soil felt cold to him, even through his gloves. "Thank you for being my friend," Mopti said and handed the bundle to Brenda.

"You want me to—?"

He nodded yes.

She smiled nervously then handed him the light and bent down next to him.

"Mopti, are you sure you want to do this? Because once we open this, you can't unring the bell."

"Open it," he said, his voice full of what he didn't anticipate.

"I'm trying but you're shaking the light. Hold steady."

Mopti was so weary but giddy, he didn't have the energy to argue or crack a joke. He waited as she unwrapped the cloth that covered it.

"Oh," she said and unraveled the fabric. "Ooh, this is wonderful. It looks like spun gold and water. But it's just a little damp. No telling how long it's been here." She pulled out another bag hidden inside. "Mopti!" She handed the album to him. "This was your uncle's dream. You should open it."

"I don't think I can. I didn't know how I would feel, but now..." his voice trailed off. "My aunt Aminata died, young. Her death left a mark on my family. My uncle's choices left a mark on my father and he in turn left one on me. I am not sure I want to hold his dream."

Brenda knew something about marks, had lived under the burden of scars her whole life. To know that she had passed them on to her daughter was another burden she would always bear. She held the album, heart aching, unsure what to do.

"Just open it," Mopti said wearily. "It's okay."

She took a deep breath. The album sleeve was not something

she'd seen before. Not paper, plastic, leather. It was made of a textile she didn't recognize. A message in a script she couldn't read was woven in the fabric. She pulled it off, resting it atop the beautiful covering.

"Wow."

They both leaned over to see it better.

It was black and coppery gold, splattered, watery waves staring up at them like an iris.

"Not bad for something we found buried under the roots of a pecan tree."

Mopti shook his head in wonder.

"There's a message here, in the dead wax." Brenda rubbed her thumb across the space.

"In the what?"

She pointed. "The part where there ain't no music. Between the end of the last song and the beginning of the label."

"Let me see." She handed him the record.

Let the light set you free, it said in English. Mopti turned it over, pointed the light so he could see. "This side looks more worn, but I think I can make it out."

"Bet you could read a whole book if you got out these woods." She swatted at some unseen predator. "Talking 'bout 'the light.' You know these mosquitoes out here are about as big as your head. I said I would bring you here, not get eaten alive while you sit up in the dark gawking."

"I'm sorry, Brenda, you're right. Let me get you home." He held the album then placed it back in its covering. "I'm sure it's been a long enough day. And you'll want to get back to Shanequa, I know."

Brenda nodded, fatigue in her voice. "Thanks." Brenda carefully repackaged it and tucked it gently inside its protective swaddling.

"Well, it's time to get our great asses going," she said. "I wonder what it sounds like."

Though he was ashamed and did not want to admit it, Mopti could not wait to hear what he had found. Giddiness and sadness guided him as he rode the car hard, barreling in the darkness, back through the flat, winding road.

"Mopti?"

He glanced over at her. "Yes?"

"I know you're happy to have found this thing you say your uncle left y'all for, but if I were you, I wouldn't tell nobody I found it."

Mopti turned down the radio. "I'm not sure if happy is the word. You know, my father was angry with Uncle Oumar because he left my aunt. Aunt Aminata, like I said, was their only sister. The youngest, she was always very ill. The family sent him to America to continue his education, but something happened. Now I have an idea of what. I wish I could have talked with him, known more about his life. For me, my uncle's biography is as illusive as your Robert Johnson. He was supposed to become a big time doctor, doing research and maybe one day help find a cure. But he abandoned his studies—and," Mopti sighed. "According to my father, he abandoned my aunt, too. And all that to pursue this folktale legend. All those years, searching. And here it is." Mopti motioned at the bundle in Brenda's lap. "We've found what my uncle could not. He was so close before he died but now what?"

"So you really believe he left everything to find this record? For you to find it?"

"Not any record, apparently, a legendary record," Mopti said, grief making his voice a hoarse whisper.

"Well, whatever his reason, Mopti, you found it. I have a feelin' a lot of other folks are gonna want what you got. Better keep it to yourself."

They drove thoughtfully in silence until he almost ran them off the road avoiding a deer.

"Damn, Mopti!"

"I'm sorry! I didn't see it."

They had no sooner corrected course when a truck shot out of the darkness, crashing right into them.

"Brenda!" Mopti yelled.

The car spun in the darkness, tires screeching disapproval. For Mopti it seemed like everything happened in slow motion. They spun down the road forever, and then, in seconds, everything happened very fast. Mopti didn't know how long he had lain there, his head pressed against the air bag, before he realized he heard nothing in the passenger seat next to him.

"Brenda," he whispered. "Brenda!"

She rose her head, eyes focusing in the dark. "Stop hollering, Mopti. I'm alright, I think."

"I'm so sorry! I don't know what happened," Mopti said. "It just came from nowhere."

Brenda rubbed her jaw, then stopped. "*Shhhh.* Do you hear that?" she whispered. "Where is the music coming from?" She was staring over his shoulder when her eyes widened. He saw the scream before he heard it.

"Run, Mopti, run! Get that thing out of here!"

"What?" Mopti's voice was confusion, pain.

"The record! He's coming for it. I knew it was no accident

way out here."

Mopti was caught between two impulses, neither included leaving Brenda, possibly broken up in a car that he was driving. "I'm not leaving you."

"You ain't got to," she said, and wrenched herself from the seatbelt. Brenda kicked open the door, was gone before he could stop her.

"I'm okay, Mopti, just grab the record and run!"

Mopti reached in the darkness for it. It had fallen on the floor, beneath the seat. When Mopti felt the burlap wrap, he half-suspected the album would be in pieces. To his surprise, the record was whole. He snatched it up, exited the car and took off.

"You can't hide, Moby, I see you. You shining!"

That voice, the butchery of his name. Mopti ran alongside the road, heading for the woods. Old Player limped behind him, shouting curses.

"You don't know what you have! Undeserving. Give it to me, boy!"

"What is wrong with you?" Mopti cried. "Why would you do that? You could have killed us!"

Old Player laughed. "Yeah but what you got in your hands could have healed ya. Play your cards right and I might heal you yet."

Mopti panted, struggled to see as he stumbled through the woods along the road. There was a field up ahead, not much to hide behind.

"You're crazy. Are you the one that tore up my uncle's house? Looking for this old record?"

"That old record is worth more than you, your uncle, or anyone else you know, put together. None of that other stuff he got off me was worth a damn."

Mopti stopped running. He had to. Could barely see in front of him or see his way out of this.

"Did you hurt my uncle? Are you the reason he died?" He turned to face the man who would have killed him and Brenda, too.

"Natural causes, well, natural enough," Old Player said. "I told you, the album is supposed to heal but it's also cursed. Folks who get after it don't fare too well."

"So why are you chasing it now? You rammed a truck into us and ran us off the road for something you claim is going to kill you, too."

"Desperate times require desperate measures. You new to the game. Don't know what you got, let alone what to do with it," he said.

Mopti's head ached. His neck was stiff.

"And what do you plan to do with it? You sat back and let my uncle, me, do all the work, for what purpose? You couldn't possibly want to heal anything or anybody."

Old Player stood in the field, his hand at his side.

"You won't have to worry about that. I'm going to take good care of *The Great Going Song* and make sure it is never lost again."

"It doesn't belong locked up in your safe, like one of your finds. If it can do what you say it can, this belongs to everyone. It belongs to the world."

"The world isn't good enough. The world can go to…hell," he said and aimed at Mopti's chest. Without thinking, Mopti used the album as a shield. The bullet must have rang through the air and hit the album, because Mopti suddenly felt a tremendous force. It vibrated through him, knocked him off his feet. He didn't even know Old Player had a gun.

Another Shotgun Lullaby

Later, when he finally caught up with Brenda, who managed to flag down another motorist and came back to find him, Mopti played the moment over and over in his mind. He knew Old Player had shot at him. He heard it fire and then he felt its force. But then a bright light lit up the darkness, illuminating tiny coppery-gold flecks in the air. The space around Mopti warmed, heating up until he wanted to release the album but he found he could not. The bullet ricocheted off its black and coppery surface, a vinyl he surely had never seen. Old Player had cried out, then disappeared, replaced with fiery dust, like shooting stars.

That night when Mopti played the album at his Uncle Oumar's house, something once broken and shattered grew whole and wanting inside him. For the first time he understood what hunger was and what it meant to be truly fed. Hunger gave his mind something his body could neither eat nor keep. Home was no longer on the other side of the ocean where he left it. He listened to the song with no name and realized he had starved himself in ways that went beyond hunger. Who was he now, Mopti wondered, far away from his orderly desk and how could he go back to whatever he had been?

Holes in his heart cried out to each other, one by one. And one by one they were filled. Strange cymbals, shouts, and snares floated through the air around him. Mopti felt a great presence slip inside his skin. The music simmered in his blood, walked in his bones. Mopti rarely sang beyond prayers. Now his voice was a choir. The sound of his own tongue hitting notes he never heard of frightened him, deep down in his soul.

He reached with shaking hands and snatched the needle up. It took a while for his heart to slow down, back to its normal beat, for his mind to catch up with his breath.

Old Mopti would have been too frightened to accept a gift so grand, a love supreme. Later when he found himself standing inside the hospital room's door he could only agree.

"You live too much inside yourself, leaving everyone else alone," Brenda said.

"Not everyone, friend," he said.

Brenda turned away, hummed the song she always hummed at Shanequa's bedside. She sang it for Shanequa, for her roommate, the other children who were hanging on the thread of life.

"So, you brought it," she said after a while. "Play it for me. I want to hear it, this *Great Going Song*. When I got home, I couldn't believe it. Got me out in the woods, about to get killed, feeling like Barnaby Jones and Nancy Drew. That's the *last* road trip I'm going on with you, Mopti Cissé."

Before he arrived and parked his rental, Mopti had it all in his mind. But now that he was there, listening to the child's tortured breathing, the machines wheezing, the other child also "resting," fear gripped his spirit again.

He wants to throw the album away, instead he tries to break it. He pulls it out of its faded sleeve. It feels strange in his hands as it warms with his touch. Where there should be faint glimmers around the folds of vinyl, this time there is red copper and orange gold, silvery threads of light like circuit boards. He holds the album in his hand, then throws it hard. Instead of lying on the floor shattered, the

shiny black pieces float in the air, rotate, and reassemble, returning
to its protective covering as a great hum fills the room. Mopti
stumbles back, shock on his face. His hands tremble.

Brenda cries out, disbelief struggling with fear,
with faith.

"I don't know what we brought out of that ground, but
somebody planted that seed years ago, and your uncle left it for you.
I don't know if it's a curse or a blessing and this may be a bell I can't
never unring, but if you ever loved somebody, anybody as much
as I love this child," Brenda says, her voice even, measured, "you
would try anything, too." She shakes her head. "No. Try wouldn't be
enough. You'd do it."

She has mastered the tone that conceals pain, but her eyes,
her eyes give her away.

Mopti unwraps the shimmery gold and blue fabric, slides
the album out again and let its warmth guide his hand. The small
portable LP player he'd hidden in his messenger bag now rests on the
night stand. He puts the needle to the vinyl, realizing how much he
has grown to like this ritual, of needle in wax. He waits for the lisp
and hiss. Watches Brenda's eyes as the record turns and Shanequa's
right leg trembles. He hears the most beautiful sound.

"Mama."

The album spins and spins, scarab wings furling and
unfurling. Only three pressed in the whole world. Somehow his uncle
managed to find one. The initials/press markings are symbolic. He
knows without knowing how he knows that there are two hidden
tracks on the album. One plays at 45, the other at 78. *The Great
Going Song* plays three speeds.

Time will pass. Time passes. Time passed.

Mopti's thoughts were one long spiral, moving from the outside to the inside, then back again. He would have to unlearn silence to be a true friend to her. He knows without knowing how he knows. Mopti wasn't sure if he could do that fully, but he would try. He looked at Brenda holding Shanequa. Or maybe it was the daughter who held her mother up. No, he thought, watching them together, watching as the other child opened his eyes. He thought of his Uncle Oumar, his father, and their sister, his aunt. He thought about all the years of love missing between them, because they did not try. Trying wouldn't be enough. Mopti let the strange music play and play, let it replace fear with faith.

Unlearning silence was the only way to do it.

MADAME & THE MAP
A JOURNEY IN FIVE MOVEMENTS

Madame's Map

I t was Madame who had such a passion for pork that she kept seven cooks slanging pans and pots around the clock. And what a kitchen that was, a fireplace as wide as a room with the dishes scattered as far as any eye could see and the skillets stacked up like Jacob's Ladder, teetering and tottering so high we knew the angels could smell the pork and dumplings way up in heaven. And the tables, what a mercy, with hogs in every state of undress, some still cold and bloody, hung over heavy hooks sharp as dogteeth, some turned so slowly on the black iron spit, the skin crackled and crumbled, popped and sizzled, a haint whispering in your ear. But most of the pigs lay in bloated piles, wasted because the Madame was ever busy, eyes bigger than her stomach. No matter how much food we piled on her plate, her endless hunger was never quite fed.

Strangeness it was, for her heart to be ruled by the belly, for her belly to eat and eat and never be full. It was her hunger that made Madame the slave and her belly that set me free.

My first day out of the hot, sweating field, I thought one of them sweet chariots we'd sang about in the praise house had swung low and was carrying me home. I had started my first day on Breakneck Hill as a hog hammerer. Madame was the one that called me. She didn't know my name, and truth be told, nobody else did either. They'd called me so many different things, you'd think my mama never bothered to name me before they snatched me from her tit. But that day Madame turned them blind mole eyes toward me. I lowered my own, thinking nothing good can come when slavery see free. I lowered my eyes, fixed them on the sun shining on a mouth full of yellow teeth.

"That one," she said and pointed, finger gnarled as an old oak. "The one with the tree trunk hands. Tree!" she said and from then on, that's what they called me. Tree. Nobody had to say nothing because they all knew she was talking about me. I'd been teased since my mama dropped me. Said my hands was so big I could carry the whole row by my own self. Said my hands was so big I could change the course of the river, just by waving. They didn't know the power of them hands, nor did I. None of us could have known that someday them great hands would carry all of us to freedom, or somewhere close to it, carry us far away from here.

"Too big and clumsy to be out here, murdering my cotton." Madame searched my face, but I avoided her eyes. I did not want to see whatever would look back at me. They said she was a neglectful owner. That she was hardly present at Breakneck Hill, always off on mysterious trips for long periods of time. Folks still worked as if she

was there, though. 'Cuz when she come back, overseer tell it all. And
she come back with strange things that don't make no kind of sense.
But she look at me and her stare feels like hunger and I look away,
not sure what to do with my hands. Then she turned to the one she
called Whistle, told him to make sure I came to the Hill. And that was
the last time she ever looked right at me. I like to tell myself that I
was too bright, like staring at the sun.

Truth is, I am ugly and she always fixed on my hands.
Madame liked oddness. Gathered it about her and sometimes treated
us like her special toys. My hands were my pass out of the cotton
fields. Guess they were larger than any she'd ever seen and Madame
was said to like big things. She had the biggest plantation East of
Stovall in Coahoma County, Mississippi. She had the biggest horse
on both sides of the Mississippi River. The biggest plantation, the
biggest number of slaves, house or field, and she lived on the Hill,
the great break your neck hill. Madame had plenty. Eighty heads,
one hundred sixty hands in the row. Though she could not see, she
seemed to know each one. New to the Hill, I wondered how Madame
could call each by name, sometimes without us even speaking a word.
I did not know how her great gray eyes, murky as the river, watched
us, hungry, sucking us into her sight, or how Madame sucked spirits
dry, as if sucking sweet marrow from a bone.

Despite her fondness for bigness, no one over five two ever
served Madame on the Hill. She kept wee servants and slaves around
her big house, little bitty people, strong and low to the ground, and
big horses, great big running things. She loved speed as much as she
loved to eat. The horse she loved best was nearly seventeen hands
high, maybe fourteen of my own, with a tail that could wrap round a

grown man three times and still make a wig for Madame. Plato was
what she called him, another old name from one of her even older
books, the books she never read but coveted. Her dead eyes watched
us greedily, for fear we'd discovered the secrets within skin. Plato was
what she called him on the Hill, but Plate Eye was what we called him
in the field. With eyes wide as plates, round as saucers, he stared and
rolled about as hard and as wildly as Madame's old cataracts. That
horse, dark as soot, twice as dirty, had the evil eye—was no question
about it. For there'd been almost as many dead grooms in Madame's
stable as pigs on her great bloody table. The ones the beast didn't
outright kill dead itself with a silent kick, swift as wind and quite as
deadly, its mistress had disposed.

Ole Scratch, Papa Death visited the Hill often, during all
seasons, for reasons great and small—because Plato's coat didn't
shine like the gold coins they said Madame kept in a red root bag
under her pillow, because the apple wasn't ripe and the horse refused
to eat. Death came because Plate Eye's long, midnight mane was
tangled or was braided too tight or too loose. Papa Death came and
went and collected more bones—our bones. Some Madame gave to
him and some, they said, she kept for her soup.

To eat and eat and your belly never grow full. Such hunger!

And when death did not come soon enough, Madame would
grow weary. And down, down the Hill you'd go. She'd sell the poor
souls downriver to New Orleans or deep down in Texas and all
because Plate Eye's precious bit was moldy and green.

The horse she loved like a lover. And for all we knew, Plate
Eye was Madame's man. We'd never seen anyone come courting
Madame, nor had Madame ever had any man, free or otherwise, in

her giant, empty bed. At least not none we knowed.

"A lone woman in these parts, planter or pauper, must dazzle, must amaze," she said, her teeth in neat rows, kernels of corn. Bread and circuses, death and swine. Old world conjure and Mississippi mojo. Was no surprise that when we finally did find a groom wily enough to out devil the demon, they say he came from a traveling medicine show. Mama Zig Zag's Curiosities, Odds, and Ends. He carried himself straight, like a broomstick and stood no higher than the horse's flank. Madame said that he was so little that if she closed her eyes, he'd disappear, and so she named him Blink. When Blink brushed the beast with a boar's bristles, he used a stool with a stout bottom and held it with a firm grip. Plate Eye was stealthy and would try to buck and give the stool a kick, but when the groom rode him for exercise, he took a great leap and flipped in the air, his tiny body arcing like a lark. Blink would leap so high, we thought he would take flight, but then he'd land squarely on the glossy back while Plate Eye reared and snorted, bucked and danced, pounded the earth with his great black hooves but could never throw him, not even with his nose in the dirt and his big ole back legs pointing straight at God.

The old ones said Blink was a natural born conjureman. That he came from somewhere far in Guinea, where they know the old ways. They said Blink grabbed dirt from the boneyard, from a newborn's grave and sewed it up in a sack, tied it round his waist so can't no man or beast throw him. Plate Eye didn't know nothing about no conjure or no goober dust. He tried to wrestle Blink all the same, and when he was in a special humor and Blink would land on his back just so, digging in his horse flesh with his big toe, Plate Eye would whinny and shout and they'd vanish in a cloud of dust and travel for miles, the dwarf clinging to the horse's mane, hooping and hollering in that odd *click-clack ticking* noise nobody understood but everybody knew was his own special language.

Nobody could make heads or tails of what he said, but Blink spoke many tongues, horse, hoodoo, his clicksong—and Madame. Nobody understood Blink but Blink understood everybody.

He made Madame laugh so hard, you could see the pink of her throat. Made her laugh so long, the gray clouds would clear from her eyes and we would think she could see. Blink made the Madame laugh and the black horse be still or go at his will and old evil Plate Eye couldn't throw him, so Blink stayed. He stayed at Breakneck Hill and I stayed. And one night we became friends.

We were in the kitchen, my apron bloody as childbirth, when the night bell rings loud and long like Ole Scratch himself standing on the other end. We nearly jumped out of our skin. Me, hands waving, I knock over two bowls of cowpeas. Such a ruckus and racket. The hammer leaning in the corner fell over, and the wee man Blink toppled off his sturdy stool. Cooks One through Four rushed to the spit while another spat on the Madame's silver. I wiped my hands, tossed the soiled apron, and pat down my dark blue headwrap. Cooks Five and Six were gone to take a great pot of juba, leftovers—chitterlings, collards, and cornbread—in the quarters, and Cook Seven never can be found when found means she's got to work, so that left me, the hog hammerer, to trudge up the spirally steps. I'm mad because them old steps Madame claimed she shipped from Paris are too prettified for me. They creak and they crack and my poor mama, God rest her soul, had enough troubles without me breaking her back.

Blink wobbles his big head leaning left, so big on his little body, it looked like his neck might surely break. "Heh," he laughs and sets his stool upright. He plops right down, scratches his ear like a cat and squints up in my eye. "Rather race that hellish horse than face the Madame at this hour." He smiles and clicks something that sounds like, *child, you sho'll in deep*. I don't smile back but give him my *never you mind* face. I'm hungry and I want to eat. I been hammering hogs all day and my hands ache, my ears ring with their screaming. By the time I come back, my grits will be cold, hard as rocks and all the bacon will be gone, too. Nothing will be left, not even the grease.

Outside it's drizzling snow. Little pinfeathers flutter through the night air like plucked chickens. My steps are slow and heavy, silent but sullen. I have to screw up my eyes and shield the lantern's flame with my hand. The house is grand but drafty, might as well be standing buck naked outside. It was cold in the quarters, cold but we slept bundled together. With all its finery and lace curtains and store-bought picture frames, the house on Breakneck Hill got as much heat as two rocks rubbed together. I want to eat and then sleep in my own pallet, with my head resting in my great tree hands.

I do not want to stare at Madame's rooster bottom feet.

Her toenails are curled like a stag's horns. All five feet five inches of her are laid up in that great cavern of a bed like she is the Queen of Zenobee. From that moment on, I call her Madame Queen in my head. When I step into the room, the lantern make haint shapes all along the papered walls. Madame Queen doesn't notice. Her wig is off and sits on a stand by her chamber pot. Her red strands stick up all atop her head, a bright rooster's comb. And she has the whole world, the whole wide turning world in her hand.

The book of maps was a sight I'd never seen. It is tan as sunbleached bone, blue as a Mississippi sky, and red as blood. Fine lines cover it like cracks in an ashcake, bend and curve as the sun and the years in my mama's face. Figures and words cover it. The book has thick pages, maps and strange drawings. One map is said to be more powerful than all the others. Folk say the map made out of skin, our skin. Some say all of Madame's books made out of folks' skin. But Madame's map is old, ancient as the Good Book, wise as God. Folk say the map lead you to heaven. Folk say the map lead you to hell. For all I know, the map lead you somewhere we can be free. In all the Hill, it is the only thing of Madame Queen's that I covet.

I want the book although I know I cannot read. Desire for the map fills me up until I cannot see. I find my eyes following Madame Queen's movements when she bustles about, when she is restless and gathers the book of maps up in arms like it is her own born child. Whether from the sky god or the earth god, I want this heaven or hell. Cook One says the map is spelled, the book, the map, and every solitary page in it. They say you have to give something to get something, but I was born with nothing, and in my life I have made nothing. My hands feel bigger and more useless because I know I have nothing to give. I watch Madame Queen and wonder how we come at such crossed luck.

She doesn't notice me but goes on smoothing and unrolling the edges of the map. Its ends keep turning up like the horsetail ends of her going to town wig. She goes on turning the map, rolling and unfolding it tenderly, stroking it with her gentle hands as if rubbing oil on. I cough. She looks up suddenly, shame in her face.

"Tree." If Madame Queen is surprised, her voice does not betray her. "Put it there," she says and snaps up the map, rolling it so expertly, swiftly, it disappears like Blink and Plate Eye in a cloud of dust.

"You want me to carve it, Madame?" I ask and have to shut my gums to hold back the *Queen*.

"Carving is delicate work, Tree. Save your hands for hammering."

I am dismissed. As soon as my heel is on the stairs she will lift the lid and pick the meat with her fingers, leaving the silverware on the tray. She will pop the moist, fat meat in her mouth and let the pork grease drip down her chin. She will push and push and cram the pink meat down deep in her mouth and she will not drink. Madame Queen wishes her whole head was a mouth. Madame Queen wishes we all were fattened pigs, waiting for slaughter. Madame Queen will eat and eat until her nightgown is soiled and her white pillowcase is stained. She will eat and dream and wake in the hollow of the night and eat some more.

In the morning when day finally comes, I will be lucky to find even a wishbone.

There is no heat, only certain degrees of cold. There is only cold and not even the memory of heat. I don't remember the feeling of a fire against my thighs, against my knees. Even in the kitchen, the warmest place in any hovel, even in the quarters at the bottom of Breakneck Hill, the heat is too thin to rise and the great cast iron skillets and the great copper pots rust and cloud over, like a cataract eye. I have no socks but I have shoes. In a pallet in the back of the kitchen, I sleep in my hard bottom shoes. We are black and blue but the pigs stay fresh. Madame Queen uses the cold like a lash, like a slaver's iron collar. At Breakneck Hill, even the winter is not free. All belongs to Madame Queen. All hail the Mississippi Queen. She who holds the map of the world in the palm of her hand.

I'm telling you lies, but what I tell you is true. All versions of stories can be true. Trust me?

Mama's Mojo

There is a city surrounded by water, a river to some, a creek to others. There is a city that is surrounded by land, a mountain on one side, a valley and plains to others. On the first, the streets and roads are backwashed, alleys only river rats can cross. Miss your way, an easy task to do, and you may find yourself staring cross-eyed at glittering teeth guarding a palace of burlap sacks and bone. Find your way, a harder task to do, and you may meet an elder on the crossroads wheel of time, lost, forgotten, and found again. She stands, hovering in the backdoor of where you come from and where you gon' end. Mojo, sign, and symbol, she ain't got but two questions to ask—pass through or will you try again? She'd been listening to the answers longer than she can recall. How she first come to the crossroads is a tale all its own.

In this place her own voice frightened her and made her want to run. She moved along the dark paths of forest, a swift shadow, passing through sudden clearings with grass that brushed her ankles and slapped her thighs. She blended with the insect flickers of gold and blue as the wind lifted the leaves, as the trees stretched their limbs, great bark covered hands as if to say *amen*.

Before she became Mama Zig Zag, she was simply called Zilla, and before she was Zilla, well, that she didn't rightly know. The long road she traveled hurried on to nowhere and had no end. Everywhere she stood made her want to be somewhere else again.

Her eyes were full of dust and her hair was stiff. Everything inside her made her feel old as the soil that caked her heels, but no matter what plagued or what sorrow struck her soul, her body with her heart and limbs never grew old. She'd long since stopped trying to find the source of it and credited it to some forgotten prayer her mother had raised before she flung her into the sea. Her mother arrived on the killing ships, the wood and sails full of death. Her father was left in the land of many waters some called Guinea. She set Zilla free in the sea. Zilla wished she could shake loose her skin, heavy with sweat and dirt. Step out of it like a winter coat grown too small, but there, on the outskirts, was the road that always beckoned ahead. It gleamed like water. Offered no purity, slaked no thirst, and yet, Zilla wanted a taste.

She should have gone humbly by.

Should have turned her backside up to the meandering road that scuttled in the dark clearing of the strange and whispering wood. A road that looked as if wild cattle or a whole herd of miniature buffalo had stumbled and kicked up all kinds of bugs and dust, running like they stone cold crazy just to get out of the gleaming road's way.

She should have gone but she didn't. Zilla scratched a scab that had healed up a hundred times, would heal up a hundred more, gathered what was left of her sagging dress tied with what remained of the hangman's rope and stumbled on down the side of the winding hill, under a dark canopy of trees, wild bushes, and cicada hush.

Some history you can't kill.

The six black wagons of Aunt Dissy's Traveling Medicine Show seemed smaller by daylight and not frightening at all, but fragile and flimsy as dead leaves. The purple and gold draperies were gone and they were adorned with burlap sack cloths and giant, jute cotton bags, snatched from bales along the river docks and dyed the most pitiful shade of indigo, faded tears. Stubby black ribbons twitched and fluttered in the breeze. Aunt Dissy's covered wagon slumped in the center of a pentacle of larger wagons that looked more like cages on wheels. A large, tattered flag emblazoned with a hand painted giant black crow crowned the center wagon, but Aunt Dissy, whomever she might be, remained unseen.

The turbaned one called Hannibal was in a brilliant cape covered with bejeweled elephants. He led a straggling crowd of country folk slowly from one wagon to the next, commented on the motley group within. A group of scraggly musicians armed with banjos, mouth harps, and amber jugs stretched and bounded like crickets. Zilla had arrived in time for the walk around.

"Juba Dis and Juba Dat. Come and see the Gold Dust Twins." Hannibal banged a curved tree root walking stick against one of the wagon cages, and the air was suddenly filled with shimmering light. Out leapt the oddest thing Zilla had yet to see besides herself. Two cherubic fatback twins spinning like little tops, covered from curly head to stubby toe with gold paint. The color was so vivid it looked almost real. The country crowd gasped and stepped closer.

"Look, ma," a child cried and yanked on her sleeve. "It's gold nigras!"

Only their dark eyes blinked. Zilla thought the gold twin on the left winked at her, but under all the gold, she couldn't be sure. In fact, the closer she got, the less sure she was that it was even paint. The shade seemed to shimmer and sparkle in the shifting sun, as if the gold color was part of them. Zilla shuddered.

She knew all that glittered ain't gold, but she also knew that everything golden don't shine. Good or bad, the twins were made from something else. She was drawn by power, but could it match her own? Zilla looked around her, drew the tattered scarf closer around her throat. Dark scarred rings rippled like water eddies down her neck. The air that settled over Aunt Dissy's Medicine Show was thick with magic, hushed with hoodoo. Aunt Dissy, or whomever she claimed to be, was no ordinary peddler of elixirs and wizard oils. It had been many years and Zilla had traveled far and wide across this strange land. She had forgotten much of what the Old One had taught her, but there were some things a spirit never forgets. Zilla knew real power when she sensed it, even when it tried to hunch its shoulders and walk 'round with its head hung low. Somebody in Aunt Dissy's was working more than herbal roots and tonics.

Somebody was hiding in plain sight, working a mighty mojo.

Zilla tightened her head wrap and stepped through the tall, pin-wheeled stakes in the ground, past the silent blue banners, past the grinning gold twins. Somebody was hiding all right, and Zilla was determined to find out who.

Scalawag's Scuffle

Forget what they tell you. There ain't no such thing as a *limited victory*. Every victory leaves some kind of a resentment. A bitter feeling in the defeated, humiliation in the heart, and loss on all sides. Triumph is just the name of another place to watch, to guard, and defend. To fear.

What I learned about war in the years before I came to this

lonely place were the things that any child could have told me. War means fighting and fighting means killing. Ain't no getting around that, no matter how you twist and turn. I traveled a broken road of stone, had all kinds of men following me. I traveled by foot, on horseback, dropped thirty in the fields, traveled by them iron tracks and for a time, ran my own train, the Selma, Marion, and Memphis Railroad. Yes, when the war started, I'd made more than a million—and all that from peddling and gambling and trading flesh—but I'd also known bitter poverty. Vowed never to drink from that cup again. But that's how it is. All that groundwork only to find out that all them roads we call ourselves building in life, all them iron tracks, well, they just lead you back where you begin.

I'm told Sherman called me the very Devil. That old me would have thanked him kindly. True I aimed never to surrender. I'd have bust hell wide open to see our way through. Damn what they tell you, all this talk about heritage and honor. That war wasn't about no battles and bones. It was about flesh. Pure and simple. About the very idea of flesh—where it come from and who it come through. More to the point, who owns it when it gets here. Can you own flesh, the way a man owns a beast? Can you breed it and seed it and bend it under your will?

I did.

The North didn't invade us. The North turned on itself. All the lies they tell. Like them Eastern ports ain't bring all that flesh through. Like their whole cities, their ivy-topped towers, the nation's very industry ain't built atop all the flesh and bones buried under them cobblestoned, walled streets. I sold them right there on 87 Adams Street between the city's first town square. Historical markers won't tell you but them old street names surely will—Exchange, Market, Court and Auction—Memphians dealt in flesh. The sign outside our building told the story plain, Forrest and Maples Slave Dealers. I knew exactly what I was fighting for. We marched out of those fields, leaving all that White Gold to rot. The weevil ate what the scalawags came and stole. All this talk of contraband—fancy talk for flesh. Black flesh. Nigra flesh. Flesh I claimed in my youth just as surely as my daddy. We fought with our fists, our boots fell apart. We slept two, sometimes three hours a night and died by the thousands in the hot glare of day. Four years of war, fighting so we'd never have to fight for flesh again. I was wounded four times, had thirty horses shot beneath me. I stood in the middle of the river, on a dead horse, made my way across because there was no going back.

Did all that struggle, all that gambling only to lose it again. What I'd gambled and won before was worth nothing after the war. I should have vanished the way them deserters did. I should have taken a new name, left Forrest back in all that blood and cannonballs in the weeds. Should have set up shop in something quiet-like, bending sweet grass to seat rocking chairs, good honest work set up somewhere small, away from the river and the City of Good Abode. But everything I touched after the war turned to dust. When dark deeds outweigh the light, the only thing people remember is the darkness. I tried to reconcile, in my way. I keep asking for forgiveness but with each step I take, my path leads me further away than where I began. The only difference between Hell and Memphis is that Hell's river runs right through it, while Memphis' river runs alongside it. I thought I had closed my eyes at last to rest, but when I woke I found myself cold as stone.

I find no warmth where I tread. I wander around this river's banks, still seeking that forgiveness, redemption. Towards the end, I can't tell you which hell I am in.

I know one thing. I didn't expect to come here, to this place where the river run all around, where the river runs past you and you can't get through. I've been walking and walking on this island, this mountain of sand and stone. The map that black haint showed me was cursed. I should have listened more carefully, to the venom beneath her words. She said I would meet my rest here, to follow the muddy path where the river flows. The faces of the dead haunt me, horses and men. Flesh. All flesh. I follow but rest refuses me. My shoes about to bust, and I can't find my Mary, can't find my children, my sisters, my brothers, and no matter how long I search, I can't seem to find my way on home.

Stone Telling

It's true and then it ain't. What they say about the dead. No, the dead don't talk—well yes they do, but not in the way you think and not about anything you want to hear. Silent as their grave until they wind up again, then it's what they could have done, what they should have done, what they had and what they should have had, who they were, and what they wished they had become.

I'm tired. Tired of their testimony, unwanted witness as I am. Here in this city park, the dead are talking all the time. Nonstop nonsense. Especially since they went and put up that fence. It sounds like the wind sighing, like a branch creaking, like the crackle of dead leaves on an overgrown path. On this here rock, where all the wind is up, I can hear them. If you listen hard, you can hear them, too.

Like that last one. I remember when he came here. Never thought I'd see the day when they finally finished that monstrosity they call a monument. Can't be nothing more pitiful than carving a broken man's spirit right into stone. Trapped the poor thing forever and forever more. Or at least until he gets the story straight. Seems like he's fixated on some things, still wrassling with the rest. And that's his problem.

The dead don't forget, not a mumbling thing. Or they forget and just remember what they want to. And that's the other problem. They say the truth can set you free, but if you ain't willing to face that truth, you lose your path. And then you just wondering in the wilderness, a lost soul good and lost. Another problem is some of the dead got funny ways, and they can't help that 'cuz they had funny ways when they were living. They remember what they want to, in a way so twisty-twisty, they can't help but be lost. And some of the dead slick-like. They try to clean their conscience by burying their dirt—knowing full well it don't work that way. Or at least they ought to know.

I've watched souls wonder round still telling the same lies that got them killed. Just 'cuz you die don't mean you suddenly get good sense. But it don't mean you got to stay the same, too. There is movement in death, change even. It's just real slow for some. For others, there ain't no changing at all. And that's not because they can't but because they ain't. That's when they run into the biggest problem. You can't leave this realm until your spirit is at rest, until you have released all the lies and you only left with the truth. And you can't rest if you are still running. The truth can set you free or it can trap you. That Forrest man been trapped, buried in lies of his own making. Sometimes he speak so, it bring water to your eyes, but then you remember what he trying to forget. Sometimes out in the wilderness, the truth so cold, it makes the tears freeze on your face. If you're ready, you face it and let the tears come until the truth carries you away. But if you ain't, all you can do is just wipe your eyes and keep walking.

River's Reply

None can walk on water, but they surely wade through it. *Wade in the water. Wade in the water, children. Wade in the water. God's gon' trouble the water.* Whoever sang that spiritual, sang the truth. The angel who troubled my waters is long gone, but all those who come through, who make it to this side of the river, they don't study war no more. They don't study pain and fear no more. They lay down their shield and spear. I wait here and listen for their footfalls. I listen and I wait. See who will wade through and see who don't—stuck on the other side—and those stubborn, remarkable ones who will dare to try again. It's true, some drown. Some dip their big toe in and the icy raindrops fall like great arrows from the sky, and their spirit is soaked through with sorrow. Some get so heavy, so rain drenched, they can't lift, they can't carry, they can't wade through their troubles no more. Sink down to my bottom and dream with the catfish, or they mess around and wake that sleeping 'sippi serpent. A dragon from the old times, he will drag you off for your last earthly ride.

That girl with the great big ole hands, she try. She carried many through. You got to respect that, give the gal her diamond due. She is carrying them one by one to a promised land that she herself may never go. She likes the journey now. She knows its ways. Its ins and outs, the ripples of time. The map has not led her to hell or heaven. She occupies a space in between. I've seen her time and time again. She will stand there at them crossroads and hold every drop of sorrow, hold it hard and squeeze it if she can until the sky breaks, and all their memories and mistakes fall like hail from the sky. She squeeze and they crumble like stones, hard rocks in her hand. Then they cross over.

Me, I take them all back in, let their troubles drift to my river bottom, let the pain build up like a levee and keep listening. Their troubles keep me company. And the troubles they tell. Here she comes now, carrying another one. O, listen to the story, listen to the love and the fear. Somebody got left behind. Somebody want to bend it straight. Somebody want to make it hold tight. There is a frost tonight that will brighten the ground, harden the stars here in this city of sinners and saints. In the morning webbed nets of ice will fill me, like stones in my ear. But I will hear them. The stone tells his story, reinventing his place in it, like all the rest. The stone wants to look good, monumental. But I am. Good or bad, I am. I exist outside of time. My waters see the story's beginning, middle, end. I enter where I please. No matter the season, my waters will keep flowing, and if you're quiet, the serpent will keep snoring. Wade in, wade in, listen.

I'm telling you stories, true tales. All tales are lies, all lies are true. Trust the River, for a river knows how to bend with the best.

Madame's Map

I could hear Madame Queen's snores as I climbed the steps. I left Blink sleeping below, *click-song-clicking* in his dreams, and all that whistled through the great house was the wind and the cold, my hunger and my regrets. I had dreamed this many times before, how I would steal away in the night, but in life, none happens quite as one would dream. First, I knocked over the quill and ink with my big tree hands, then my hands burst into bushes of fire. I had only meant to take the secret book of maps and go. But the moment my hands held the book, a patchworked reddish-brown and not bone-bleached at all, the dark lines of my palms ignited in flame.

I screamed and felt Madame's milky gray eyes on my back before her hands. She spun me around. Flames shot from my palms to my wrists. The bright red strands on her scalp fluttered like plucked pinfeathers.

"Tree! Would steal from me? Thief!" she cried, spitting through her kernel corn teeth. She leapt from her bed and shattered one of the lanterns, kicked over her chamber pot. Her crimson wig lay in a bloated pile on the floor. The lacy curtains swayed with rage, but I feared the map's flames more than any punishment she might decree. To my horror, the flames burned not with heat but with images. Pictures I could not make heads or tails of. I tried to pull away but my hands were melded to the covers of the book. My palms ached. I felt the blood pour out of me. It spilled through the dark grooves of my hands, stained the book's covers. Its cursed pages flipped back and forth, creating a mighty wind, a sound that made me want to cut off my own ears.

"Give it to me!" Madame screamed, her nightgown soaked with sweat and pork grease. The room still smelled of her meal and my stomach ached from hunger. She punched and scratched me. Her nails raked my back as sharp as the lash. Despite her cries, I held onto the book of maps as it held onto me. Bound together, I now knew why her palms were scarred, why it looked as if she had taken a knife and carved out her own lifelines. *Carving is delicate work.*

The book of maps had taken its price from her flesh, too. *Spelled,* Cook One had said. *The map could lead you to heaven, the map could lead you to hell...*Where had she gone, I wondered, on the long months away from Breakneck Hill? What marvels, what horrors did the book of maps reveal to Madame Queen? Where in the world did she want to go, she who reigned over Breakneck Hill and all within it, supreme?

My head ached with seeing, my hands burned with futures I could not follow. Visions of smoke and fire, of black gold and green. I wished that I could turn my eyes back in my head, but I could not. First, I saw Blink lead a group of field hands away from Madame Queen's house. We rode a black cloud over a trail of silver and green, the house engulfed in red flames. Winter, icy and silent all around, the fields were barren, but the tree where my mama was buried, was ablaze. Next, I stood on a hill and watched a purple caravan of wagons lurch by. Strange people with faces as if from a dream. Children made of gold, their bellies fat and shining. They held the hands of an old young girl. Her eyes held the sadness of a hundred years. She looked up and through me, her neck corded with scarred flesh, but then her smile was the light of a greater sun. She made me feel something like hope.

The next picture made me holler and cringe, made me try to pull away but the book of maps held me fast. It burned figures beneath my closed lids, figures I could not unsee. A dark-eyed, bearded man with a sharp widow's peak stood by a river. Piercing dark gray eyes you can't easily forget. Soldiers, colored soldiers nailed to logs, their screams engulfed in flames. Black and blue, the figures kept coming while Madame Queen pummeled me with fists and curses.

"You think you'll be free?" she cried and hopped on her rooster bottom feet. Pork grease glistened on her lips and chin. She tried again to wrest the book away from me. "These maps were not made for *you*." Smoke filled the room. I could hear a ruckus below. Cooks One and Two stirred from sleep and Blink would be waking.

Madame Queen coughed and spat out blood. The veins in her neck pulsed and writhed with fury but I had anger of my own. "You may leave Breakneck Hill and you may escape me," she said, "but your big tree hands will never carry you away to freedom." She stared straight at me and laughed as if she knew my fate.

Ghostly pictures moved across my mind like memories or dreams. I had never had a vision, except for my mama's face. A blur that comforted me and was taken. Never held onto a dream except for this—what might life be if ever I was free? Longing, deep and wide as hunger, opened up inside of me. As black smoke swirled around us, I imagined wide open air, earth in my great tree hands, dark, rich soil that brought sustenance not pain. I concentrated on green, on a field so lush I could smell the roots of the grass deep in the ground, as the book's flames spread up and out, engulfing the room.

Madame screamed. She dropped her hands in horror. Her claws did not sting anymore. I watched her scuttle backward, her hateful murky eyes filled with resignation, then with shock as the flames leapt from the book and spun a fiery web around her. She stumbled and screeched, a red gold spinning top, then dropped.

The air in her bedroom chamber changed.

I held the book, the book held me. I was now mistress but the book of maps set her free. I watched Madame burn. Her skin turned so slowly, as if on a black iron spit. She crackled and crumbled, popped and sizzled. *You'll never be free.* She was a haint whispering in my ear.

The papered walls burned, erupted into fiery blossoms that bloomed up the ceiling. I stared and swayed as if in a spell. The fire was like looking at the sun. The scent of burnt flesh overpowered me. Hard feet stomped on the creaking wood stairs. Muffled shouts below.

"Tree!" It was Blink.

Black clouds made it difficult to see, to breathe, but the book of maps burned brightly. Pictures reeled through my mind, a wide, unfolding vision. A statue that sees, stone witness to all. A river that weeps, rambles, remembers, its currents running in and out of time. I saw my people chained in fields, some surrounded by muddy water. White and black stripes clung to sweating bodies. I saw them hang from trees. Frayed ropes twisted in darkness. I saw them lying face down in black roads. Silver monsters with red eyes roared past them. The air filled with screams. I saw them huddled in strange vessels, dressed in bright orange garments. Capsized, they fell in big water, desperate hands reaching up at me. And just when I thought I could see no more, the figures faded. A new vision began.

Voices raised together, marched hand in hand. A woman with a star-shaped hole carved in her right temple led hundreds of cheering families on flat-bottom ships. Children dressed in fine clothes and shoes, real shoes, entered buildings grander than any I'd ever seen before. A silver-headed man buried a golden gift beneath the roots of a great ancient tree. A sweetfaced woman dressed in the strangest garbs floated in the air like a spirit. She was surrounded by contraptions, giant roots and pale white limbs. When I peered over her shoulder I had to take a breath, felt like I had seen the face of God Himself.

Is this what it look like to be free?

The map had shown me strange, frightful wonders I hoped one day to understand. By the time Blink pulled me out of Madame Queen's burning room, I knew I would not let go of the book of maps—even if the book let go of me.

We raced down the spiral staircase, but my feet didn't touch the groaning floor. Cook Seven showed up with a big black pot of water. Blink knocked it out of her hands and clicksong-motioned for her to follow us out the door. I darted back in to get my hammer. When I tumbled out into the icy air, the entire plantation was awake. People were screaming, running in every direction in stages of undress. They held their heads in their hands. Some stood, trembling in the cold, and prayed. I knew just as well as anyone else.

A dead mistress on a burning plantation meant death not freedom.

Breath ragged, I opened the book. The pages turned, moved by unseen hands. I watched strange figures and symbols emerge on the pages in blood red. A black cloud spun like a cyclone on the page. It swerved and dipped on its side, appearing on one page, then disappeared only to reappear on the next. Blueblack swirls and muddy curves spread out before me, unfolding into green. The hill. Not Breakneck but the strange one from the vision.

"Blink!" I cried and turned the book so he could see. The black cloud swirled on the pages. It darted through what looked like forest and then along the muddy brown banks of what could only be the 'sippi.

His eyes widened and he took off, past the frightened and the confused, past the women, men, and children who carried water, still trying to save Madame Queen's big monstrous house.

Suddenly a shout rose from the crowd of hands. Blink was

sitting atop Plate Eye. The black horse snorted and reared its great head, looking as ornery as ever. Blink clicked for me to join him. I shook my head no. He clicked again and pointed. It took me a minute to understand what he wanted. I dropped my hammer and ran through the paths that led to the rickety shacks and returned with a cotton sack.

"Here," a young woman I didn't recognize said to me. "Blink say we going on a long trip."

"We?" I watched in wonder as she filled the sack with pecans and all that she had in her food rations. I thought I would spirit my own self away to freedom, but what I had done put every life on Breakneck Hill in danger.

What is freedom if we ain't all free?

I looked at my hands, my big tree hands holding the sacred, cursed book and the cotton sack. I was born with nothing, and in my life I had made nothing. But in that moment my hands felt bigger and everything more possible. The girl stared at me, watching, waiting.

"Tree, we goin' now?"

Blink was sitting on Plate Eye, fingers entwined in the black horse's great mane, clicking up a storm. The popping sounds emerged rapid-fire from his tongue on the back of his teeth. They say his language is the oldest in all of Guinea, that each click contains a century of memory. But Blink's not telling stories now. He saying *run or die, don't matter which—make it quick!*

His body is a hinge. I feel his fear open inside of me. They have put down the water pots. No one moves as Madame Queen's big house burns. All watch with eyes full of hunger, eyes full of hope. The book of maps was transforming before my eyes. It burns more pictures in my mind, but I push them back. Replace the figures with one of my own. Red flames erupt from the covers. The others back up, cry out. My palms bleed again, but I don't feel no pain. Blink reaches his little hand down for me. *Take it,* he says. I close my eyes and imagine the green hill. I can see the purple flags, the fatbelly gold twins marching below. The young old woman stares up at me and smiles, as if in a dream. I don't know where we are going, I just know we got to go. I close the book and climb onto Plate Eye's black back. He rolls his big head and snorts. I wait for him to throw me off but he don't.

"If you coming, gather round," I say to the others. "Hold hands and think about freedom."

Freedom somebody say. *What that look like?*

I listen to the murmurs, the low grumbling like thunder, then the shouts that fill the air, red black shiny embers of joy. A mighty wind picks up all around us. Most people run, they are so afraid but some stay. They clasp hands. The girl who gave me her food places her palm gently on Plate Eye's shoulder, and we are one long curving line of flesh and faith. Blink clicks and hums a song I've never heard him sing before. It sounds like gentle rain on red clay earth, thirsty, bursting, clouds about to break.

Plate Eye charges forward, the shout rings through the smoky night air. *My sist'r Mary boun' to go. My broth'r Luster boun' to go. Everybody's boun' to go!* A black cloud swirls around us, a dark tunnel spinning above and below, in the middle of the starless sky. We ride the black cloud, over silver and green. The pictures in my mind blur and fade into one until we are sucked inside the tunnel. The girl who gave me all her food reaches out her hand, but the picture dissolves with her touch. They are all singing now, not just the regretful and the afraid. A deep hum down in their bellies. The sound comforts me as we ride the rope of wind.

We arrive on the other end of the wind tunnel to stand on a patch of green. The old young woman from my vision smiles as the flames from the map of books sputter out. The black tunnel disappears, sinks into dewy wet grass. The scent of fire and ash and the faint hint of basil fills the air. She squeezes the gold belly twins' hands and one points up at me. She laughs.

"Yes, dear," she says. "That's what it look like to be free."

Mama's Mojo

This is the one Aunt Dissy foretold before she left us, and the one Mama Zig Zag saw before she left us, too. The one with the big tree hands. Pockmarked and puckered, I wept in Mama's lap, afraid to lead the others on my own. She pulled me up and looked dead in my eye. "You won't be alone, Zilla. A great tree will comfort you. And I will be with you, too, just changed." She stroked the scars on my throat, the ringed deaths I had escaped. She wiped my cheeks, each tear for the lives I saw come and go. "They will gather you up and all my children here. They will lead y'all on to freedom, and you, my ancient newborn, will finally get your rest."

Get your rest.

A motley crew, they blended well with the Curiosities. I wish Mama Zig Zag could stay to see them. She didn't have the same gifts as Aunt Dissy. Mama's gift required her to change. She was resting in the back of the wagon, wrapped in cloth. No one knew what she would be when we unwrapped her again. And few other Curiosities remembered well our leader who protected us before. Aunt Dissy, who could travel folks' dreams and read their souls. I traveled with her for nearly a century.

I did not know what gifts Tree's people might bring, if any, but whatever they brought was welcome here. Some carried food rations in gunny sacks. Some carried fiddles and other handmade instruments. Some carried tools and some carried just themselves. From their tattered clothes and the weariness that curved their bones, I could tell they had worked rain-wet, sun-dry all their lived days. I knew well what it was like to walk with a mouth full of dust and have no drink. To be whipped and starved and yet, asked to dance. I lived that life until Aunt Dissy freed me.

Now they stood in the tall grass. Their eyes glittered hard as jewels. I watched the emotions ripple across faces worn smooth from hard labor, like stones in the wind. The wee one sighed, clicked his tongue and made soothing noises against the great horse's neck. Mama Zig Zag said he would be coming, too. The horse was one of her Curiosities, stolen, she insisted by a wretched one. Mansamusa would never run away and now he was back with the one I waited for, Tree.

Exum was beside himself. He kept squeezing my hand and pointing up at them, sunlight reflecting gold. Axsom expressed her excitement with a flurry of questions. Her eyes shifted from amber to iridescence.

"Zilla, where we go now? They come too? Who the wee wee man?"

"Hush now," I say. "That one carrying the book will answer all."

Axsom snorted. "The way she hold it, I think she got more question than answer."

Exum chimed in. "She do look fearful. Can we go to her?"

We walked along the trail carved by ancient ones, the Mississippians who roamed this land many years ago. No one with any sense lived here, where the elders buried their dead, but that didn't stop the others from turning burial ground into a bustling river town. We walked with the bluff on our left, the river on our right. Tree and their people peered down at us, still shivering from their journey. The great horse stamped his feet and snorted, then bolted down the hill right at us.

"Mansamusa!" Hannibal cried. "He is returned!"

At Mama Zig Zag's Curiosities, Odds, and Ends, behind each mystery hid a hundred more. How we traveled between worlds, the enslaved and the free, the whole and the broken. How we stayed in the light when so much of the world trafficked in darkness. Mysteries. We traveled along the river's brown hips, a vista of green and dandelion weeds, crooked trees, unharassed most days because everyone liked oddness. Some gathered it around themselves like garments to make their lives seem more normal, more true.

Hannibal, our strong man, knew more about the world's appetite for oddness than most. And he knew Mama's horseflesh as well as his own. He tended it and grieved when Mansamusa was taken. Man and beast were bonded, friends who shared the same blessed malady. Unapologetically black and big, both refused to be broken. A friendship Mama Zig Zag said only magic could have parted. For folks' curiosity about Curiosities was eternal. They coveted the strange, the unusual, the freakish with the same appetite as they hungered for food, water, flesh. Of the many eyes who had seen him, one craved the beast's oversized blackness more than most. It seems the Tree returned what had been stolen, but they also returned with a gift I would have to help them understand.

When Hannibal saw Mansamusa, he was pulling the wagon that carried Mama Zig Zag's current body. It was wrapped in colorful cloth. Brown and white feathers poked out of the fibers, here and there. Hannibal was so big, it took three of us to measure him for clothing. But as big as he was, it didn't stop him for stepping lightly on his feet. When he saw his old friend, he sprung into action, leapt in the air. Man and horse united at the bottom of the grassy hill. The wee man atop laughed and held on as the two embraced.

"He let you ride him," Hannibal said, breathless. Admiration broadened his handlebar mustache. His colorful cape fluttered in the wind, the bejeweled elephant stomped and raised its trunk, swirled around his shoulders.

The wee man smiled and tapped out a greeting that made Exum and Axsom clap their hands. Gold sparks flickered in the morning air. We all breathed green and took solace in the scene. Puffs of cotton floated across the road like drifting snow.

Over the slope of earth, I could see their faces, open, expectant. They thought they arrived in a place where they could reach for warmth. They left the scent of fire behind but not its heat. The flames burn in their faces as they crest the hill. Down by the river, where the water is brown-black and slippery, where the cobblestones whisper with the fallen trees, the morning belongs to the open sky. The morning belongs to all of us. I know this view. You look down and everything looks possible, like the whole world is a floating barge, and all yours dreams just drifting on a bend in the river.

They walk first then run down the hill's side. Squeals turn into laughter. They are joyful. They are light. They think they are finally free. They look to the wee one for guidance and he is telling them a story. He calms their fears and reminds them the gift of laughter. I can tell by the Tree one's face that they are not sure but gathering hope.

"Where are we?" they ask. Their voices don't sound like I imagined. "They will come through a door," Aunt Dissy had said. "That tree holds a book. Guard both with your life," Mama Zig Zag said. What Mama didn't say was that the tree would be beautiful.

"Welcome to Mama Zig Zag's Medicine Show." Three Strands extends her dainty hand in greeting. Her four mamzelle dragonfly wings were bound in an exquisite, custom made robe. Her trademark hair was tied up in a voluminous bright scarf. Excited, Three Strands hopped in tiny circles, hopped so much, the robe and the scarf come loose. When her wings shot out and all that hair, the people gasped, then clapped their hands.

"Formerly known as Aunt Dissy's," I added with an awkward bow. I wasn't used to greetings. Hannibal bows his head and the other Curiosities bend low, too. They sing thanks to the original founder of our haven.

Aunt Dissy built the groundwork, rescued an abandoned child who could not yet settle on a single form. Later, that child, our Mama Zig Zag, grew up and welcomed other folks too odd to go unnoticed amongst the masses. Regulars loved to see firsthand what they would never be, reveled in seeing the extraordinary. They wobbled between being scared and captivated, watching us achieve strange feats they would never attempt. But Mama knew us odd ones, her Curiosities, needed family. She who could take on many forms herself, needed family more than most.

The wee man, the one the Tree called Blink, hum-clicked a tune. Exum and Axsom joined in, and soon all added a note to the song. Music cast a spell over everyone gathered in the new circle. Sometimes the family you choose is better than the one you get by blood.

Exum pulled away from me and ran right up to the one Mama Zig Zag called the Tree.

"What's your Curiosity?" he asked and chewed on the tip of his gold finger.

"Hush, Exum! You got better manners than that." I ran my fingers through his thick curls.

"Jes being friendly," Exum said and stared at the Tree's hands. The Tree reached out and stroked some of Exum's golden curls. Shock clouded their eyes.

"Gold?" They whispered, the great fingers curved round Exum's plump, shiny cheek.

"Gold!" the twins said in unison.

"From the rooter to the scooter," Exum said and balanced on one leg, his fat belly bouncing.

I stared at the Tree's hands. "It's they strength," I whispered.

"Like Hannibal?" Axsom asked.

I nodded. Axsom looked skeptical.

"We'll see," she said. "Don't look all that strong to me. Look tetched!"

I laughed and waved my arm for the others to join us. "Y'all welcome here. I know you've come a long way."

Tree's people listened as the Curiosities told stories, one by one, until each voice became a whisper as silence deepened in the night. They sat on the edge of our camp, their faces moved in firelight. Families unwrapped their small bundles and lay their dreams out beneath the stars. Their journey through the whirling tunnel of time was another dream they would examine under another day's light. But that night, after we fed and comforted them, I listened to the Tree's tale of how they got the book of wonders Aunt Dissy foretold, that book of maps Mama wanted to behold. It is a tale that makes me marvel. Courage or foolery, the Tree took a gamble and gained a chance at freedom.

"What do you plan to do, now that you think you are free?" I asked.

The Tree narrowed their eyes, fatigue and learned fear shadowed their face. "We free from Breakneck Hill. The rest I don't rightly know. The book," they paused, chose their words carefully. "The book of maps showed me figures, visions and things I can't understand."

Tree looked away. I knew that look.

The first person I knew who spoke of visions was the Old One who fished me from the sea. He brought me back to the death ship my mama tried to spare me, so many years ago, when they had not yet fashioned chains for children on the ships. Said I was a wonder, that the spirit of the water blessed me and made me float. The men on the ship heard me wailing in the water after my mama threw me overboard and drowned herself. They watched me sink, then float in the wake of their ship for three whole days. Alive when others had drowned. Whole when others were torn to pieces, ripped by the harsh teeth of the sharks and the sea. Frightened, they ordered the Old One to fish me out. Bad omens, good omens, they didn't know which. They knew someone meant for me to live.

I live.

I've been drowned, smothered, stabbed, shot. Hung. Come off the hangman's ropes and marched right pass the terrified eyes of those who would lynch me. I live. That is my blessing. That is my curse. My Curiosity.

"What kind of visions?"

"Things that made me wonder and things I wish I'd never see."

The Tree set those eyes on me, and I felt seen in a way I can't explain.

"The map showed me you, standing with the others at the bottom of the hill. Then Plate Eye took off, fast as lightning."

I laughed. "Plate Eye? That's what y'all call Mansamusa?"

Tree nodded, offered that hide-your-teeth smile. They stared at their hands. I saw strength in the fingers, kindness, too. The darkness around the half-mooned edge of nails, the skin marked by old scars and the palm lines burned as if they had been branded. They picked at the raised flesh, traced the memory carved in skin.

"We entered the mouth of that tornado at Breakneck Hill and before we knowed it, came out here. We traveled faster than a bird can fly. Don't know how we made it through."

Over time, the Tree and their people began to believe in their new life with the traveling show. They no longer leapt up, eyes wide and fearful, when the little ones suddenly shouted with joy, playing. The curved bones in their backs began to straighten, the muscles in their faces relaxed when strangers from Memphis emerged from the bayou to visit us in Voodoo Fields. But revival is fragile, a delicate prayer, and some resurrections must be held on higher ground.

A constellation of fireflies flickered over our heads. Laughter and the unmistakable *shimmy-she-wobble* flutes of Exum and Axsom's drum and fife music floated through the air. Only a few stands away from the Mississippi, the night was dark moon and high tides.

"Be at ease," I said, sometimes our meaning falls short. I searched for the right words, of comfort and caution. "I don't mean no harm. It's just that you have a powerful gift and you want to think powerfully on it."

"They said the map can lead you to heaven, the map can lead you to hell," Tree said, as if in a trance. Sadness settled in the space between words.

"Not just that. When you arrived, you said you traveled faster than a bird. Can't no bird we know travel cross that much time."

The Tree's jaw stiffened. They watched me like I had been tricked, crawling on my belly. We had tried to provide comfort and ease them into life in the medicine show, but we had already stayed in the city longer than we planned.

"I have seen such things I never heard tale of before," the Tree said, "the night Madame rang the bell, but crossing time... when the sun chases the moon? We were in that tornado for only a few breaths. The map carved that tunnel out of the night sky and it looked like it saved us five days walking if not a week."

"It saved you more than walking. You crossed more than days, Tree. You crossed years. You say you're from Breakneck Hill in Mississippi. Well, that plantation was burned down and abandoned thirty years ago."

"Wha—" The Tree's mouth was slightly parted, revealing a row of mostly straight teeth.

"You're in Memphis, Tennessee but you skipped right over

the path of war."

"War?"

"They battled over our freedom. You didn't know?"

Confusion then sorrow stared back at me. The Tree looked as if they remembered something that pained them. I ran my fingers over the cool, wet earth, pulled up slick blades of grass. How could I forget bondspeople's lives were ruled by seasons not by years? Even those who had somehow figured out how to cross time itself.

"And who won?" The Tree asked after a while, their voice so quiet I had to strain to hear them. "When I held the book..."

Win, lose. We were still *between*. What are the right words when meaning falls short?

I chewed on a dandelion weed. The bitter root numbed my tongue. I wished Mama was here to make the crooked straight. In most medicine shows, the talent was crackpots, dazzlers, and imposters. At Mama Zig Zag's, every one of us was real, far too real. I had to think of a way to make the Tree see what was hiding in plain sight, the truth staring right in their eyes.

I pointed up at the sky. "No matter how long night, dawn will break."

The Tree just looked at me. That was a very Mama Zig Zag thing to say, but it didn't sound half right coming out of me. Clearly, I wasn't as good at this as Mama. I had to try again. Didn't realize how much invisible work she did until I had to take it on myself.

"If you guide it, the map can set you into a steady circle of light, or..." I closed my eyes, rubbed the thick scars on my neck. "Or you can stay where you is." I looked at them. "But hell is not always out there. It can be right here."

They looked at their hands. The book of maps rested in their lap.

"What you saying then, we have to go?"

"What I'm saying is that we *all* got to go. We can't stay in this bayou forever. Memphis full of change, you can see it all around but it's going through the fire and if we're not careful, we're the ones gon' feel it. Some places burn 'fore they learn."

The Tree held out their hands, burnt palms facing me. "I brought us all here. Now I don't know what to do."

The pain etched in skin was hard to turn away from. I was wrong. Strength was not the Tree's Curiosity, but their vulnerability. The Tree thought with the map their journey would end. But the book of maps revealed an open wound that may never be healed.

They turned over the book of maps, held its flesh-covered spine and dark-stained covers away from them, as if afraid to open it. They brushed its uneven pages, touched memory with their fingertips.

The wind whistled through the treetops and in the distance a barge floated, a silent serpent, in the darkness down the river.

"I know you hoped to stay here, but there is discord, bitterness still in the air. Three Strands says there is much anger down in the Pinch. It grows each day."

"You mean the little girl with the wings? The dragonfly?"

"Yes. She sees danger ahead," I said. "Senses it really. Like Mama Zig Zag she can penetrate the veil. She says bad things make her wings ache, and frightening as it is, our little mamzelle is usually right. When she gets anxious like that, I know we don't have much time. And I heard whispers, down by the Freedmen's School. Something hateful is amiss."

"Can we ride with you?"

Now it was my turn to look at the Tree as if they had been crossed.

"I was hoping we might ride with you. We got wagons, but wagons only travel so far. In these times, we need to travel by more ways than one. That book you got, it brought you here. I don't know how but it did. I saw you ride the wind. If it can bring you and all your people here, nearly three decades in time, then it can bring you just about anywhere—any time."

The Tree's silence stretched into the starless sky. I tried again. I had to.

"We'll help you anyway we can. Between Hannibal and Three Strands and some of the other Curiosities, we can try at least to keep you all safe."

"But I don't know how I did it. Everything was on fire back at Breakneck Hill."

"Everything gon' be on fire here," I said under my breath. They stared at me and once again, those eyes made me feel like they could see my every gift and fault. But you didn't need to be a Curiosity to know that I was afraid. Without Mama Zig Zag guiding us, I was more frightened than I had been in a long time. I could taste my fear, deep down in my belly.

"If you want freedom, Tree, you're not going to find it here, at least not now. We gon' have to leave and find it somewhere else. And that book of maps, whether you believe it or not, it's in your hands because *you* know the way."

"A few days ago, I was just a hog hammerer. How do you know I know anything?"

"Because Mama Zig Zag told me. She saw you before you come."

"The one y'all ain't buried yet?" The Tree looked

uncomfortable. Not quite judgment but close.

"We can't bury her 'cuz she ain't dead. She changing."

"Changing into what?"

"I don't rightly know," I said and chewed my nail down to the quick. "Could be what, could be who. She was someone from her memory last time. The time before that, she was an owl."

As if on cue a screech owl scared the life out of us. I laughed, nearly jumped out of my skin.

"See. A sign and a symbol. Mama Zig Zag believes in you and I do too. The question is, do you believe in you?"

The Tree let my words rest in the night air. They ran their fingers over the cover of the strange, spelled book, as if for comfort. From the terrible marks on their hands I knew they'd paid a heavy price for their journey. I stroked the necklace of scars that circled my neck. I had, too. We all had. I hoped by joining the Tree, this new journey wouldn't cost us everything we got.

Scalawag's Scuffle

Not everything in a body has a price. Though creation knows I tried my best to name one. We could weigh the flesh, oil it up and stand it on the auction block. Depending on the profit, we could add stones or whittle away at its years. But the soul was one thing we could never quite contain, no matter how many cages and iron locks we'd build. Blacksmiths don't make irons for that. And that was the problem. We couldn't hold the soul, no matter how much we tried to break the spirit. Somehow they'd manage to break chains, even in death. No matter what the tongue said, you could see it in their eyes—a part of them was already, would always be free.

We tried to keep the natural world from them, allowing them to see only what we wanted them to see. Some kept not only an education but the Word from them. Does a tool need to read? Does a tool need to pray? A tool was ours to use and to own, to mend and to break.

But some things are harder to break than others. At first, I never believed in nothing that I couldn't hold with my hand. Gods and monsters, souls and spells, none of that held sway with me. But I've known superstitious nigras in my time. They walk with red pepper in the bottom of their shoes, silver dimes between their toes. Freedom didn't make them change those country ways. No matter what we did to them in the hooded cover of night, they still believed they could break free and make new their own world. Back then I didn't believe in nothing but might, in a show of arms, in the way our world was ordered. For me, everything depended on maintaining that order, and anything we did in that name was right. I didn't come to believe in Spirit or a world after life until I was damn near about to face my own death. Facing your own mortality has a way of forcing you to break your old bonds and values, see your life anew.

And Lord knows I have seen my share of Death and raised my hand to pass it on. Death follows me now like it did all those years. I lost my father, a blacksmith, from typhoid, and five brothers and sisters. I lost my uncle when them Matlock boys murdered him, and I barely had whiskers when I murdered two of them. I lost my twin sister Fannie when she died in childbirth. Lost my baby daughter named after her. I've seen death and death has seen me. Though I lied and left it out of my dispatches, I can't wipe my eyes and unsee it. Blood, human blood, gathered in pools. Black bodies floated along the water's edge. Eyes punched out by bayonets, back-shot twice in the head. They tried to hide in holes and the cavilles along the river's banks. Hunted, they were ordered out, and the river ran red with their blood. At the fort, men hacked to pieces by sabers. Nailed to logs, crucified. Burned alive, bodies consumed by fire and all around the stench of death and smoke and hate.

Enraged, my men enforced the death penalty, fury against the nigras who dared enlist in the Union army. *If we ain't fighting for slavery, what we fighting for?* We knew why they took up arms— Freedom. The two could not be reconciled. Women and children slaughtered. Massacres and murders in cold blood. Hundreds threw down their arms but were not spared.

Fierce, bitter animosity. Don't say I didn't try to warn them. They could have surrendered when I told them to but that damned fool they called their commander tried to stretch the terms. *Should my demands be refused, I cannot be responsible for the fate of your command.* My man tidied up the words but Booth refused. Think I was going to rear back and let them figure a way to weasel out some kind of victory? We needed every win we could get, and they had placed themselves in a fort that, truth be told, wasn't nothing but a prison and a trap. No comfort from that pillow. The stone was their witness, their final headrest.

I never got much of an education but I know advantage when I see it. They called me the Wizard. Strategy was my strength. Enlisted as a private, I was promoted to general with no prior military training. I didn't follow the rules if the rules didn't satisfy. Everything was at stake. Thought I had fortune on my side, fate on the other. But after, when I reached out my hand, I learned that I had lost more than the war.

The railroad company went bankrupt, but it surely wasn't

because I didn't try. I even went North to get investors, but all my gambling and speculating fell short. Fact is, poor as I was born, all the wealth I'd ever had came from flesh, black flesh. I'd fooled myself, thinking I could do something different. Before the war, I had acquired thousands of acres worked by hundreds of black hands. I didn't know nothing about pulling wealth from cold iron and steel. Though they looked the same, the men I worked with weren't like the men I used to own and sell. Something in their bones had changed, the way the words came out their mouth, the way the skin curved around their flesh. Like they weren't filled with just blood no more, but with that something we worked hard to pretend we couldn't see. Spirit. Human dignity.

I watched my old life until it passed out of sight into the black. And when that sank out of view, I followed the words of a colored who had that same look about their eyes. They had great big ole hands that looked like they could carry a world. The group presented a most curious picture on Beale Avenue, the oddest passel of nigras I'd ever seen. And that's saying something, since the city was overrun with freedmen after the war. They stood outside one of the notorious dress shops that everybody knew was a brothel. All of the handsome dressmakers were gawking out the windows instead of hawking their natural wares, and who could blame them? If you saw that raggedy band of nigras, *you* would stare.

One fellow wasn't knee high to a duck. I stopped to listen as he made the most astonishing sounds. They were all gathered around him, their faces leaned in as he spoke. They didn't look like musicians but something right out of one those traveling medicine shows. The little fellow nodded at me and then the one with the great big ole hands stared at me as if they had seen a ghost. The whole group froze and the look they gave me, felt like cold fingertips running under my skin. I shuddered and would have dismissed it, to go about my day but when I looked up, they were staring at me. Didn't look familiar, like none of the ones I'd owned, nor anyone I sold. But there had been so many back then, wasn't no telling. I was one of the richest slave dealers in the South. Made my fortune from the thousands who came through my mart.

Superstitious nigras, looked like they'd been crossed. The big-handed one pulled out an old battered book from a satchel they carried on their waist. I watched as they flipped through it, their great hand trembling. The others stared. Their eyes burrowed holes in my skin.

Then the trembling one said just as plain as day, like they knew me, "You'll get your rest on an island with kings. Ancient land where a serpent sleeps."

"Beg your pardon?"

"Here," they said. Their eyes scanned the page as if the words were scattered about. "This is where you will go." They turned the book to face me.

It was a rudimentary map of Memphis. I'd recognize the outline of that river anywhere. Where they pointed was three and a half miles from the city proper. Wilderness really, mostly untamed woods and high weeds, a big strip of land in the middle of the Mississippi. Freedmen had worked it before, where the Yankees set up a camp. Then the strange one closed the book and stared at me as if they could see my thoughts as they formed in my head. I was surely thinking on rest, fretting about how Mary and I would start our fortune up again. After the war, I told my men that I didn't know where they was going but I was a-goin' home. What I didn't fully know was that home was never going to be the same again. I thought I could rebuild through the railroad and speculating, but none of that took. I put our frustration on the free, the ones that had broken up the natural order of things. No matter how much we dressed it and rode into the night, lighting fires we hope would break their spirits and put the vigor for voting out, it was clear that for all of us home was ever changed. And after the firelight and spectacle, the unspeakable scent of burning flesh, I had grown weary of death.

"There are no kings here," I said and made ready to take my leave but they gripped me with those eyes. Deep set, hooded eyes held me as tight as any hand. I could feel them on my back as I walked away, past the streets that once held my offices.

But the idea was like a dark seed that took root in me. How to make my way again, me who once made millions, was a spell that was hard to break. That kind of rootwork, the thirsting kind that sinks its roots in your soul, is what I had no defense against. I believed in the power of the coin and aimed to have it again.

Mary and I tried to make our new home together close to the last one, on an isle, President's Island. Not a king's but close enough. Right out in the middle of the Mississippi, the river where I had once watched Union gunboats go by. It had been ten years since the Union set up those so-called freedom camps. Where the men worked in sawmills and farmed the land and the women were set about learning to sew and cook before they moved on. Ten years and the land was left, the camp abandoned. Nature had taken over again. I knew what I would do.

It didn't take much convincing to get Shelby County to lease out prisoners for my farm out on the island. Corn, cotton, sweet potatoes, millet, and other vegetables was my focus. I was a planter after all. I still had not forgotten how to pull a profit from the black earth and flesh. They weren't doing much of nothing for nobody sitting up in the prison, so why not put them to good use on fertile land? I leased 1300 acres and 117 convicts—thirty-five white males, sixty black males, four white females, eighteen black females. Do you know how many black bodies came through my auction house before the war? How many worked my land? There is no way I could have remembered them all, not by name or deportment. How was I to know that one of those nigras had never forgotten me?

When I first started emptying my bowels, they said perhaps I had taken in bad water. Mary and I lived humbly on the isle. We made a double log cabin from the bones of our former house, and there we lived until they had to carry me away to my brother's house on Union. I thought I might make it through, but it had been twelve months of uneasy living. I was lying flat on my back, drinking beef tea. My health declined week after week and I started feeling that old familiar presence again. Death followed close by me, day after day, tried to catch me by my shirtsleeves. Dysentery they said, diabetes. What ailed me was a mystery. No one suspected the truth. One or more of those black bastards I leased poisoned me.

Guess I should have seen it coming. Can't nobody say I didn't earn it. I'd done worse to others and then some. When you live the life I lived, evil is just a thing done in degrees. But I thought when a soul asks for forgiveness, you supposed to be forgiven. I might have been late coming, but the doors of the church were surely open when I came through. Mary was my witness as was my old chaplain who served with me in the war. Mary had been praying up on this since we married. Chaplain Stainback had been praying up on me since he met me. I made Mary a promise and I delivered, even if it was mighty late. Told her I would change my ways after the war—listen, it's hard to be churching while warring. I tried to walk in the ways of the Redeemer before the poisoned waters washed over me. I know it was a good year at least, before I was fully sick, so don't say it was only because I was dying. Say it was mostly because I thought I was dying, or at least running out of time. Still, a lot can change in a man's spirit.

I thought I could make it through.

A colored girl kissed me on my cheek once and gave me flowers. Can't say I smelled any more sweet. They asked me to give a speech and I said what I could. Vote the way your blood beats. Do what you got to do. We are all striving together. We are here now. Let us be friends. I told the klan to disband. Is it my fault if they didn't listen? I tried to make an honest living. I did my best. What else is a man to do when you walk and walk and your spirit still can't find its way? When the field of vision turns, withholding its secrets from you? When light keeps its shadows and all you can see are cobwebs and the corpses of dead leaves? When the trees turn their branches away from you?

I've seen sunlight copper the sky. On a hill far above the battle's roar. Such a glory over the fields. The sun looked like spun gold. What I wouldn't give to see the gold of the sun reflected in my Mary's eyes. To love is to leave no one behind. She is gone away from me. I am gone away from myself. All I have for company are these creaks and sighs, the occasional grind of metal, the echo of voices, strange names from disparate tongues and far-flung places, the

breath of memory. Every life I ever took haunts me now. Every body
I put a price upon beats me. Every bond I ever broke buries me with
grief. My bones should be dust now. The darkness in this room is
silent as a stone tomb.

Redeemer, hear my prayer.

Stone Telling

Breath. Bone. Stone. Prayer.

Here in the dark, Forrest is all chest and bone, fleshless
breath and skin. Outside time is falling, falling far into the night.
He no longer hears the thrashing of bones. He no longer hears the
stories of the other ones, buried in the ground longer than him. Not
even the burrowing of vermin to feast upon what is left of departed
souls. He lingers in the darkness, his spirit afraid beneath the tarp
and the sounds of the caul come down all around.

This is the tomb legacy built. This is the mausoleum heritage
and history built all around that man and the city. How was he to
know his legacy would become another trouble put to rest?

Now he leaned under a tarp, the white and haint blue fabric
weather-stained and faded. Dirt and dried up leaves collected in its
many folds. With the dust of many years resting on his head and
shoulders, he tries to maintain the statue's straight back stance. But
King Philip rears his head no more. And he is long past his horse-
riding years, when he was the wizard of the saddle and controlled
horse flesh as harshly as the rest.

Sometimes when he stretched his spirit wide, pressed his ear
under the dark gate, he thinks he can hear the river's sluggish flow.
River taunts him, reminds him of his schemes that turned to dust. He

wishes he was still there, lost under the curve of the moon, treading and retreading the same steps all along the river on an island empty of all life but his.

Sometimes he curses, when he sorts through the years that make up a life. He believes it is the great-handed one with the haunting eyes that fooled him.

No matter how much his thoughts wander in the silent room that is now his resting place, slipping into the corners and crevices of his life, they always return to those hands pointing at the book of maps, a curse and a blessing. Anger, resentment, regrets blow across the storage facility's concrete floor with the rotten leaves that remind him that outside, life continues on without him. He no longer counts time by the songs of birds or the whiskey hum of cricket limbs.

Instead, he counts time in spider webs, in the scuttle of insects or rodents who wonder in the storage space that has become his own prison. He remembers when he used to purchase and sell flesh, when he leased out convicts to farm the lands on the island. The first grand wizard, ku kluxer, a wizard of the saddle reviled as a war criminal, slave trader, peddler of flesh, the first to mete out a profit from prison labor out on the island where he hoped to rest.

In the end, the pulse of life beat weak and low in his fevered veins. He choked on his own breath, poisoned by deeds that could not be undone. Legacy lit his lungs afire. If only he could return eyes that no longer see. Repair holes in flesh and bone in crowns that shine no more. Restore wood and skin reduced to ashes. Reunite blood and kin torn apart by avarice and greed. Resurrect the lives that were lost in the battle between those who would enslave and those who would be free.

River's Reply

After slavery, was the Jubilee, the great-wandering-down-the-road time, the where-I-go-is-my-own time. And during the Jubilee, there was plenty of names. People shuffled them like cards and drew new ones out the deck, tried names on their tongues like new year clothes, whispered and shouted them into the bright clean air to see how they fit, licked their lips to see how they taste.

Names like Mercury Lincoln and Josiah I. M. Freedman, names like Hallelujah Williamson and Blessedbe Jones...

And some kept them old slavery time names, but not out of loyalty, no indeed. Not out of remembrance but out of hope. The old names was a bead in a prayer of the same longing, a map to the future, a map to the past, leading lost ones and loved ones and never forgot ones, sold or stole away ones, back home to them.

Have you seen Thistle? Do you know a Milkweed? My child, my brother, my husband, my sister, my mother

Do you know...

In this way, all the names, the new and the old, were a witness, to the beginning of a prayer long lit on the candle's wick, to the changing of hands in the new land they called Freedom.

But Freedom didn't come easy to the one with the tree hands and the book. Freedom was a destination always slightly out of reach. Each time they turn the book's pages, the map sends them somewhere else, the picture of a place just out of view. Some fellow wanderers, a rag tag bag of Curiosities, traveled with them and some begged to be left behind. The winds of Time wore them down to just a *nib-nib* rib of bone. They'd rather take their chances where they stand, they said, weigh them up and set'em down as they come. And anything was better than Breakneck Hill or the endless wandering. Any future, great or small.

But that Tree! Never settled for a sometimey, mayhaps kind of freedom. Part-time freedom whatn't no freedom at all. Tree kept placing them carved up palms on that book of maps and it spun them off like a top into a newborn world. But it wasn't long before they started to realize no matter how much Time they crossed, the new world had the bends and curves, the gap-toothed smiles and holes of the old. For broken promises taste sour in any mouth. And Freedom, that great big hand Tree kept reaching for was still ever out of reach.

It got so that only a few old friends remained, steadfast, stubborn, sure. But like the first families and couples, one by one they tipped their hats, begged off and bent low. Weary, they asked to be left in the different folds of time they'd rambled to. Strange places far removed from their origin on that miserable break-your-neck hill. New grounds with new seeds to be planted. In time Tree lost even the wee one, the big tall, the gold dust twins, and even the black horse that was once a king and now a god. Tree walked on hard bottom soles, same as they always did, but missed having the oldest friend, Blink, *click-song-humming* at their side.

And when the future rolled by, wave after wave, Tree looked and realized they was almost alone. Only that gal, the Zilla one remained, the ancient newborn still looking for her eternal rest. Together they moved from place to place, from time to time. The years unfurled like the ends of the map in the book. Haunted by the visions that dried before they were grasped, visions that danced in the moonlight, Tree's hope stretched across the long floor like sunlight. For Tree, Freedom was a thirst as strong as the memory of water.

And my waters are nothing to be played with. Plenty ships have sunk in my depths. Ramshackle boats broken within seconds. I have surged levees and listened to the lone witness moan. No train could escape my wrath. I tore away lines, left tracks standing straight up like picket fences. Waves washing families apart. Mothers gave birth in my waters, sisters and brothers washed away weeping. So many dead, for years fishermen pulled up skulls and bones in their nets. Anyone foolish enough to plunge their faith in me, may come away bone-soaked and disappointed. Yes, there is hope present in my waters, and consequences, too. But I ain't never been fickle as Time.

Time did Tree wrong. Yes she did.

I ain't gon' lie. I watched Tree and that one that calls herself Zilla, wandering hand in hand, as they searched for their ever after, rooting for a place they can settle down and experience that true, true Freedom. Together but seeking separate ends. A Life for one, Death for the other. Now, some places were closer to the destination, but look like them two were never quite satisfied. Can't say that I blame them. Mortal souls are something to behold. Curiosity or common. Fire spark and miracle, they trifling as they come when they want to be. And look like somebody always got to be lording over somebody else. Whether it's year one or twenty-one twenty-one, if they take one step forward, somebody will make sure they take three steps back. When you're fooling with mortals and flesh, it's a neverending journey of progress and regress.

So I admit it. Stone is my witness. One year, when they stepped through Wind and somehow found themselves back on my muddy banks, I listened as they walked by my side, trading their dreams and their laughter, their tears for another vision. I am River, but even I know sometimes a soul got to be still. You need to stand on the grassy bluff and let the wind beat the longing out of you. Let it heal your centuries of wandering.

Marked by old scars, Tree's palms once riddled by grooves and blisters that had hardened to toughness, now settled into smoothness. Love will do that sometimes. As they walked down the hill, those hands still remembered the prick of cotton plants, the shape of wood, the coldness of the hog hammer's iron, and the weathered flesh of the book that was always within their grasp, but now the years had added a new memory, the warmth of a dear one's touch.

I listened to their weariness and the hope that still steered them forward, ever forward, wondering for that space and time that would reveal true Freedom. The sigh that escaped Tree's lips when they sat down on the grass, just within reach told me that the endless wondering had worn a groove in their heart. To stay or go from this place that had bonded them in ways that only those who love and sacrifice together can comprehend. The city with the beautiful green bluff where Zilla had first seen the great hands that would carry so many out of bondage. Now they sat together as they did so many years before, pulling slick blades of grass from the damp earth. To stay or go, together or alone, one to learn how to live and the other to discover how to die.

I listened to them weigh the future. The weathered book rested in the great Tree's hand. Wind beckoned, urging them onward, in search of a more perfect freedom, but when the Zilla one planted a weary kiss on the Tree's forehead and said, "We've traveled far but I don't think I can go on with you," the Tree dropped the book.

They reach with those great big hands, impossible long

fingers like the branches of a tree.

"You are the only family I have left." Something in their voice knelt down inside of me. Strong currents and high tides, storm surges, vast inundations, damage. I can't say if it was right or wrong but I knew what I must do.

So I whispered to the Wind and the Sky and Sky answered back. The clouds up above called to me. And with a murmur and a shout as quiet as the first drops of rain, I threw back my head and kicked out my legs. Every now and then I raise my skirts and walk a while, if only just to wiggle my toes. Those old sandbags and cobblestones could never truly hold me. Nor could data and dykes and determination. I walk among the land I used to know, searching for the trees and grasses now replaced by concrete, asphalt, glass and tar. Sky answered and finally Wind rose around me. I walked and reached, climbed and stretched. And while the Tree and the ancient young one wept in each other's arms, I raised my watery fingers and stole away with the magical book.

Here since that Second Day, when my waters broke, I have rambled far and wide, across an ancient terrain that is always changing but some truths remain the same. When you are given Life, at some point in Time you got to live it. And Freedom is not something you find, it's something you make.

Whether the two lovers decided to stay or go, is a part of the story you may never know. Or maybe it is just the part I refuse to tell. Some secrets hold themselves. And some knowledge and pathways are best left to waterlogged memory.

But I will tell you this. Them two were mighty surprised when they looked up and saw that ole book gone. At their side one minute, in my waters the next. But don't judge me! If they wanted it, they could have plunged in my waters, swam through my depths. I would have been happy for their company, especially Zilla. She was such a pretty baby, but she didn't belong in the sea. So I kissed her and sent her back. She has always had my protection. I am waiting for her, whenever she is ready.

But that book of maps, I let it float a while, just so they could think hard on their next steps. The book floated gently down the riverside like a babe in a basket, like Zilla when her mama tossed her overboard that abominable slave ship and gave her to me. I could hear Tree and Zilla's cries over the downpour. Their voices hung in the air, like entering a song and the sound—surprise, fear, relief, hope—pleased me. Such music in the din. I let it spin and spin, a leathery top, then tilted the book on its side. Water-soaked and heavy, the signs and symbols merged and blurred on the pages. The blood-stained ink mixed with my muddy waters until the only sign that remained was one I will commit to memory. With a final spin, the book of maps burst into blue flames, then spiraled down and disappeared. Down, down, and down again, the book of maps floats yet, in the winding river, in the river of the great bend.

And now the tears have dried. Mama Zig Zag taught that girl well. Zilla has the gift of seeing the insides of a thing. "You don't need a map to know the way to freedom," Zilla tells Tree. "And you'll find your rest here," Tree says and points at her heart. Them two together let me know my people gon' be alright.

Good or bad, I am. The force that swirls beneath the surface. She who connects Sea to Sky. I carry the future in my hands. And Stone is my witness. These sweet waters will keep flowing. Wade in, wade in, listen. Can you hear the future calling you?

Listen, I'm telling you stories, true tales, tomorrow tales. All tales are lies, all lies are true. Trust me, the future is in good hands, for I am River, the Infinite Mother who Reclaims you, and a river knows how to bend with the best.

TEDDY BUMP

Down down baby, down down
a rollercoaster
Sweet sweet baby, sweet sweet
won't let you go...

Melanie kicks her skinny legs out. Her ashy elbows and arms pump and pump, ricochet off the cool wintry air. She wears summer clothes, a flowery church dress that billows around her, like a pink upturned umbrella, and cornrows, neat and lustrous, her Easter Sunday best. Melanie swings from a frayed brown rope. Her ankle socks must have looked good in her shiny black Mary Janes, but one shoe is missing. Her giggles bounce off the shards of ice atop the frozen red earth of Miss Dinah's playground. They echo around her, crimson crystals glistening beneath her tiny feet. One shoe on, one shoe off, locked

somewhere in an old dusty box, the label is faded, her name long
since unremembered, unread.

KeKe blows bubbles in her left hand and waves them around
like a magician, pops them like iridescent smoke rings. The bubbles
float over her shoulder and drift past the slide that is still and silent
for now, then disappear into the surrounding trees. The rusted
merry-go-round spins ever so slowly behind her. It creaks and
growls like the sound of Miss Dinah's laughter. KeKe sits with her
back against a green glacier rock, denim legs splayed out in front of
her, like a giant black baby doll. Miss Dinah smiles down at us, then
floats from her perch in the willow tree. I shudder then wave from
my spot on the prickly grass and hope Miss Dinah doesn't land near
me. Melanie laughs and pumps her little legs harder, swinging from
the sturdy oak. Even if someone finds the other shoe Melanie is not
wearing, somewhere across the red-stained layers of time, as far as
the world beyond is concerned, we are all still missing.

The word ricochets in my mind like a stray bullet, and I
rub the side of my head. It hurts sometimes to be, just thinking.
Sometimes, when the sky is flesh and Melanie's dress flies and
flutters like a hollow-boned bird, like the butterfly that once carried
me far away from home, I wonder if we are truly missed, missing.
Those words hurt, the words Miss Dinah is so careful to never say.
When it is cold outside and all the land is grieving, when Melanie
is swinging like the first days of Spring, I wonder. Are we missing if
no one in the world is looking for us, if we are just another random
group of little black girls lost?

"Halloo!" Melanie cries and leaps from her swing, arcing
through the air, a giggling brown grasshopper. "Come on, Ruby,

KeKe," she says. "Turn for me?" The rope spins slowly, unseen hands, a question mark waiting in the air behind her.

I groan. I was just getting comfortable. It's not Melanie's fault that she is the youngest among us, that she still finds some joy in this place. Somehow our littlest playmate holds onto hope, but we've be here so long with Miss Dinah, I'm not sure what that means. KeKe coughs, doesn't even look up. Amber, as always, is carving her name furiously in the bark of a tree. What's left of her dress hangs in dark shreds. We pretend like we don't see the wounds beneath them. I pretend the ice on my back is a sailboat. I pretend it will rock me away like a grandmama's arms, like sleep, drifting down through the river of air, spiriting me back to where I belong, fighting my way back to my own tree-lined street, where the sky is Mama.

"Ruby!" Melanie whines and I can feel Miss Dinah's eyes frowning down at me. Her eyes are so big, they hold a whole river in them. If I knew how, I would climb up in those eyes and kick and swim. If I knew how, I would snatch that rope and find my own way home.

"Leave me alone, ole wor'sem girl."

"I ain't wor'sem," she says. "I'm 'sistent."

"Persistent," Amber says. Her sparkly scrunchie and messy bun dangles on the side. Amber is always whispering in that child's ear, as if new words could change our story. Amber was like a house where the lights are always off. You knew someone lived there, but they were never seen. She carves, destroys whole trees with her big seeking words, hiding in the dark bark of her weird scriptures. As if prayer would save us now, trapped on the other side of Miss Dinah's trees. "You're too old to talk like that," I say. "Didn't she teach you how to read yet?"

Amber rolls her eyes, brushes away pieces of bark. I watch as she wipes the knife on her bare thigh. I am cold just looking at her. There is no heat from the Jackball sun that spins in the sky above us. It pulses and shimmers, the colors swirling with every move Miss Dinah makes.

Melanie digs her big toe into the hard bright earth, kicks at one of the many weirdly shaped rocks that litter the playground. Her head hangs low, lace white sock buried beneath the ice and snow.

"*Be nice,*" Miss Dinah says. Her white teeth glisten like new bones, the words whispered this time, not quite a hiss. Why girls always got to be nice? I huff and puff, and imagine a big gust of wind blows all their asses down, like the house in the story Mama once read to me. I feel my eyes swell up, the pressure behind my closed lids rising, an electric black cloud. I bite my lip hard but as usual I don't taste anything. Not even blood. I don't wanna be, but I'm mad now. Madder than Amber, who is slaughtering another tree. Madder than KeKe, who is always crying and picking at the frayed threads of her jeans, saying how she used to be fine, so damn fine, Teddy Bump fine and pretty. I want to snatch Melanie by her shiny naps, kick Miss Dinah in her sparkly teeth, her dusty shin. Everything was so good, so right before .... Why they make me remember? It's cold enough as it is, here. It hurts to remember, and Melanie's little baby girl voice now feels like a cold fire running through my head, burning right into my brain.

"*It's alright, Ruby.*"

Miss Dinah reaches for me with Mississippi Missionary Baptist white gloved hands. Stiff and clean, she looks like an usher at Granddaddy's old church. I turn and roll over. Don't want her touching me, rubbing her hurt all over me. I trusted her once, Miss Dinah and her Double Dutch lies promising a new way home. *You'll play all the time,* she said. *Never grow hungry, never be cold.* If I could count all the lies a haint told me, I'd be counting forever.

The icy grass stabs and pricks, tickles my belly. Sometimes I envy Melanie. Even if it is just one foot, at least she gets to feel real air, feel real grass tickling her toes, her heel and her sole. The one not wearing the patent leather shoe. Me, I feel nothing but pain. Miss Dinah says she thinks Melanie went missing in her sleep—as if she does not know how. And who does that? Goes missing in their sleep, like a bad dream except when you wake up, you don't exist? Only Miss Dinah would tell a lie like that, sing you a lie and make it feel like truth. But for me, it is always the same. My right pinky toe is squenched up in Emerald's shoes. The black ankle boots are so tight I can almost feel a corn growing. All my big sister's hand-me-downs were too little for me. My too early breasts were too big, crushed inside her too small shirts. My butt, my height, my mouth, everything too much. Mama called it, "mighty inconvenient." And though my feet hurt and my heart hurt too, I would laugh, we would roll and gasp together, laughing so hard I could not breathe. Being a little black girl can be mighty inconvenient sometimes. I laugh every time I think of it.

And that is what I miss most. Not the thinking but Mama's laughter. She looked so pretty with her eyes all big, not full of worry, and her perfect doll baby lips turned just so. She could make the biggest hurt sound like a joke, make you laugh so hard the pain disappeared in your throat. Not like Miss Dinah. When she laughs, the sound is a splinter in your big toe, glass in your ears. She is the crow in the tree, mocking us, each girl one of her *shiny things,* her own special jewel, a collection she has picked through the ages. When she laughs, you want to hide and disappear all over again.

"*I found you,*" she crows. "*No one else did, maybe no one else will. Remember that.*"

What I remember is Mama's absence. What I remember is spending my first twelve years missing Mama, missing her laughter. Mama worked so hard, but when she laughed you wouldn't know it. I guess everybody's got mamas like that. Working so hard to make you the woman they think you should be, can be, worrying so hard that only a little bit of them is left. The girl part almost gone, disappeared. But when Mama laughed there was no more worry. She sounded like light. And though it never grows dark, night never comes here, I wonder if Emerald still turns all the lights on, if she still spends each breath waiting for Mama to come back home, waiting for her to return from work or sleep. Waiting for the sun sound of her laughter, so we could all feel light, pretty, free, safe.

But we are not free and there is no *safe* here. We just *is.* We exist, between who were once were and whatever we have become. I've been here so long I don't know if I am a girl anymore, grown, or something else in between.

"Push me!" Melanie says, her face twisted up in a little brown knot. I want to push her and hold her at once. I want to push and be pushed, to hold and be held. None of that should matter here, but it does. No matter how many scars Amber carves into the tree, no matter how many holes KeKe digs out of her denim pants legs, as long as I've been here, this loneliness, this ache is always here.

I push myself up from the ice crystal grass. The sound is soft wind chimes in the cold air. I can hear KeKe shivering, sniffling behind me, and Miss Dinah—her cold eyes bearing holes into my back, the top of my head. The Jackball sun is a sickly green, a bruised blue now. Miss Dinah is mad. When she looks at you, you feel like you will disappear all over again, and whatever little peace you felt before her eyes is gone.

When Mama was gone to work, Emerald knew I was afraid, so she pretended she was her. She used to sneak into her make-up drawer when Mama was off to her second shift, and make moon faces in the old timey mirror. Emerald said Mama ought to throw it out. Get something black lacquer and new. Emerald would say this and then pucker her lips. "Mama got a lipstick mouth," she'd say. "Perfect shape, perfect size for wearing any color she wants." She used to stand in front of Granddaddy's old green painted dresser and mirror, making faces that looked like her stomach hurt or like she was some kind of strange clownfish. Mama's mouth didn't look nothing like that. It was perfect, like the kind they used for the scratch n' sniff stickers plastered all over my Trapper Keeper notebook, perfect lips that made every hurt feel whole again.

But I don't know if I have Mama's lipstick mouth, or if Emerald's little bitty feet ever caught up with me. I don't know why my Mama named me Ruby but my favorite, favorite color is blue. I don't know when real girls start or stop growing. When the pain ever ends. For Melanie, for KeKe, for Amber and me, maybe Miss Dinah, too, for all of the others lurking behind the trees, crying under the stones, waiting in the river, on the side of the road in a ditch, waiting in a hotel's deep freezer for somebody to come carry us out, every day changes but every night is the same. Nothing grows here, not even our dreams. We are visible and invisible. Just the layers of red dirt, full of time and all of it so full of our tears, the red clay looks like its crying, like the whole earth bleeding, too.

"You're daydreaming today, better keep up, better keep it lively," KeKe says, mimicking Miss Dinah. She wipes snot from her face with the back of her hand. She talks so funny, half the time I don't even know what to say. She talks like Mrs. Aldridge, KeKe's favorite teacher, the one she used to imitate for us. Said she used to stand in front of the classroom, discussing worlds they had never seen, every detail a new language, then she would weave around the neat rows of their desks, an exotic bird in constant motion. KeKe used to make us laugh so hard, but now she don't talk much anymore, not since she realized Miss Dinah never plans for us to leave here. KeKe just holds herself now, and cries, digging at her denim jacket, her jeans, the last outfit she chose for herself. When she does talk, she tells us about her friends going to the shows, and the cute boys, and the slick girls who smiled in her face and did her wrong so wrong, and then sometimes, she will tell us about high school.

Mrs. Aldridge sounds nice. The only thing about school I liked was the first day and lunch. But when KeKe talked, she made it sound like some kind of adventure. KeKe is the only one of us to make it to high school, but she missed her prom.

"What is a prom?" Melanie once asked. For a moment, KeKe stopped crying.

"A prom is a promise," KeKe said.

And after she described getting your hair did, the pretty

dresses, the decorations, and drinking ice cream punch, she grabbed Melanie and pretended to dance. The only prom I'd seen was in that scary movie when the mean girls covered the magic one with pig blood. Watching KeKe and Melanie dance was one of the few times since Miss Dinah brought her here that I'd seen KeKe look happy. But she don't look happy now.

She has placed snow-covered ice blossoms in the four holes in her matching denim shirt. It looks almost pretty, like her blouse was made that way on purpose. I don't feel like arguing so I just dust myself off, even though I know my parachute pants can never get wet. I'm so sick of them. I wish I could take a knife and rip them up, too. But whatever I do to them, they just turn back the same way they were when I came here.

I can't think of anything more embarrassing than dying in some bright red parachute pants that barely fit, dying in some too shiny polyester nylon that don't even cover your ankles good. Even Michael Jackson wouldn't be caught dead in that. And Melanie might be a wor'sem baby who can't even read but at least she looked right when she went missing, even with her one little shoe. Me, I am trapped here in Miss Dinah's world looking like Who-Done-It-and-What-For forever. But then I think of Amber. Poor thing. Can't get more pitiful than that.

Shimmy, shimmy cocoa pop
Shimmy shimmy down
Shimmy shimmy cocoa puff
Shimmy shimmy break down

"I said, who wants to play?"

"I do!" Melanie raises her hand, hopping around like a cricket. Amber, KeKe, and I just look at each other. "I do," we say in unison but it's not enough. Miss Dinah wants razzle and dazzle, but I feel like my voice has seeped right out of me, or frozen under the ice. I don't feel like playing. I don't feel like singing. I don't feel like....

"Oooh," Melanie says. If her eyes weren't so big, her little hand covering her mouth, I would've thought I'd only imagined it, but the shock on Amber and KeKe's faces says everything: I messed around and said that aloud.

The Jackball sun darkens and the air feels like fire.

"I don't understand!" Miss Dinah roars. "I do everything for you. I take you from that scary darkness, I carry you in my arms and bring you to the light. I fill your world with toys and games, and none of you can still bring me laughter? None of you can show me gratitude?"

As she speaks her ropes hiss and sputter, twisting like serpents. The frayed edges shake with electric flares. Miss Dinah grabs one rope in each hand and begins whipping them in the air, lashing them out right near our feet.

Melanie screams and dives into my arms. I hold her and cover her eyes so she will not see which one of the stone ones, the stone dolls would be brought back to whatever it is Miss Dinah calls our new lives.

Miss Dinah's right rope sizzles and sparks as she whips it across a small boulder. When I first arrived and crossed over the blueness into Miss Dinah's light, I thought the wet stones were just part of the park. But now I know they had once been little girls, too.

Miss Dinah had turned them into stones that remained wet with tears. I once saw her turn a new girl who had never learned to play jacks. She turned another because she could not keep time well. She always stumbled and missed during our hand-clapping games. Clapping when she should've been sliding, stomping when she should've been crossing her heart. I can still hear her screaming.

Miss Mary Mack Mack Mack
All dressed in black black black
With silver buttons buttons buttons
All down her back back back

The new girl was still screaming when Miss Dinah's rope hit her and her face turned gray. Her raised palms froze mid-air and her body changed shape. All that was left was her tears on a stone. After that Miss Dinah had us clapping "Miss Mary Mack" so long, it felt like my whole hands were on fire, the skin blistered, red and sore.

To survive Miss Dinah, a girl had to have rhythm, had to have a good memory, too. Little Melanie had neither, as long as she had been beyond the blue, but Miss Dinah kept her anyway.

"All I ask is for a little affection, some cooperation," she says. *"Joy is what we are supposed to be here! Joy!"* The sky roiled above her head, covering the Jackball sun.

"All I ask for is just a little love, a little companionship, a little 'thank you, Miss Dinah,' for all I've done for you, but you have the nerve to fix your lips to tell me what you ain't gon' do, how you

feel? Let me tell you about feelings..."

Melanie trembles and KeKe shakes. Amber grips her knife, the blade digging into her hand. The rope writhes back and forth in the air, a spinning cyclone one moment, a whip the next. As it cracks through the air, we wait for Miss Dinah's anger to pass, her black hole eyes an ever changing storm. She hovers above us, her stained palms raised upward, toward the sky, their redness trembling against the black and blue.

"Fast tailed girls, now you've ruined my gloves."

There is no sound, only the dry rattle of our watching breath trapped in terrified throats. Our tongues and voices turn back on ourselves. Now Melanie moans. KeKe curses. Amber bites her lip, grinds the blade into the tree's hard flesh. Still the red hands remain outstretched, a prayer or a curse, we cannot tell. Miss Dinah lowers herself until her bare feet touch the floor. The church shoes now gone, I turn away from the dark, curled nails on her toes. Miss Dinah spins slowly, turning her head to stop and stare at each of us, her wintry eyes great gaping holes of rage, her lips frosted popsicles. She walks stiffly, her long skirt and bare feet dragging in the stiff, frozen grass with a sound that chills me, makes my bones ache. Long toenails scraping across ice.

Melanie twists out of my arms, and turns to face me, her eyes pleading. She grabs my hand. "Turn for me?" she asks. She presses her palm into mine and tries to get me to begin the game.

"Ruby," Miss Dinah says, waving my name on the bitter tip of her smile. *"Join the circle or the circle will join you."*

The rope spins in the air behind her, a warning. It spins then splits into two.

I rise and take my place. The ropes feel like fire in my hands but I hold onto them. The rhyme is the same as before. Miss Dinah likes the old games.

KeKe bends down to pick up the frayed ends of the ropes from the icy ground. She drops it, as if she is burned. Sucks her fingertips. "Why can't Amber turn today?" she cries. I glance over my shoulder at Amber. She is gripping her blade with two hands, stab, stabbing at the heart of Miss Dinah's favorite tree.

"You are wasting your time, Amber. That is not where my heart is buried, child."

The smile on Miss Dinah's face makes me grip the ropes tighter. "Come on, KeKe," I say. "Begin."

"High John saw the mighty number," she sang. "High John, High John."

"High John saw the mighty number, High John, High John..."

Miss Dinah is a master jumper. No one can beat her jumping. We start off easy then speed the doubled ropes up. She gets real mad if we turn the ropes too slowly.

"High John was a mighty number, High Jo—"

"Enough of that wearisome ditty. Sing something else," she cries.

We are just about to turn the ropes when I hear Amber whisper behind us. We are so astonished to hear her speak, that we let the ropes drop and fall slack. They hiss and groan as they touch the cold ground. The ropes only like heat, they hate the ice crystals prickling their frayed little bellies. The faster we turn, the hotter they get. I hate the ropes. They hiss and move like snakes and shed like them, too.

Miss Dinah whirls, turning to face Amber. *"What did you say, Amber dear?"*

Miss Dinah is trying to resume her nice voice, the friendly voice that comforted me when I awoke to find myself waiting in the dark blue.

Amber takes a deep breath, her eyes intent, her mouth a straight line, unsmiling.

"I said, can we hula hoop here?"

"Hula?" Melanie is confused. We have been jumping rope and pattycaking so long that we barely remember other activities.

"*Is that another way to turn, another way to jump?*" Miss Dinah asks.

Suddenly, I catch KeKe's eye and motion for her to lay the crying ropes all the way down. They hiss in protest.

"Yeah," I say. "Yes," with more enthusiasm. "Can we, Miss Dinah? I haven't hula-hooped in a long, long time."

"It's so fun," KeKe says, finally catching on. She sounds corny as all get out, but she fixes her face to something that looks like excitement.

Melanie hops over to us, her shoeless foot lightly skipping over the snow and ice. "I wanna hula, too! Me, me, me!" she cries, tugging on Miss Dinah's tattered dress.

Miss Dinah narrows her eyes into sharp slits. "*What does this hula look like?*"

"Like a big skinny, hard donut," Amber says. "You spin it around your waist and keep it spinning with your hips. You can spin it as fast or as slow as you want, but you can't let it touch the ground."

"It's so much fun, Miss Dinah," I say, trying to sound bright, light.

"And there are songs, too!" KeKe says.

"*Songs?*" Miss Dinah cocks her head like a bird of prey. "*Try me,"* she says, both a warning and an invitation.

Amber walks to the center of the playground, away from the ropes that have finally quieted down. She adjusts the ragged remains of her dress that barely cover her chest, the strips of dark-stained fabric around her waist and begins to sing. After a while, we join in.

"Hula, hula, now who think they bad?"

"I do!"

"Hula, hula, now who think they bad?"

"I do!"

"I think I'm bad 'cause Amber's my name. Yellow is my color don't you worry about my lover, honey."

"*Mmmf*, she think she fine."

"Fine, fine, fine enough, fine enough to blow your mind."

"*Mmmf*, she think she cool."

"Cool, cool, cool enough, cool enough to skip your school!"

"Hula, hula, now who think she bad?"

Miss Dinah's face, first pale with anger, now darkens and shines with pleasure. Her long teeth recede back into her mouth as do her claw-like nails. She turns back into the motherly creature that had come to the blue oneness and smiled and grinned and lied to our face, the haint that claimed us like a fairy godmother in a bad, bad dream.

"*I will get this hula,"* she says and rises to go. Her ugly feet levitate off the ground.

"We need five," Amber says quickly.

"*Five?"* Miss Dinah lowers herself, looks at us, suspicious. "*Why can't we share the one?"*

Amber glances around uneasy. KeKe begins to stutter. I start to speak but then Melanie interrupts me. Any other time I'd be annoyed by that but not this nightday.

"Because I want a pink one with sparkles on it! Sparkles and stars! And Ruby," she raises my hand. "Ruby wants a red one of course."

"No," I cut in. "Blue."

"I want blue," KeKe says, her voice soft, quiet.

Miss Dinah smiles, revealing normal teeth now. "*Yellow for Amber, RED for Ruby, Blue for KeKe, pink for my Melanie, and... and gold for me!*" Delighted, she shoots up into the air like a witch without a broom. She is heading straight for the Jackball sun, the bright colorful sphere that seems to embody her every mood.

"That's it!" I say.

"That's what?" KeKe asks.

Amber motions at the ropes. I signal agreement.

"I know where she buried her heart." I point up to the fake swirly, swirly nebulous sky, the spinning Jackball where Miss Dinah disappears.

"We've got to get her ropes. Quick, KeKe, I know you hate turning, but we've got to hide them and keep them quiet somehow. Distract her with the new game."

"There are three ropes now. I know just what to do," KeKe says. "I can twist anything, I can braid anything, I just need a little help."

We sneak up on the ropes while little Melanie distracts them and grab them by their tails. Before they hiss and holler, KeKe ties one set of their ends into a tight knot.

"Now turn!" she says.

"Turn?" Melanie asks.

"Not you. Keep watch. Amber, Ruby, help me braid this."

The ropes jerk and yank, trying to get free. They sparkle and sting us but we keep braiding, one loop over the other loop, under the rest.

"It hurts," Amber says. We nod, yes it does, what doesn't here, but keep folding over and over until we are done.

Melanie hops over one of the rocks to us, the little pigtail ends of her cornrows shaking, frantic. "Miss Dinah is on her way back here. She has the hula hoops."

"Back to your places," I whisper. Melanie runs to Amber, then runs back to the me.

"What you doing over here?" I ask.

She looks worried. "I don't know how to hula hoop."

"It's easy," I tell her. "Just watch me."

"What if I drop it?"

"Miss Dinah loves you."

Melanie screws up her little chubby face. "Miss Dinah don't love nobody."

I think about this as she lands, spinning on one foot.

"Hulas, hulas," Miss Dinah sings. She hands them out, one by one. *"Now let's get started,"* she says.

We sing, each girl stepping into the center of the ring, spinning the hulas, singing of personal glories. Melanie drops her hula many times, but Miss Dinah only laughs and orders us to play again and again.

Finally, when I think I can't sing another note anymore, when I can't think of another boast to share, Amber steps forward to take my hoop.

"One hoop is easy. It's really for beginners and babies," she says, cutting her eye at Miss Dinah.

"*Amber, you know I hate babies.*" Miss Dinah hates babies because babies can't survive here. What would she do with something that needed more attention than her?

"A real master hooper can spin one, two, maybe even three hulas at a time."

Miss Dinah looks curious. "*Are you a master hooper, Amber?*" She is always ready for a challenge.

"I am," Amber says and Melanie gasps. She plops her hand to cover her mouth.

"No, Amber, you're going to drop them," Melanie whines.

"No, I won't, Melanie. Watch me!" Amber wraps her bun tighter in her scrunchie and smooths down what is left of her dress. She adds my red hula and KeKe's blue to her own yellow hula, one by one. She begins to spin around and walk as she hoops.

"Teddy bump, teddy bump! Teddy bump, teddy bump!" she sings as she swivels her hips, the hoops spinning slowly at first, then faster and faster.

Melanie looks like she's thrilled and terrified all at once. Her little eyes are about to pop.

"*Oh, you want to try me, I see,*" Miss Dinah says. She unfurls her razor sharp fingers, her flat palm up. "*Give them to me.*"

Amber shakes her head no. "Miss Dinah, if you think you can beat me, get your own."

Miss Dinah throws her head back, surprised at Amber's tone, her newfound confidence. But she loves a challenge more than anything. What is a game worth if there is no risk? Her explanation for why she mixed danger and pain with all her playground games. But Miss Dinah liked to win every game. The weeping rocks were all that was left of the girls who lost.

Before Melanie can speak, Miss Dinah shoots back up to the Jackball sun. When she returns, she has hula-hoops stacked on her arms and waist. She doesn't even wait to land before she is spinning like a top.

"*Hula, hula!*" she cries. We cheer her on. "Miss Dinah, Go Dinah, Miss Dinah, Go Dinah!" The more we cheer and clap, the faster she spins.

Miss Dinah spins so fast, she and the hulas begin to sparkle and glow.

She is really showing out now. Doing a little shimmy shimmy limbo shake while she flows.

"Go Dinah, Miss Dinah!" Amber cries, then she nods at me. "Ruby, KeKe, add the heat!"

KeKe and I have unbraided and untangled the ropes. We crack the spinning Miss Dinah Ball like rodeo whips. Miss Dinah squeals with delight at first. "*More! More!*" she cries. She holds herself tightly, spinning as the hula hoops rotate around her. "*Faster, faster!*" The ropes respond, spinning her faster than any top we've ever seen.

"Oooh!" Melanie cries. We crack the ropes harder. They rip through the air like lightning bolts. Miss Dinah's ragged, tattered gown catches afire.

"*Wait!*" Miss Dinah screams, panic spoiling her smile. She tries to slow down, but she can't.

We have her and we have her ropes.

We lasso her with the remaining hulas and the Dinah Ball hovers in the air, just a few feet above the ground, crackling and rising the angrier she gets.

"*What have you done?*" she screams and levitates a few feet higher, trying to escape but the hula hoops are weighing her down. She can't go far.

"No!" I yell. "We can't let her get to the sun. If she makes it out of here... "I don't finish. We all know if she does escape, we are all finished. If we lose this game, we will become wet stones, or pebbles, or worse, dust.

"Give me the ropes," I say. KeKe looks confused. Melanie is wailing, and Amber takes out her blade. I think she understands.

She carves a deep groove into her favorite tree. I steer the Miss Dinah Ball with the ropes and use the tree to wrap the ends of the spitting, hissing ropes and anchor myself.

"You are going to have to climb up and ride the ball like a bull."

"Like a skateboard!" Melanie says.

Surprised, now even Amber looks unnerved.

"There's no other way out of here. You'll have to ride her evil tail right up through the Jackball sky. All of you." They nod, recognition slowly registering in their eyes.

"But what about you, Ruby?" Melanie wails. I don't answer.

"And Amber..." I say, yanking the ropes. "Be still you evil thangs." They sputter in protest.

"Yes," Amber says.

"When you get to the Jackball, to the sun, I need you to carve out the heart she has buried there and toss it down to me.

Don't let her get it. Can you do that?"

"Yes." Amber is crying. Melanie is crying, KeKe, all the wet stones, we are all crying. But I know what I have to do. I've seen a lot of movies, and in the movies folks, especially black folks, don't always get free. I've been knowing for some time, but hoping all the same. Truth is, I might never see my mama or my sister again. I'd already gotten used to that, but these girls, these plain little black girls missing just like me, they were the only family I had here.

⟋⟍

The Jackball pulses, its colors flickering from bright blood reds, oranges, and yellows, to purples and blues so dark, they look like bruises. Each time Miss Dinah winces with pain, the Jackball changes colors and seems to wince, too. The Jackball is not only where Miss Dinah hid her heart, it is her heart.

I wrap the ropes even tighter around my wrists though it burns, and I scream, "Run, now!"

Miss Dinah has managed to get a few of her bony fingers loose. She's trying to cut through the hula hoops with her nails but they are too strong. The see-saw, the merry-go-round, the slides on the dark playground are twisting and undulating. Soon the metal will transform and they will run after the girls, after me.

KeKe takes Melanie by her hand and they take a running start before they leapfrog onto the Dinah Ball. Amber follows, slips and runs to try again.

"You better stop playing girl," I cry, "and get on out of here!" I don't know how much longer I can hold onto these ropes, how long before Miss Dinah manages to take over the tree.

I yank my arm in a long rippling motion, bouncing the Dinah Ball up, up into the sky, like one of those Atari games. Amber, KeKe, and Melanie are holding onto the hula hoops, clutching them like a ladder. "Now climb!" I say, "climb like they monkey bars!"

Melanie is the first to get free. She pinwheels up and out into the force that circles the Jackball sun. KeKe and Amber follow her. Amber grabs her knife.

"*Noooooooo!*" Miss Dinah screeches, her face contorted, her lips and mouth stretched out like a bottomless hole. "*You can't leave me! Never, never leave me! I cannot bear this place alone.*"

And there it is. Miss Dinah, a creature as powerful as she, is just as lonely as any of the children she pretended to befriend here in the in between world.

As much as I hate what she has done to us here, I wonder if Miss Dinah was ever missing. I wonder if she is not only a trapper but is trapped here, too.

Amber plunges her blade deep into the center of the Jackball sun. KeKe and Melanie sadly wave goodbye. None of us know what is on the other side of the Jackball sky or the big, wide blue. I do know I will never see them again.

Maybe out there in the blue, there is more than darkness. Maybe in its depths there are more than scary things that just want to run you down. I realize I didn't linger long enough to find out. Miss Dinah had called to me, maybe before anyone else had a chance.

When Amber tears the sky in two, and rips the Jackball sun to shreds, Miss Dinah lays in a smoldering heap, and the ropes fall asleep in my hands. The stinging stops, the burning, too. Real light, real warmth returns to the playground. I watch in wonder as ice melts for the first time in what might have been many ages. First the air is filled with the sound of exhalations. Then laughter. The music of little girls awakening from a long, cold nap. Silver and gold rainbow bubbles float in the air above our heads. Then I discover what the ropes can truly do. We each take turns, turning, each take turns, jumping, changing. I reach inside the memory of my oldest girlhood dream, of Trapper Keeper notebooks, scratch n' sniff stickers, new back to school clothes, freshly done hair—fried, dyed and laid to the side—and Granddaddy's old dresser painted green. I hold the rope and remember my sister Emerald and my Mama's face, then I lay the ropes down and skip all the way home, thinking of the color blue.

ORIGINS OF SOUTHERN SPIRIT MUSIC

"There is no theory, you just have to listen." Claude DeBussy

I n a faraway land, far from a chosen people, was an old music man with a strange music shop. Shop was too kind a word, shed more truthful. But in faraway lands of forgotten people, sometimes the truth is best faced with a gift of magic. And where the music man lived, on the end of a dirt road that curved to nowhere, truth and magic, music and night, lived side by side. There, on the edge of the woods, the old man's little dirt road was the place where the forest skinned its knobby knees. It was the place where the river stretched her toes, and the mountain rested its head as he drifted off to sleep.

The music shed was made of earth, river, and stone, and it was filled with the remnants of the offerings the forgotten ones salvaged. From the salvaged bits of metal and trash, the old man fashioned the strange instruments whose music was the breath of life. Some of the instrument parts he found and some the children gave him. Whatever the origin of the gifts, he took the discarded bits of everyday life and wrote a song from them, made the doubters dance and the shamed ones sing, all sorrows turned to an orchestra of joy.

One night a series of pipes and flutes pierced the air, and as the door cracked open, a child poked her head in. She walked as if waking from a dream. Her hair fluffed on the left side of her head, a dark puffy frown. Tears glistened, starlight on cheeks that were full and brown. "Papa Othar?" Her voice was cool water, like the sound a mountain river makes when she wakes. "Mama sick," was all she said. Water moon eyes told the end of the story.

The elder sighed, welcomed her with the wave of his dark, gnarled hand, the skin like weathered leather, tree bark split by the wind. His movement sent the golden disks and wind chimes to shimmer and wail, spinning from strings that dangled from the rootwork ceiling. The wind whispered in the corners of the room, set the water pipes to whistling. And the air in the shed vibrated like a one-string Diddley board.

"She eating?"

"No," the child said, and stood weeping by the door. "She sleeping, say she not hungry no more."

The old man lowered his eyes, nodded his head, picked up a vagrant flute and placed the metal to his lips, and said,

"Rest for the weary and souls too tired for a crust of bread."

"But a body got to eat," the child insisted. "That's what my teacher says. To live long, she says a body got to move, a body got to play, and we got to put good things in it. Mama won't do none of that no more."

The old man chose a mallet and waved it in the air like a baton, then handed it to the child. He chose another and beckoned her to carry on.

In the shed whose walls grew taller, floors wider with each step they made, the sound of distant scales filled the air thick with memory and iridescent light. As they walked, the child's tears formed into crystals, C-notes that shattered on the floor, beautiful and bright.

Together they walked with the strain of necessity, yearned for the strain of freedom. But the instruments in the old man's shed lived by their own strange physics.

To the untrained eye, the shed was full of junk. But to those gifted with eyes that do more than see, to those who listened with more than their inner ear to hear, the shed was a wonderland, a black rabbit hole in a forgotten corner of the cosmos. Lyres made of garbage lids filled the room, and strange nautilus shell-shaped instruments made from roots, designed to be plucked with fingers or stroked with a bow, dangled from the root sky. T-bars and wrenches, hacksaws and files, grinding wheels and gears spun like strange planets against the dark light of the shed.

Some of the instruments looked like great metal machines with teeth that could chew through any note. Others with buckets and pails looked as if only flowing water would make them go. Drums made from cooking pots and cymbals made from pans, dark blue glass bottles hanging from metal stands.

The old man, wizard and muse, was a master of chaos, drum major of dissonance, and the proud maker of many-stringed curiously harmonized musical things. He strummed a low harp with a satellite dish body and resonator and plucked its piano strings, vibrating the pickup on the backside under its bridge.

Sometimes the river came and visited him. Sometimes

she tap danced on the roof, as raindrops from the river's bottom. Rain was another way the river chose to travel. She sounded out a symphony of sand and silt. She sang of all that she had seen in her journeys, of misery and mayhem, of courage and kindness, riots and revelations. She dripped, dripped her blues into the amber jug that sat on the highest shelf. He took a tree-trunk stump and climbed. Among his welder's mask and gloves, his wire brush and sandpapers, his bolts and bobbins, the old man found what he was looking for.

Held it in shaking hands, an instrument plucked from his steeple of dreams.

He stumbled over a spool of magnet wire, caught his breath as he stooped to set it right. The rattle in the gourd creaked like old bones, the bones in his back creaked with old gourdsongs. Alone he could fuss and fiddle endlessly, but the child's eyes and her mouth, a sad quivering 'O', reminded him that every soul arrived and danced at a time of its own. The song he would make night, the song he would make might hold Mama's spirit longer, excite the memory of appetite, remind her of the music that lived in blood. And she would dance again, and hold the child just so, the puffy cloud smiling under her chin, but when the time came, not even spirit music could stop the will to go.

And no matter how sweet, every song must end.

Harp in hand, the old man climbed down from the night, and returned to face the little one whose eyes were now a shroud. The child had walked past the shekeres decorated in bottle caps and net, past the lunch pail lutes, and the shimmie-she-wobble flutes.

The child stood before a great giant balafon made of dried gourds and lost and found keys. She held the mallet high like a fist and struck each note with the strength of her fear. The sound of her grief made the old man tremble and shake, made him clutch the harp because he could not shut his ears. The keys rose and fell, rolled like a silver river, the crescent moon's smile. He waited until the child grew worn and weary, until her arms grew heavy, the balafon silent and her tears spent.

"Here, dear one. Play this with all you feel inside, and Mama will hear your song, even in her dreams, where she now resides."

"And will she dance?" the child asked, and she took the bone harp and placed it to her mouth.

"You tell me, child, you tell me."

In her song he could hear the motion of waters and the play of curves in the evening breeze. As she walked away, blowing gently into the mouth harp, the wind lifted the dust around her feet and carried her song into the trees, beyond the sleepy mountain and the rambling river: if music is the space between the notes, then love is the space between lives.

And so it is, and so it was, in a forgotten land of faraway people, where music is the breath of life.

ACKNOWLEDGMENTS

First, all praise and gratitude to the Ancestors, to my mother, Jacqueline Denise Thomas and my father Eddie Larry Thomas— thank you for holding space for me. To my siblings, Terrence, Brian, Ebony, and Xavian Thomas. To my daughters, Jacqueline and Jada. I love you!

Love, light, and many heartfelt thanks to the wonderful editors, readers, arts organizations, educational institutions, publications, and dear friends who have supported my work! Special thanks to Third Man Books, my *Nine Bar Blues* editor Chet Weise, Caitlin Parker, Maddy Underwood, Jordan Williams and to Kiini Ibura Salaam for supporting my neaux new! Continued love and light to my dear family and friends, Andrea Hairston and Pan Morigan, Wild Wimmins of the Beyon'Dusa Writers Collective, James Emory, Arthur Rickydoc Flowers, Danian Darrell Jerry, Daniel Coates, Isaiah Coates, Ronda Racha Penrice, Evens Smarth, Jacqueline Johnson, Duriel L. Harris, Reynaldo Anderson, the BSAM fam, Clairesa Clay, Celeste Rita Baker, Daniel José Older, Jaime Manrique, Rob Costello, Danielle L. Littlefield, Metta Sáma, Patricia Spears Jones, Julia Rios, Cindy and Luis Alberto Urea and the Guerreras, Jaquira Diaz, Jamey Hatley, Ephraim and Sheila Urevbu, Celia C. Peters, and Tobacco Brown for offering encouragement, insight, and a listening ear. Many thanks to Bread Loaf Environmental, The Millay Colony of Arts, the Virginia Center for Creative Arts, Smith College, and Artspace for creating beautiful realms for my imagination to soar while I wrote these stories. I reach and grow because of all of you!

Sheree Renée Thomas
Photo by Gabby Rodriguez and Wisdom Dewberry

BIOGRAPHY WITH SELECTED WORKS AND HONORS

Sheree Renée Thomas is an award-winning short story writer, poet, and editor with fellowships and residencies from the Millay Colony of Arts, Bread Loaf Environmental, VCCA, Ledig House, Blue Mountain Center, Cave Canem Foundation, NYFA, Tennessee Arts Commission, and Smith College where she served as the Lucille Geier-Lakes Writer-in-Residence. Her work has appeared in numerous anthologies and literary publications, including *Sycorax's Daughters, Do Not Go Quietly, Memphis Noir, Stories for Chip: A Tribute To Samuel R. Delany, So Long Been Dreaming: Post-colonial Science Fiction & Fantasy, Revise the Psalm: A Celebration of Gwendolyn*

Brooks, Luminescent Threads: Connections to Octavia E. Butler, Mojo: Conjure Stories, Revenge, Ghost Fishing: An Eco-Justice Poetry Anthology, Lightspeed, The Ringing Ear, Bum Rush the Page: A Def Poetry Jam, Apex Magazine, An Alphabet of Embers: An Anthology of Unclassifiables, The Moment of Change: Feminist Speculative Poetry, Memories & Reflections On Ursula K. Le Guin, StorySouth, Hurricane Blues, African Voices, Drumvoices Revue, Fiyah, Fireside Fiction, Strange Horizons, Obsidian, Renaissance Noire, Harvard's *Transition, Callaloo, Essence,* and *The New York Times.* Her work is also forthcoming in *The Big Book of Modern Fantasy.*

She edited the *Dark Matter* speculative fiction volumes that won two World Fantasy Awards and first introduced W.E.B. Du Bois's work as science fiction. She was the inaugural recipient of the LA (Leslie) Banks Award for outstanding achievement in the speculative fiction field. Her hybrid, multigenre collection, *Sleeping Under the Tree of Life* (Aqueduct Press) was longlisted for the 2016 Otherwise Award and honored with a *Publishers Weekly* Starred Review. *Shotgun Lullabies* (Aqueduct), was described as a "revelatory work like Jean Toomer's *Cane.*" She serves as the Associate Editor of *Obsidian: Literature & Arts in the African Diaspora* (Illinois State University, Normal). *Nine Bar Blues: Stories from an Ancient Future* (Third Man Books, 2020) is her first fiction collection. She lives in her hometown, Memphis, Tennessee.